Praise for the *New York Times* bestseller

FUTURE SHOCK

"A cyberpunk tour de force thrill ride that aptly provides urban fiction, sci-fi, and mystery. This is a guaranteed hit recommended for all young adult collections."—*VOYA*

"A tense tale of predestination and paranoia, fleshed out with a diverse cast and an intriguing premise."—*Publishers Weekly*

"This is an entertaining science fiction murder mystery that should appeal to James Patterson fans along with readers of Michael Grant's Gone series."—*School Librar*

"An intriguing take on time travel g

"The author refreshingly swaps teen
the edgy, brooding girl with the heart of gold, and he's the adorable, inexperienced good guy."—*Kirkus Reviews*

"Intense, romantic, and gripping...you won't want to put it down."
—Amy Tintera, author of *Reboot*

"Buckle up—*Future Shock* is a full-throttle thrill ride of a murder mystery."—Karen Akins, author of *Loop* and *Twist*

"A page-turner that'll keep you guessing until the very end."
—Melissa Landers, author of *Starflight* and the Alienated series

FUTURE THREAT

BOOK TWO IN THE
FUTURE SHOCK TRILOGY

ELIZABETH BRIGGS

ALBERT WHITMAN & COMPANY
CHICAGO, ILLINOIS

For my father, Peter,
who always believed in me

Library of Congress Cataloging-in-Publication
data is on file with the publisher.

Published in 2017 by Albert Whitman & Company
ISBN 978-0-8075-2684-2 (hardcover)
ISBN 978-0-8075-2686-6 (paperback)

Printed in the United States of America
10 9 8 7 6 5 4 3 2 1 BP 20 19 18 17 16

Design by Jordan Kost

For more information about Albert Whitman & Company,
visit our website at www.albertwhitman.com.

PART I
THE PRESENT

THURSDAY

There are three things that make the memories stop, if only for a moment.

This is the first.

The needle bites into my skin, but I welcome the pain. It's less of a prick and more like a wasp stinging me over and over, buzzing deep into my skin. The vibrations travel through my bones, across my upper body, and I grit my teeth. I've hit that point where I want to pull away, where I don't know if I can take it anymore, but I force myself to be still.

I close my eyes and let the pain block out everything else. It builds and builds until it crests like a wave, breaking over the shore. My mind goes blank. There's nothing but the sharp pressure and the hum of the tattoo gun, and in that instant I'm numb.

For a few seconds, the past disappears.

When José pulls the needle back to examine his work and wipe away the extra ink, the memories all come back in a rush. The salty smell of cold ocean air. An echoing boom of a gunshot. Blood dripping down bone-white tiles.

"Está bien, Elena?" José asks, jerking me back to the present.

My mouth is too dry to speak at first, so I nod. He brings me a mirror, and I turn my arm to get a better look at the design from different angles. The lines of ink are thick and stark black against my brown skin, which has turned red and blotchy around the tattoo: a stylized image of the origami unicorn Adam made for me six months ago.

"Perfecto," I say.

José covers the tattoo in saran wrap, but doesn't bother giving me the standard instructions on how to take care of it. This isn't my first tattoo, and I doubt it will be my last. But other than the tattoo of my mother's name, this one might mean the most to me.

"Gracias," I say, doling out a hefty tip on top of the fee he quoted me before. José used to tattoo me when I was younger, back when it was technically illegal since I was under eighteen. He's the older brother of the guy I was hooking up with when I got my first tattoo, the spiderweb on my other arm. Now I'm old enough to get them done legally, and I have money to pay him right. For once.

I head out of the tattoo parlor, and the bell on the door tinkles overhead while it swings shut. But as soon as my foot hits the sidewalk, I tense.

There, across the street, is that damn black car again.

I've seen it on and off for the last six months, ever since I was part of a "research project" that sent me—and four other teens—to the future, with deadly consequences. At various times the car has been outside my apartment, in front of my kickboxing class, or in a parking lot on my college campus. One time I swore I saw it waiting outside a restaurant when Adam and I were on a date.

It's Aether Corporation. It has to be.

The car waits, its windows tinted so dark I can't see inside, but I get that skin-prickling feeling like someone is watching me. I don't know what they want, but I wish they'd make a move already, instead of biding their time and following me everywhere I go. They're probably monitoring me, making sure I never reveal their secrets. Keeping tabs in case I ever get out of line. Getting ready to pounce when they're good and ready.

Maybe they want me to know they can get to me whenever they want.

There's a harsh, brisk wind in the air, heralding the fact that Los Angeles is finally switching from summer to fall after a hard-fought battle to hang on to those hotter temperatures. I pull my black hoodie over my hair and shove my hands in my pockets while I walk down the sidewalk, trying not to make it obvious that I'm watching the car while it watches me.

As I near the corner, it creeps down the street behind me. They're not even trying to be subtle anymore.

I turn onto the next block, but a flash of electric blue hair makes me freeze in place. A girl ahead of me, getting out of her car.

Zoe?

My vision blurs and panic shoots through my veins, but it's not her. It's *not*. I saw her body. I know she's dead. But I can't move, can't breathe, can't do anything but ride through the flashbacks.

Her limp body in the tub.

Blood and water mixing on their way down the drain.

The sound of my own cries as I realize I'm too late to save her.

The girl's head swivels in my direction before she walks into a sandwich shop, and my brain snaps out of it. Her hair isn't even the right shade of blue. Zoe is dead and gone for good, and no matter how many times I relive that moment, I can't go back and change the past.

Here's the thing about having a perfect memory: it makes it

really hard to move on from the shit you've been through. And God knows I've seen enough death for a lifetime.

I check the time on Mamá's watch, rubbing the smooth face back and forth with my thumb. The familiar gesture grounds me in reality again, in the present moment. 4:18 p.m. Breathe in. Breathe out. Move on.

I shake the past off and continue forward like nothing happened, trying to ignore how I'm breathing faster and the way my muscles are twitching to punch something. I clench and unclench my fists, wishing I was at my gym in front of a bag.

The second thing that makes the memories stop?

Fighting.

In a few steps I reach my car, a Toyota so new it doesn't have plates yet. Once I'm inside, I grip the steering wheel hard until my pulse slows and I catch my breath. The therapist Adam convinced me to see told me this kind of thing is normal for someone who's been through a traumatic experience, but that doesn't make it any easier to live with.

And at the moment, the flashbacks are the least of my problems.

The black car hovers in my rearview mirror, dark and dangerous. As I pull away from the curb, it follows. I could try to lose it, but what's the point? They know where I live. They know where I go to school. They can come for me anytime they want, and there's not a damn thing I can do to stop them.

* * *

The car quits following me two blocks from the tattoo parlor, but I don't feel safe until I'm inside my apartment with the door locked behind me. Even then, it's only the illusion of safety. Today they let me go, but I know it's just a matter of time before they come for me.

I toss my keys onto the table in the entry, drop my bag on the hardwood floor, and collapse onto the soft, gray couch in my living room.

I love those words. *My living room.*

After years of being in foster care, moving from place to place all the time, and having zero control over where I lived, it's the greatest feeling in the world to finally have a home of my own. One that *I* chose.

It's nothing special, just a small one-bedroom apartment I'm renting for a year. I could have bought a condo or even a house with the money I got from Aether Corp, but that felt *too* permanent. I'm still getting used to a life where everything isn't temporary.

And with that black car following me around, I don't trust Aether not to take it all away.

I stare at the popcorn ceiling and run through my memories for the hundredth time, trying to figure out if I missed something, hoping to find an explanation stored away in my brain for why Aether is watching me.

Six months ago, they sent me—and four other teenagers—thirty years into the future for twenty-four hours. The goal was to collect data and technology so they could reverse engineer it after we returned. But it didn't work out that way.

We broke the rule Aether gave us to not look into our own futures and learned we were going to be murdered when we got back to the present—and all evidence pointed to *me* as the killer. Only by trusting Adam, one of the other time travelers on my team, was I able to uncover the real murderer.

Lynne, the project manager for the time-travel experiment, had been secretly working with Adam to bring back something his future self developed: the cure for cancer. Lynne wanted it for her daughter, who was dying and didn't have much time left. But once

Adam brought the cure back to the present to save his mother, the three others on our team—Chris, Trent, and Zoe—stole it. They thought they could use it as leverage to ensure they wouldn't be killed, but Lynne tracked them down and shot them to get it back. The final step of her plan was to kill me and frame me for the murders as a cover-up.

With Adam's help, I was able to change the timeline and stop Lynne, but I wasn't able to save Trent or Zoe—and their deaths continue to haunt me. I failed them. I have to live with that. Forever.

Lynne's death is on my hands too. I'm the one who shot her. It was self-defense, but that does little to ease my conscience in the middle of the night.

Even though Aether Corporation had nothing to do with Lynne's secret agenda or the others' deaths, they could be trying to dig up the truth about what happened the night of the murders. Or maybe it has nothing to do with Lynne and the murders, and everything to do with Aether's other secret: future shock.

Our team discovered that Aether Corp sent time travelers to the future before us, and the ones who returned suffered future shock, which causes paranoia, memory loss, and delusions. They chose the five of us because they believed teenage brains might be immune to future shock—and they were right. None of us had any of the side effects when we returned to the present. But to protect ourselves, we lied about everything and told them we *were* suffering from it.

Now I wonder if Aether knows, or at least suspects, that we lied. Are they following us to see if we've recovered our memories or if we're suffering from any side effects? Or are they making sure we don't break the confidentiality agreement and tell everyone what they did—and how three people are dead as a result?

No matter how many times I go over it, I have no more answers than I did before. Until they come for me, I won't know what they're after.

I grab my bag and pull out my statistics textbook to read this week's assigned chapters, hoping that will distract me. Maybe if I pretend I'm just an average college student, I'll start to believe it.

At 7:14 p.m., there's a knock on my door. I jerk upright, and my textbook hits the floor with a thud. My fists clench, my heart thunders, and I'm instantly in fight-or-flight mode.

Knowing me, it'll be fight.

I already suspect who's on the other side, but I can't help this response. Ever since I came back from future, this is how my body reacts to everything. I'm always on alert, ready for an attack, expecting the worst.

I open the door. Adam waits outside my apartment, carrying a bag of takeout, and the tension drains out of my body instantly. His dark hair is messy and wet, hanging down almost to his black-rimmed glasses. A faint trace of stubble lines his jaw, like he forgot to shave for a day or two. My heart lifts as his blue eyes meet mine and a grin crosses his lips.

"I brought dinner," he says, holding up the large brown bag. Chinese food, from the smell, probably from my favorite place down the road. Even though I knew he was coming, it's still a surprise to see him. I keep expecting that one day he'll stop showing up. Or that he'll walk out of my life like everyone else has. But he hasn't vanished yet.

"My hero." I take the bag from him, leaning close to give him a kiss. I mean it to be quick, but he slides a hand around my waist and pulls me closer, against his chest. With my free hand, I grip his shirt, clinging to him as our kiss grows deeper, and everything else fades away except this moment. The past can't hurt me, not when I'm in his arms.

Adam is the third thing that makes the memories stop.

"I missed you," he whispers as we pull apart.

I should say it back, but instead I reach up to grab a dark lock hanging down his forehead. "Your hair is wet."

"I did some laps after class."

Adam's a swimmer, but like me with kickboxing, he doesn't do it to stay in shape. He does it because he says it helps him think. Or, I suspect, to forget.

We each have our ways of coping with what happened to us. Adam swims laps for hours. I beat the shit out of things.

He steps into the apartment, and his dark eyebrows jump up. "So did you get it?"

"Yeah." I pull back my sleeve to show him the tattoo. My arm throbs with a dull, yet constant pain, similar to a bad sunburn, but the design looks good. The origami unicorn is just like the one he made for me when we first met, like the one his future self gave me as a clue.

"Wow. I can't believe you did it." He adjusts his glasses as he examines the tattoo but doesn't touch the angry, inflamed skin lined with black ink. I can't tell from his expression or voice whether he likes it or not.

"I have lots of tattoos." I shrug and turn away, but my throat is tight with unsaid emotion. Maybe I shouldn't have gotten it. I'm not sure what I was thinking, anyway. I'd do anything to forget what happened to us, and instead I got a reminder branded right on my skin. But Adam is one of the few things in my life worth remembering.

Once in the kitchen, I pull out some plates for the food, avoiding his eyes the entire time. Adam moves behind me as I unpack the plastic containers, sliding his arms around my waist. "It's beautiful," he says. "Like you."

I close my eyes and lean back against him, relieved. He brushes my hair away and presses a kiss to my neck, his hands skimming up and down my sides. Adam is the first guy in a long time who can touch me without making me flinch. The only person I let get this close.

"I love it." He spins me around to face him, and his eyes are intense as they search my face. "And I lo—"

Every muscle in my body tightens up, and I jerk away from him. "I'm starving," I say, forcing a smile. "Getting tattooed always makes me hungry."

His face falls, but he's used to me pushing him away by now and he recovers quickly. "That's probably an aftereffect from the endorphin rush of getting a tattoo. Your blood sugar—"

I place a finger on his lips. "I don't need a science lecture, Dr. O'Neill."

"I don't have my PhD yet."

"You will soon enough."

"True," he says, but his voice has shifted. He begins opening the plastic food containers, but his face is tight. Closed off. Because of me.

We serve ourselves and sit on the couch in silence with our plates. He's ordered all of my favorite dishes without even having to ask. He's the perfect boyfriend, and I can't help but keep him at arm's length. Especially when it seems like he might break out the *L* word.

As I eat, I notice he's distracted, staring off into the distance with a frown, but I get the feeling it's not only me he's upset with. There's something else on his mind.

"What's wrong?" I ask.

He blinks and then he's back with me again, giving me a small smile. "Nothing. I told them not to put peas in the fried rice 'cause I know you hate them. But it's just not the same."

"Liar."

"I'd never lie about Chinese food."

"Not that." I study him for a long moment. "Is your mom okay?"

"Yeah, she's fine. She went to the doctor the other day, and he said the cancer has completely vanished from her system. The cure really worked."

Despite his words, his frown has returned, and I lightly bump against his side. "Tell me what's bothering you."

He sets his plate on the coffee table, his food untouched, and scrubs his face with his hands. "I was volunteering at the hospital today, and another girl died. She was only eight."

I almost drop my fork. Not this again. "Adam..."

"If I'd created the cure already, she'd still be alive."

"It took your future self over ten years to create the cure," I remind him for what feels like the hundredth time. "It's only been six months. You haven't even finished school yet!"

"My future self spent half his time trying to solve your murder, but I can focus solely on developing the cure, and I can get it done faster. I know I can."

"After you get your PhD—"

"Over eight million people die every single year from cancer. In ten years, that's almost a hundred million lives I could save. I have to do it sooner. I *have* to." He runs a hand through his hair, his eyes tortured. "If only I'd kept some of the cure we brought back, I could have studied it. I could have—"

"Stop." I rest my hand on his knee. "Some things can't be rushed.

Not if you want to do them right."

"I know." His shoulders slump, and the fight seems to have gone out of him. After a moment of staring at nothing, he picks up his plate again and starts eating, but I know he's not going to listen to me. Adam will never give up trying to save the world, even if he pushes himself too hard in the process. I just have to make sure he doesn't burn himself out by trying to speed up the future.

"How was your day?" he asks, wisely changing the subject.

I hesitate, but I can't bear to bring up the black car or my near panic attack, not now. Besides, it's not like anything new happened today with the car. It follows Adam too, although not as often as it follows me. If I mention the car, it will only worry him. And he definitely doesn't need to know I thought I saw Zoe in the street.

"Fine, except I swear my statistics teacher is trying to confuse us on purpose so we all fail," I say, keeping my tone light. "Nothing he says makes any damn sense."

"Hmm. I always liked statistics."

"Of course you did. Maybe you can explain it to me."

He points his chopsticks at me. "Since when do you need my help with school? You're the one with the eidetic memory. Pretty sure you could ace all of your classes without even trying."

"My other classes maybe, but not this one." I stab my fork at my kung pao chicken. No chopsticks for me. I still can't seem to master them, no matter how many times Adam has tried to show me how to use them. My fingers just won't cooperate. "Just 'cause I remember what he says doesn't mean I understand half of it."

"I'd be happy to tutor you after dinner."

"Thanks." There he goes again, being too good to me. My stomach twists, and I set my fork down, unable to eat another bite.

Adam and I shouldn't be together. We're total opposites with completely different lives. He's a genius who graduated from college at sixteen with two degrees, and his future involves curing cancer and winning a Nobel Prize. Me? My father's in prison for killing my mother. I've spent the last couple years living in a different home every few months. And until recently I didn't have a future at all.

If we hadn't been recruited by Aether Corp for the time-travel experiment, we never would have met. The fact that we're dating—that he could possibly be interested in someone like me—completely mystifies me. Every day I worry he's going to wake up and wonder what the hell he's doing with a wreck like me when he could do so much better.

This thing between us can never last. I should end it now before I get hurt. Before *he* gets hurt. But I can't let Adam go. I care about him too much.

And so we remain, trapped in this strange limbo where he takes one step forward and I take another back. A never-ending dance that leaves us both unsatisfied.

* * *

The dream is always the same.

There's a bloated, white hand in the dumpster. The stench nearly overpowers me, but I reach inside, digging through the trash and rotten food, trying to find him. I have to get him out. I have to save him before it's too late.

The hand suddenly jerks to life and grips my arm in its stiff, icy fingers. I scream and try to pull away, to pry them off me, but it's no use. No matter how hard I fight, the hand won't let go—and then it pulls me into the dumpster with the body. I see it clearly now as the trash surrounds me: the too-pale skin and glassy eyes of this thing that used to be Trent. He opens his mouth, the teeth all black, and says, "You're too late, Elena."

And then the dumpster is a bathtub, but the water is as cold as his hand was. Not just water, but blood. It drips down bone-white tiles and fills the tub like thick, red paint. In only seconds I'm drowning in it, choking on it, struggling to get out. But as I try to stand, another clammy hand pulls me down by the ankle. Zoe's head emerges from the bloody water, her skin almost as blue as her hair, her eyes bulging. She whispers, "Help me, Elena."

And then I'm in the ocean, drowning in pitch-black salt water, my bones so cold I can barely move at all. My head crests the surface and I take a deep, ragged breath of air, but another dead hand grips my neck, and the face in front of me is Lynne's this time. Panic shoots through me and I fight, but she's too strong. She chokes me with frozen, bony fingers and her mouth opens—

"Elena, wake up. It's just a dream."

Adam's calm voice breaks through the darkness, and I open my eyes. We're on my couch, where we fell asleep while watching a superhero movie. His warm arms are wrapped around me, holding me to his chest. The water, the hands, the death…none of it is real.

The dream releases its grip on me, and I bury my face in his neck, clinging to his strong, solid presence. Cold sweat soaks through my T-shirt. Adrenaline pumps through my veins and makes me twitch, like my skin is about to jump off and run away without the rest of me. I'm safe, but I can't convince my body of that.

"Adam," I whisper, needing to feel his name on my tongue, to hold on to the one good, normal thing in my life.

He kisses my forehead, his arms tightening around me. "It's okay. It's over. I've got you."

I take a long, shuddering breath and try to relax. Adam rubs a hand up and down my back. Thank God he's still here. It's so much worse when I wake up alone.

"Was it the same dream?" he asks once my heart rate has returned to normal and I no longer grip him like he's the only thing that will save me from drowning. My throat feels too scratchy to speak, so I only nod. "Maybe you should see that therapist again," he says.

I sit up, loosening myself from his arms. "I can't do that."

"Why not? It seemed to help."

It did help, at first. The therapist convinced me to try kickboxing as a way to manage my rage and control my tendency to punch first and think later. She explained that I was suffering from a form of post-traumatic stress disorder after what I'd been through, and my eidetic memory only made it worse. She gave me some tips for dealing with it, but could only do so much for me when I couldn't be honest with her about *why* I was having the panic attacks, flashbacks, and nightmares. If I told her I'd been to the future, she'd think I was having delusions and would probably make me take all sorts of pills or something. I wasn't doing that. And if I couldn't talk about what had really happened, what was the point?

There are only two people in the world who can possibly understand what I've been through. Adam is one of them, but he's also the last person I want to talk to about this. If he knew how messed up I was, he would leave me in an instant. And Chris? He's moved on, as best as he can anyway. I won't drag him back into the past.

When I don't answer, Adam takes my hand in his. "You can talk to me, you know. About anything. Maybe I can help."

I pull my hand out of his grasp. "You can't fix me, Adam."

"Of course not. Because you're not broken."

That's where he's wrong. But I'm too tired to argue, and I appreciate that he's trying, even if I suck at showing it. I lean against him and close my eyes. "Stay tonight. Please."

Adams's eyebrows shoot up but without another word, he takes me into the bedroom. I slide under the covers, and he takes off his shirt and curls up against my back, his arm draped around my waist as if he can shield me while I sleep. I don't usually let him stay over, but as much as I hate admitting it, I need him tonight.

His breathing evens out behind me, but I can't fall asleep again. Every time I close my eyes, I see blood and pale hands and dark water. I stare at the clock beside my bed, watching the numbers tick over, minute by minute.

It wasn't always like this. For a while, everything between us was perfect. We'd spend our long summer days after my high school graduation doing something fun, pretending we were a normal couple. Picking out furniture for my brand-new apartment. Binge-watching his favorite TV shows with his dog, Max, sprawled between us. Doing all the silly tourist things people who grew up in LA never actually do. We even scheduled our college classes this semester so we'd both have Fridays off.

But after that day at the beach, something shifted between us.

It wasn't the same beach where I was supposed to die, of course. I still can't go back there, or to the pier. But I wanted to prove I had moved on, and Adam knew of a spot north of Malibu that was secluded, where we could have a romantic picnic in the sand.

Bad traffic on PCH made us late, and the sun had set by time we got there. I braved it anyway, pretending I was fine, but when we passed the lifeguard tower, the memories came back in a rush. Fighting Lynne while the black waves reached toward us. The gun going off in my hand and echoing across the stars. Her body slumping down into the pale sand.

I had my first panic attack that night.

The nightmares started after that. The flashbacks got worse and worse. I started pushing Adam away, ignoring his calls and texts, declining his invitations to hang out, and was distant when we did see each other. That's when Adam convinced me to talk to someone, and I began to spend my Fridays with the therapist. The rift between us started to heal, but it wasn't enough. I stopped going to therapy a few weeks later.

Going to the future was supposed to fix everything—and on paper, my life probably does seem perfect. For the first time, I have money and freedom, a loving boyfriend, and a future.

The problem is me.

FRIDAY

The red numbers of the clock read 6:06 a.m. I've tossed and turned all night, grasping at sleep but unable to catch more than a handful of it. I might as well get up. I can hit the 7:00 a.m. kickboxing class and burn off some of this frustration.

I run the shower at a near-scalding temperature, and it washes away the lingering cold from the dream. When I'm done, Adam's awake, tugging his shirt back on over his toned chest, his hair adorably messy. Heat flickers inside me with a rush of desire, and I'm tempted to cross the room to him, to drag him back into bed and cover him with kisses. Instead I look away, my throat tight.

"What's your plan for today?" he asks as he grabs his glasses off the bedside table.

"Homework. Kickboxing. The usual." I shrug. "You?"

"Working in the lab. Swimming. The usual." He tilts his head with a tentative smile. "Hey, I have an idea. Let's ditch all that and spend the day together doing something fun. Like we used to."

I guess I'm not the only one with the past on my mind. "What would we do?"

"We could...go to the zoo?"

"The *zoo*?"

"Sure. I haven't been there since I was a kid, and I heard there's a new koala baby."

I don't answer at first. I'm not sure if it's possible for things to go back to the way they were before, but it'd be nice to have one day where we pretend everything is normal between us. "Well, how can I say no to that?"

"Exactly. You can't. No one can say no to baby koalas. We should grab breakfast at that diner on the corner with the cinnamon pancakes and then head over."

His enthusiasm makes me smile, and when we head outside, I start to think it might be a good day after all.

But the black car is waiting for us.

It's parked on the curb, right in front of my apartment. The passenger door opens. My hand grabs Adam's, and the other one clenches into a fist. They came for us. I knew they would.

A man steps out of the car. He's Indian, with hints of gray in his wavy black hair, and he wears a white lab coat. Dr. Rajesh Kapur, a scientist from Aether Corporation. One of the people who sent us to the future before.

He gives us each a nod. "Adam, Elena—we need you to come with us."

"Why?" The word escapes my lips in a rush. I always knew they would never let us walk away from the project. It was too easy, too fast, too clean. Something like what we went through never completely goes away.

"What's this about?" Adam asks.

"We'd like to speak to you about some potential complications," Dr. Kapur says. He clasps his hands behind his back and appears calm, but his eyes survey the street at all times.

"What complications?" I ask. Does this have to do with my flashbacks and nightmares? Or something else entirely? A thousand possibilities run through my head, each worse than the last.

His gaze sweeps the area again. "Please, get in the car. This isn't something we can discuss out here on the street."

I shake my head. "I'm not going anywhere with you. Not until you tell me what's going on, and why you've been following us all this time."

His face is a mask, his voice even, betraying nothing. "We'll explain everything once you reach the facility."

"But—"

Adam squeezes my hand. "I think we should go with him and hear them out."

My mouth drops open. How can he be so calm? He's always trusted Aether more than I have, but I can't be the only one with the creeping sensation down my spine that signals something is wrong. Why are they coming for us now after all this time? What's changed?

"What about Chris?" I ask.

"Another car is picking him up," Dr. Kapur says, as he opens the door to the backseat. "This won't take more than a few hours. We'll have you home before dinner."

The last thing I want to do is get in that black car. I've spent the past six months trying to get away from Aether Corp, to live a normal life after their experiment, and to forget what they did to us—and now they're drawing us back in again.

"It'll be fine," Adam says to me. I search his eyes but don't see the same fear and hesitation currently twisting in my gut. Maybe I'm being paranoid. That was something the therapist warned me about too.

And what can we do but go with them? We need to find out what this is about. Once again, they're giving us no real choice but to comply.

We get in the car.

* * *

Dr. Kapur sits in the front with a driver sporting a buzz cut. He refuses to say another word to us during the long drive to the Aether Corp facility where the time-travel experiment—Project Chronos—was conducted. Adam and I sit in the backseat in silence, and through the windows we watch Los Angeles fade away and the desert begin.

Over an hour later, we get off the freeway and approach the metal fence. Dread fills my stomach with battery acid as the security guard waves us through and the gate opens. The facility looms before us, corporate and cold, and it terrifies me despite its benign appearance. With its gray walls, tinted windows, and perfectly trimmed grass, you'd never guess what kind of experiments occur down in the basement.

As we pull up in front of the building, I have to resist the urge to throw open the car door and start running. This time, there's no Lynne to meet us at the entrance. Instead, another woman waits outside the building in a white lab coat.

She holds her hand out to me when I step out of the car. "I'm Dr. Ronnie Campbell. A pleasure to meet you."

Her handshake is firm but not too tight. She's black, with tight curls and a nervous smile, maybe ten or fifteen years older than me and Adam. Probably just out of medical school, or whatever she did to earn the *Dr.* in front of her name.

"Can you tell us why we're here?" Adam asks while he shakes her hand.

Her smile falters, and her eyes dart behind us to Dr. Kapur. "Everything will be explained soon. Follow me, please."

She leads us into the building, and I have to force my legs to follow her inside. The lobby is exactly as I remember it: bamboo, shiny floors, big Aether logo, and a frizzy-haired receptionist behind the desk. With every step, my heart rate spikes even higher, and every instinct tells me to get the hell out of here. Beside me, Adam's face is a tight mask, but he keeps walking. We stand together as the elevator rises, and I mentally brace for whatever is coming. It can't be good, not if they rushed us here without an explanation.

During the ride here, I came up with a dozen scenarios for why they would call us back in and what they might want to talk about. I'm convinced they've figured out we were lying about future shock, or that they know about the cancer cure somehow and want it for themselves. Or maybe there's some medical risk caused by the time machine, and they're bringing us in as a precaution. But I think it's more than that.

I always expect the worst.

We walk down the hall, and they stick us in the same freezing conference room as before. At least we're not subjected to hours of medical tests this time. So far, anyway.

"Wait here, please," Dr. Campbell says. "It should only be a few minutes." She nods to Dr. Kapur, and they both leave the room, shutting the door behind them. Adam and I are alone, but we still can't speak freely—they're watching us and probably recording everything.

I scan the room, looking for clues, for cameras, for anything. But the place reveals nothing. It's set up like it was before with chairs all facing one direction, but they haven't bothered feeding us. Guess they don't need to impress us this time. They've already caught us in their web, and I'm starting to think they're never going to let us go.

Adam gives me a weak smile. "This is where we met."

"Not exactly your normal boy-meets-girl story."

"No, but it's *our* story."

My gaze snaps back to him. He's still so calm. Making jokes. Being cute. How? "You know something about why we're here, don't you?"

He holds up his hands. "Nope. I'm as clueless as you are."

I cross my arms and stare out the window at the freeway in the distance buzzing with cars. I can't tell if he's lying or if I'm being paranoid again. Am I pushing him away because of my own fears, when I should be turning to him for comfort instead? Or am I justified in being suspicious?

The door opens, and in walks a muscular black guy with a shaved head and tattoos inked across his huge arms. *Chris*. He looks pissed and just as confused as I am. But when he sees us, his face softens, and a grin cracks the surface of his otherwise hard features.

"Hey," Chris says, crossing the room toward us. "Any idea what this is about?"

"Not a clue," I say.

"Damn." He scowls, but then he grabs Adam in one of those guy hugs, thumping him on the back. He reaches for me next, pulling me in for a real hug, even though he knows I hate them. "Been too long, you two. Too damn long."

I find myself hugging him back, and realize how much I've missed his solid presence. Even though we all promised to stay close after we returned from the future, Adam and I haven't seen Chris in a few months. We used to get together regularly and hang out, but I suppose we just…drifted apart. My fault, no doubt. Like my relationship with Adam, I neglected my friendship with Chris too.

"How's Shawnda?" Adam asks.

"About ready to pop. Crazy, right?" He grabs his phone and flicks through it. "Check this out."

He thrusts the phone in our faces and shows us a picture of the baby's room. It's done in powder blue with cartoon cars all over the walls, blankets, and crib. There's even a lamp decorated to match.

"That's perfect," Adam says. Chris loves cars—he used to work as a mechanic, and now he's getting an engineering degree so he can design them.

"Isn't it?" Chris can't stop grinning. I've never seen him this excited before. He takes the phone back and pulls up another photo, this one of a recent ultrasound. "Look at my son! Isn't he handsome?"

"Very," I say, even though it mostly looks like a grayish blob with something that could be eyes and maybe some fingers. "When is Shawnda due?"

"Monday. Any day now I'm going to be a dad." He chuckles as he says it, his eyes dancing.

Adam clasps him on the back. "You're going to be a great father."

"I hope so." He runs a hand over his bare head. "I'm planning to take a semester or two off from school so I can help Shawnda with the baby and all that. Plus, she wants to go to nursing school. It might be a while before I graduate, but whatever. It's not like we're strapped for cash at the moment."

"Doing the stay-at-home dad thing?" I ask, raising my eyebrows.

He gives a slight shrug. "Yeah, for a few months at least. I don't want to miss out on anything. I never knew my dad, but my son is going to grow up with a father who is around. Shawnda and I are going to do it right."

Chris is only nineteen, but I have no doubt he'll be the kind of husband and father his son can look up to. Other than our ill-fated trip through time, the three of us have something else in common: all of our fathers abandoned us in some way. Mine's in prison for murdering my mother, Adam's dad has a second family in another state, and Chris never knew his. His determination to not become like his father is something I relate to a lot.

At first, Chris and I didn't get along. We were always butting heads, and one time he punched me in the face and I pulled a gun on him. He and Adam got off to a rocky start too. But we put all that behind us, and now the three of us have a bond that comes from surviving something impossible, something no one else could understand. We'll always be there for each other, no matter what happens next.

"When are you getting married?" Adam asks. Last time we saw Chris, he'd just gotten engaged.

Chris slips the phone in his back pocket. "Soon, I hope. Although Shawnda wants to wait 'til she loses the baby weight or something like that."

"Congrats," I say. "New house, new wife, new baby…Your life seems perfect."

"Yeah, it was." He eyes the room with suspicion, his frown returning. "Until Aether showed up outside my house this morning."

The door opens, and a man I've only seen before in the news walks in, followed by Dr. Campbell and Dr. Kapur. He takes his place in front of the room and exudes confidence, with thick auburn hair, a strong jaw, and an expensive three-piece suit. There's no sign of Dr. Walters, the other scientist we worked with before.

"Thank you for coming," the man says, addressing the three of us. "I'm Vincent Sharp, CEO and founder of Aether Corporation."

Even though I recognize him, it's hard to wrap my head around the fact that Vincent Sharp is standing here in front of us. The guy is a freaking billionaire, like *Forbes* richest-people-in-the-world kind of billionaire, on the same level as Bill Gates and Mark Zuckerberg. Plus, he's a genius, one of those guys who dropped out of college to start up a tech company that later became an international powerhouse. I read an article earlier this year about how he spent his fiftieth birthday on his own private island.

Why would he want to meet with us? Even when we spoke to some of the Aether higher-ups about what had happened with Lynne, we never heard anything from him. This must be something serious if the CEO has gotten involved. They're probably worried about a lawsuit.

He shakes our hands, one by one, with a big smile. It's not predatory but charming, friendly, like we're all equals. "You already know Dr. Kapur, of course. And I believe you met Dr. Campbell? Excellent." He answers his own question. Probably used to people agreeing with him all the time.

He leans back against the table, clasping his hands in front of him, disarmingly casual in his pose. "First, I want to thank you all for your help a few months ago, and I'd like to apologize again for the tragic incident with Lynne Marshall."

Tragic incident, my ass. I'm ready to be done with this crap and get to the point already. "Why are we here?"

His gaze lands on me. It's not hostile, but reminds me of when Adam focuses on me, with intelligent eyes that seem to see everything, like they're taking notes and calculating what I'll do next. But Adam's gaze doesn't creep me out.

"Direct," Vincent says. "Exactly what I expected from you, Elena." I must look surprised, because he chuckles. "I've studied all of your files closely. We may never have met before, but I know all of you *very* well."

He makes it sound like this should be comforting, but instead it makes me even more freaked out. I hate that he knows so much about me, probably more than I can ever guess at. They had a file on us before they recruited us for Project Chronos, and they've been watching us since it ended. I wonder how much they saw and heard over the last six months. Adam always insisted they wouldn't keep tabs on us, but Chris and I suspected otherwise. Now Vincent's basically admitted he's been spying on us.

"Where's Dr. Walters?" Adam asks. Dr. Walters was the one scientist on the other project who seemed halfway decent, and it's troubling that he isn't here.

There's a brief pause. Dr. Campbell and Dr. Kapur exchange a glance while Vincent says, "He no longer works for Aether Corporation. Dr. Campbell has taken over his position." There's a brief awkward pause, but then Vincent smiles again and says, "Dr. Kapur, can you take it from here?"

Dr. Kapur gives a sharp nod and turns to the three of us. "In the months since you returned from the future, we've learned there might be some unexpected side effects that we couldn't have predicted."

"What do you mean?" Adam asks.

"Side effects other than future shock?" I ask. We have to keep up the illusion that we all had future shock, after all. Even though I have a feeling they know we lied about that.

"We theorize that beyond the normal effects of future shock you experienced, you may also experience some...additional symptoms," Dr. Kapur says.

"Shit, do *not* tell me this," Chris says, crossing his massive arms.

"I cannot handle this right now."

"What kind of symptoms?" I manage to get out. My throat feels so tight that every word has to be dragged out of me.

"Nausea. Anxiety. Hearing or vision loss." Dr. Kapur's face is impassive as he speaks, but my gut clenches. I've had some of those. Not the vision or hearing loss, but the other symptoms for sure. "It's probably nothing to worry about, but to be safe, we'd like to run some quick tests on you. It shouldn't take more than a few hours."

"Tests?" Adam asks.

"Nothing too invasive. A few blood tests and X-rays. We'll get them done fast and have your results by tomorrow."

Behind him, Dr. Campbell's face scrunches up. She looks like she wants to say something but is biting her tongue. They must be holding something back, something she wants to tell us but isn't allowed to. I meet her eyes and she looks away, her brows pinched together, her lips tight. This worries me more than anything the others are saying.

Are nausea and anxiety symptoms of a much more serious problem? Will the hearing and vision loss come next? And have Adam and Chris been experiencing these all along too?

Everything about this feels wrong, but I'm not sure why or how. I'm not thrilled at the idea of more tests, especially when they'll tell us so little. And I don't trust a damn thing anyone at this corporation says. For good reason.

But what other choice do we have? Walk away and possibly suffer some terrible fate? Live the rest of our lives waiting for more impending problems to surface? No, better to go through with this and find out what they know—and how to protect ourselves from it.

"Let's get it over with," Chris says, echoing my thoughts.

* * *

We're led to the third floor and separated into different exam rooms to wait for a nurse to start the blood tests. I sit on the edge of the crinkling paper-covered bed and study the room, but there's not much to see. White walls. A tray with vials and other equipment on the counter. A sink and a poster reminding employees to wash their hands. Frigid air blasts down on my bare arms from an overhead vent, and I rub them while I wait.

A few minutes later, Dr. Kapur enters the room and shuts the door behind him. It's the second time I've been alone in an exam room with him, and I'm just as creeped out now as I was the first time. I keep telling myself it'll be fine, but I can't shake the feeling that this is all wrong, that I need to do something—but what?

He examines something on a clipboard, then flips to the next page. He hasn't said a word to me, like I'm not even there. Then he utters a quiet "Hmm."

"Something wrong?" I ask. Why is he here instead of a nurse, anyway?

"Not at all." He slaps the blood pressure cuff on my arm, and I barely flinch this time. After he gets the reading, he checks my heartbeat with his stethoscope and ticks things off on his chart.

"Have you noticed any memory loss since we last saw you?" he asks.

"No."

"What about any sort of physical pain or discomfort?"

"No."

"Very good."

I expect more questions, like about vision or hearing loss, but he turns toward the counter, where needles and vials are waiting to draw my blood. He instructs me to hold out my forearm and make a fist so he can reach the vein at my inside elbow, then rubs the area with alcohol. I brace myself for the prick of the needle, for the blood to flow out of me, but instead he reaches past the vials and grabs a nearby syringe full of milky-white liquid. My gut screams again that this is wrong, wrong, wrong. "What—"

He stabs the syringe into my arm and injects me before I can react. Pain shoots up my veins with the invading liquid, and I push him back with a hard shove. I jump to my feet and yank the syringe out, tossing it on the floor. "What was that?"

He stands back and watches me with narrow eyes. The world seems to go hazy.

Oh my God, what has he done? What did he inject me with?

What is really going on here?

I turn to the door, reaching for the knob, but my fingers are numb. My knees weaken. The room spins.

And then, darkness.

* * *

When my eyes open, I'm on the floor, palms pressed into concrete, legs sprawled at an awkward angle. Someone groans to my right. I blink, struggling to focus, trying to figure out where I am and what the hell is going on.

The needle. Dr. Kapur. Oh God.

I try to get up quickly, but my head throbs and I'm so tired, so weak. I crumble back to the floor and focus on breathing, willing strength into my limbs. I need to pull myself together as fast as possible so I can get out of here. Wherever *here* is.

"Elena," Adam says beside me, his voice low and rough. He sounds as dazed as I am. I reach toward him, groping around until I find his arm, his hand. As soon as my fingers tangle with his, I feel stronger. Where are we? What have they done to us?

I slowly sit up, and my vision begins to clear. Adam's on my right; Chris is on my left. Chris is still out cold, but Adam's awake, and he gazes at our surroundings in horror.

We're in a small metal dome, big enough for five people to stand in and not much more than that. It's a place I recognize, although I really wish I didn't.

We're inside the accelerator—the machine that sent us to the future.

I stagger to my feet, and something between a choke and a scream escapes my throat. No, God, no. Why are we in here again? How?

The room seems to tilt and grow darker. Panic squeezes my throat. I can't stop the flashbacks from flooding my mind, and I press my palms into my eyes, trying to block it all out. The accelerator. The future. Rain and police and adrenaline-fueled escapes. Cold, dead hands and blood dripping into water. Gunshots and salty air and oh God oh God oh God, this can't be happening again, it can't it can't *it can't.*

I rush to the door and try to open it, but it's locked. Adam's behind me a second later. Our fists pound on the door and we both yell, but no one answers. Our words are incoherent, our voices strained, our pleas desperate, but they're not enough to get a response.

I press my back against the door and sink to the floor, choking on a dry heave. I can't breathe. Tears leak from my eyes. Adam keeps pounding on the door, and the banging echoes around us: *clank clank clank.*

That's when I notice I'm wearing different clothes. My T-shirt and jeans are gone, replaced with a black jacket and tank top, cargo pants, and combat boots. Adam and Chris are wearing clothes similar to mine. That means someone *undressed* us while we were unconscious.

I cover my mouth but still gag from the repulsion at being so violated, so helpless. They knocked us out, changed our clothes, and locked us inside here against our will. Was everything they said about possible symptoms and complications a lie, just to get us in here again?

I drop my head between my knees and focus on breathing, like the therapist taught me, but I can't stop dry heaving. What I really want is to punch something. *Someone*.

Either the sound of Adam banging on the door or my panicked noises finally wake Chris. I see it the moment he realizes where we are, when he discovers what they've done to us. When it hits him what they're *going* to do to us.

He lets out a primal yell and charges the door, like a football player rushing toward the goal, but all he does is crash into the metal with a heavy *thud*. There's no way out. We're trapped.

My head clears of the leftover fog from whatever they drugged me with, and it really hits me: they locked us in here for a reason. They're sending us to the future again.

Vincent Sharp's voice is broadcast around us, echoing through the dome. "Please relax. We don't want you to injure yourselves."

"What have you done?" I force myself to my feet and spin around, looking everywhere, addressing the cameras that must be watching us. We have no way of seeing out, but they can see *us*. I'm sure of it. "Why have you locked us in here?"

"We need your help," Vincent says.

"Hell no." Chris practically spits the words, his fists clenched at his side. "No fucking way."

"Help with what?" Adam asks, his voice steady somehow.

There's no answer at first, only silence, but then the words boom through the metal walls. "We need you to return to the future."

At first I can only stand there with my mouth hanging open, too stunned to speak. His words won't sink in. "You locked us in here," I say slowly. "You changed our clothes. And you want us to go *back* to the future? No way. Not in a million years."

"I know this must be very upsetting for you, but please hear me out," Vincent says. "Over the past few months, we've been sending another team of time travelers to the future."

Another team? They promised to shut down the program after what happened with us. Dr. Walters swore he would destroy the accelerator. And yet, here we are, trapped inside it. I should have known better than to believe Aether would really stop trying to chase the future. I just never thought they would get us to help them again.

"The first few missions went well," Vincent continues. "The team brought back technology and information from the future for us to study. We had no problems at all. Until now."

Idiots. Of course they would have problems eventually. Going to the future isn't like heading to the store to pick up something for dinner. It's an entirely different world full of new technology, unknown laws, and the most dangerous thing of all—the temptation to find out your own fate.

"We sent the team to the future last night for the third time," Vincent says. "None of them returned through the aperture. We need the three of you to travel to the future, find the other team, and bring them back."

I can't help it. I laugh. A mad, wild laugh that I can't control, that sounds a lot like a sob. But really, what other response is there?

"This is crazy," Chris says, crossing his arms. "There's no way in hell we're doing this."

"What about future shock?" Adam asks.

A second later, Dr. Kapur's voice comes through the speakers. "We've confirmed that younger people can handle the effects of traveling through time much better than adults can, due to the fact that teenage brains are still in development, particularly in the prefrontal cortex. The cutoff age for future shock seems to be at about twenty years of age, so you will all be safe."

The three of us glance at each other, and Adam clears his throat. "But we *did* have future shock..."

"We know that was a lie," Dr. Kapur snaps. "There's no reason for you to keep pretending."

"How?" Adam asks.

"After studying your medical tests and interviews, we knew something didn't add up. You all reacted much differently from how our previous subjects did, and there was no physical evidence you were suffering from future shock. Your brain scans were all normal, and you showed no long-term side effects in the months that followed. It didn't take us long to realize you weren't being honest with us."

I should have seen this coming. In the future we visited, Aether shut down Project Chronos because I killed the others and myself, which they believed was a result of future shock. But we changed the timeline when we got back to the present, and with Lynne exposed as the killer and most of us still alive, Aether figured out we were lying and decided to try going to the future again with another team.

"Is this why you've been watching us?" I ask. "To see if we really had future shock?"

Vincent Sharp answers this time. "That was one of the reasons, yes. We also wanted to monitor your health and make sure you didn't break the confidentiality agreement."

"Screw your confidentiality agreement!" Chris yells. "We're not going to the future. End of story. So open this door and let us go." He bangs on it again, and the sound resonates throughout the entire chamber.

"I'm sorry, but I can't do that," Vincent says. "You *will* be going to the future."

"Why us?" I ask. "Why not get someone else to go?"

"Unfortunately, it has to be you. You're the only other team we have right now."

"Then find another one!"

"It's not as easy to find willing teenagers as you might imagine, especially with the right skills. But even if we could, I want the three of you. You went to the future and came back safely. You know something of what to expect." There's a sharp intake of breath. "And nothing else can go wrong with this mission."

"Why is this so important?" Adam asks.

Vincent pauses so long I think he's going to ignore the question. "One of the people we sent to the future is my son, Jeremy."

"You sent your own *son* to the future?" Chris asks.

"Yes. Something I deeply regret now. But I can't go back to the past and convince myself not to do it, which is why I need your help." His voice changes, softening. "I'll give you anything you want in return for bringing my son back. Anything. Just name your price."

"Go to hell," Chris says, glaring at the door. "My son is about to be born. I won't risk going to the future again. I barely made it out alive last time. Find someone else, 'cause there is not a damn thing you can offer me that I want."

Adam is silent, staring off into the distance with a frown. My hands are still clenched at my sides. I slowly open them as I consider

Vincent's words. We're trapped in this machine, and they're going to send us to the future against our will. We have no choice but to go, even if it's the last thing we want to do. And if there's another group of people stuck there, *someone* has to bring them back. We can't leave Vincent's son and those other teens trapped in the future, and I can't deny that the three of us are the best people for the job—even if I hate the idea.

But there *is* something I want in return.

"Wait," I say. "If we do this, we want you to leave us alone for the rest of our lives."

"No way. I won't do it, even then." Chris pounds on the door again. "Let me out of here! You can't do this to us!"

"Chris, I don't like this any more than you do," I say. "But they've got us trapped. No matter what we say or do, they're sending us to the future again."

His eyes blaze into mine, his anger hot and forceful. "I don't care. I can't do this. I *won't*."

"We don't have a choice. And you must have heard it in his voice—he'll do anything to save his son. You would too, wouldn't you?" I put my hand on his arm and refuse to look away, no matter how intense his glare is. "Believe me, the absolute last thing I want is to relive our time in the future. But at least this way we can get something out of it to protect ourselves and the people we care about."

Adam moves to my side. "She's right. And we can't leave those other people in the future. They need our help."

"Not sure how that's my problem," Chris says, but I can tell from his voice that he doesn't really mean it.

"We have to do this," Adam says. "If not for them, then for us. Aren't you a little curious about your new future?"

Chris stares us down for a moment longer and then spins around. "Dammit!" He yells it so loud it echoes off the domed metal walls, before he runs a hand over his face. His shoulders slump, as though he's given in to the inevitable.

But Adam's words set off a warning bell in my head. He's so willing, even *eager* to go along with this second trip to the future. I flash back to our conversation last night, to his frustrations with trying to create the cure, and I can guess why.

I lower my voice, hoping the people outside the dome won't be able to pick it up. "Did you know they were going to do this? Send us to the future again?"

"I swear I didn't."

"But you're not that upset about it either. You want to get the cancer cure, don't you?"

He hesitates, his face guilty, but then he clasps my hands in his. "Yes, but think of all the good we could do with it. Bringing the cure back would save years of research. Years!"

I step back from him, shrugging off his hands. "I can't believe you're even considering this."

His face falls. "But—"

"No. You have to develop the cure like you did before. There's no magic shortcut and no way around it."

Chris shakes his head. "I gotta agree with her, man. If you bring the cure back already made, then no one will ever actually create it. It'll just spring into existence thanks to this freaky time-travel loop. Won't that mess things up?"

"I don't know," Adam says, his brow furrowed. "Possibly. But if it works, it would save millions of lives."

"And if it doesn't work?" I ask. "What then?"

"I-I suppose it could alter the timeline or even cause a paradox."

His head drops, and after a minute he sighs. "All right. I won't try to get the cure."

I take his hand again, giving it a squeeze. "I know it's hard to wait, but you *are* going to create the cure. There's no doubt in my mind."

Chris slaps him on the back. "You're the smartest guy I know. You'll figure it out eventually and save the world and all that good stuff."

"I hope you're right." With one long breath, Adams draws himself up and meets my eye. "So we're really doing this?"

I rack my brain one last time for another solution or for a way out of this mess, but come up empty. "I think we have to."

Both of them reluctantly nod, and I turn back to the door and speak to the person I know must be listening. "We'll find your son on one condition: you leave us alone after this. No contact. No following us. No surveillance of any kind. You never come near us—or our family members—again. You forget we exist, and we'll do the same for you."

Our proposal is met with silence. I wish we could see out of this freaking dome, to know what is going on out there. Are they discussing it? Or starting up the machine to send us against our will?

"They'll never agree to this," Chris says. "And if they do, how can we trust they'll keep their word?"

"Because if they don't, we'll tell everyone what they're doing here," Adam says. "And no confidentiality agreement is going to stop us."

When no response seems to be coming, I cross my arms and raise my voice. "Look, you can send us to the future, and there's no way we can stop you. But once we get there? We can sit on our asses until the aperture opens again, and your son will still be missing forever. If you agree to this, I promise we'll bring him back."

"Very well," Vincent finally says. "Aether will never contact you again or do any further surveillance, I swear it. As long as you rescue my son."

"Fine," Chris says. "But let me call Shawnda at least before we go."

"I'm sorry, but we can't allow that. But you'll only be in the future for five hours, meaning only a few minutes will pass here in the present. She won't even know you're gone."

Adam's eyebrows dart up. "Only five?"

"We found that twenty-four hours was far too difficult on each subject," Dr. Kapur says. "With such a long time period, we had to account for eating and sleeping—but five hours is the perfect amount of time to send a team for a mission without them getting overly tired or hungry. Plus, there's a significantly lower risk of future shock with a shorter duration."

"I thought we wouldn't suffer future shock?" I ask.

"There's always a small chance." He sounds dismissive, like a small chance of brain damage is no big deal. I'm already regretting my decision to agree to this.

"How far ahead in the future are we going?" Adam asks.

"You'll be going thirty years forward, like before," Vincent says. "We're sending you an hour before the other team was supposed to return. Dr. Campbell will meet you in the future and explain everything you need to know. Do whatever it takes to find Jeremy and bring him back, along with the others on his team. If you succeed, you have my word that Aether will leave you alone forever." He pauses to let that sink in. "Now, if there are no other questions, we'll get started. Good luck."

The three of us share a wide-eyed look. We're going to the future *now*. For the second time. Even though I knew it was coming,

I'm still not prepared for how quickly this is happening. What will we find in this second future? Will it be identical to the other one we went to, except that Chris and I are alive in it now? Or will it be completely different?

"Sequence initiated," says a robotic-sounding voice. "Five."

Chris begins to swear under his breath, while we cluster in the center of the accelerator in anticipation of what we know is to come.

"Four."

The walls around us begin to hum. My throat grows tight as the machine seems to close in around me from all sides. Last time there were five of us in here, but it feels more cramped than ever.

"Three."

The buzzing grows louder, vibrating under our feet, through our bones. My head throbs, and the world starts to go dark, to tilt. But it's not the world, it's *me.* I fight off a wave of dizziness and flashbacks, pressing my hand to my forehead. I never thought I'd be going through this again, and it's too familiar, too real, too much like last time. I'm tempted to run to the door and demand they let us out, to scream until they stop this madness, except I can't make myself move.

"Two."

The floor shakes so violently I feel it in my teeth. Chris stands beside me, his face a hard mask, his hands clenched into fists at his side. Adam pulls me into his arms, and we cling to each other as the golden light appears and the earthquake stops.

The aperture is opening. The doorway to the future is here.

"One."

The rest of the world fades away into darkness. The present disappears and there are only the three of us, scared and trapped in a storm of pure gold energy. With no way out but forward, into the future once more.

PART II
THE FUTURE

00:00

The golden light dims, and the world around us starts to form. Dark shapes begin to sharpen as if someone is adjusting the lens on a camera, slowly making the future come into focus.

I blink rapidly against the brightness. I already know we'll be in the same location as we were before, in the basement of the Aether building, but now thirty years in the future. Last time we visited this time period, the place was abandoned, eerily silent, and pitch-black. Now it's full of light and sound.

Voices filter into my ears, hazy and slurred at first, but I pick out a few words:

"They're here."

"Good, they made it," a woman's voice says.

"Was there ever any doubt? It's all in the file…"

"It's still a miracle every time."

When the last of the fog lifts, an older black woman moves toward us, smiling. It takes me a second to recognize Dr. Campbell. Her curls are tied back and don't show any gray, but the edges of her eyes crinkle more than I remember and her mouth has laugh lines that weren't there before. Of course—she's thirty years older now.

"Welcome to the future," she says.

"How are you feeling?" the man asks us. He's Asian and younger, probably in his mid-thirties, and wears a bright purple tie under his lab coat. He was likely just a kid back in our time. "Do you need to sit down? Would you like a glass of water?"

"I'm not sure if you remember me, but I'm Dr. Ronnie Campbell." She gestures to the other guy. "And this is Dr. Edwin Chow. He monitors the physical and mental health of the time travelers."

None of us answer as we take in the world around us, still dazed. I don't see Dr. Kapur or Vincent Sharp anywhere, but other scientists I don't recognize stand around the basement, watching us with curious eyes. The accelerator is gone, but the massive basement is full of equipment and set up like a command center. Blinking lights. Sleek metal. Plastic and glass. I don't know what most of it is, but it's more advanced than anything I've seen before.

"What year is this?" Adam asks. His words come out strained. I don't think I could speak if I tried.

Dr. Campbell points to a wall where a dozen huge, paper-thin screens are set up, showing video feeds of different parts of the city, interactive maps with flashing pinpoints, and other things I can't begin to guess at. Some of the screens are translucent, seemingly turned off. One of them flicks on and shows today's date and time, along with a silly picture of a cat and a dog dressed up as witches. The month is October, exactly thirty years from the present, give or take a day or two. I set Mamá's watch to the current time.

Chris puts his head in his hands and swears loudly. I don't blame him. It's hard to believe we're back, hard to imagine facing another five hours in an unknown future. The more I think about it, the more I might throw up. I focus on our mission instead.

"We're here to bring the other time travelers back," I tell Dr. Campbell.

"We know. They're supposed to return here in about an hour, but we lost track of them some time ago."

"You have no idea where they are?" Adam asks.

"Unfortunately, no. They disabled their trackers and went off-mission without any explanation. We'll share everything we know so far and provide you with whatever you need to bring them back."

"I need to scan each of you quickly," Dr. Chow says. "It will only take a second and won't hurt, I promise." He raises a small white object that looks like a TV remote control and points it at Adam from head to toe. Dr. Chow studies the device for a moment and then turns it on me. I scowl at him, but he scans me anyway, before doing the same to Chris. He nods at Dr. Campbell when he's done. "Vitals and brain activity are optimal. They're good to go."

"Perfect," she says, and smiles at us. "Our files say you haven't eaten and might be hungry—is this correct?"

My stomach growls at the mention of food, and I press my hand against it. Adam and I were on our way to breakfast when we were taken by Aether, and they didn't bother feeding us. They just drugged us and tossed us into the future. "I could eat."

"We have food waiting for you. Follow me, please."

Dr. Campbell leads us to a conference table set up near the large screens. A tray of sandwiches from Subway sits in the middle of it, along with some cans of soda. It's a strange contrast—all this tech from the future, next to something I'd see in the present—but it's somehow comforting too.

We spend a few minutes loading our plates and take a seat at the table, while Dr. Chow and Dr. Campbell discuss something quietly. He hands her a smooth black box, about the size of a book, and walks away. While we dig into our sandwiches, Dr. Campbell sits beside us and opens the box, revealing a padded interior and three tiny plastic objects that look like see-through band-aids.

"Are you familiar with flexis?" Dr. Campbell asks.

"Yeah, we used them in the other future we visited," Adam says.

Flexis were computers that worked through brain waves, which beamed the interface directly into your head and allowed you to control it with your thoughts. They were nearly invisible when worn on your temple, but people in the other timeline liked to have their flexis display different images, almost like temporary tattoos.

"Good, then I don't need to explain how they work." She hands the box to Adam. "You can use these flexis while you're here. They're connected to Aether Corporation's accounts, so you won't have to worry about money or anything like that."

Adam takes a flexi from inside the box. It's much smaller than the ones we saw in the other future and thinner than a sheet of paper. He presses it to his temple, and it disappears completely from view, as if melting into his skin. He blinks once, and his gaze goes glossy as he becomes wrapped up in whatever he sees behind his eyes.

Dr. Campbell takes the box from him and passes it to Chris. "Flexis are old technology now, of course, but we keep them around since we know you don't have imbeds."

"Imbeds?" I ask.

She taps her temple. "They're similar to flexis but instead of attaching to your face, a microchip is implanted in the body through a quick, easy injection. They work similar to flexis in that you control them with your thoughts, but they've gone far beyond flexis in terms of capabilities. Imbeds can record memories and monitor a person's health, and we're starting to develop ways to use them for physical and mental enhancement, such as heightened reflexes, preventing insomnia, and shutting off pain."

Adam's eyes focus again on the real world. "Wow. Computer implants? I never imagined those would be common in only thirty years."

"It's only possible thanks to Team Echo—that's what we call the other time travelers. They recovered flexis during their first mission, and Aether analyzed and replicated them over the next few years. This allowed flexis to be created much sooner than they otherwise would have been and eventually led to the development of imbeds. Of course, many people still use flexis—just like people who refused to get smartphones in your time." She shakes her head with a smile. "Funny to think that back then people carried phones around all the time. I had a bad habit of dropping mine and cracking the screen. Now we don't have to worry about any of that."

Chris hands the box to me, and I reluctantly take the flexi from inside it. I wasn't a huge fan of flexis in the other future. Now people are injecting computers directly into their bodies? Terrifying.

I'm not thrilled about using a flexi again, but I don't seem to have much choice. I press the small, thin membrane to my temple, and words immediately pop up in my head. *Welcome, Aether Corporation employee.* They fade away, and an interface lays over my vision, displaying the time, local weather, and some icons. It's like playing a video game where stats like your health and a map are displayed in the corner—except this is real life and it's in my head.

Dr. Campbell takes the box and snaps it shut. "All of Team Echo's profiles are loaded in your flexis already, along with everything we learned thirty years ago, from when you rescued the team. Unfortunately, it isn't much."

"What do you mean?" I ask.

"Both teams gave us a report after all of you returned from this mission. We know that Team Echo went off-mission for some unknown reason, and that your team found them and brought them back. But when pressed for details, all of you clammed up. Neither team would tell us any specifics, which is why we need the three of you to track them down."

Chris snorts. "What, you couldn't force it out of them somehow? It would save us a lot of time and effort if we knew where to go."

She gives him a rueful smile. "I know you think poorly of us, but what would you expect us to do? Torture the other team members? Or you?"

"I wouldn't put it past Aether…" he mutters.

"We're a publicly traded international corporation full of the best scientists and brightest minds of this century, not some evil organization bent on world domination. We don't use torture or threats or assassins in the night. If none of you told us what happened, there wasn't much we could do to get you to talk."

Sure, they don't use torture. They only drug people and force them into time machines. But if our future selves didn't tell Aether exactly what we did, we must have been confident we could track them down on our own. And we must have had a reason for keeping our actions a secret from Aether.

"But we *were* successful in bringing them back?" Adam asks.

"You were…for the most part," Dr. Campbell says. "One of the members of Team Echo—Ken Miyamoto—never made it back. According to your report, he died in this time period and you were unable to save his life."

"He *died*?" Shivers creep up my spine. The familiar feeling of dread makes my every limb tense up. "How?"

"We don't know," Dr. Campbell says. "None of you knew how

he died, or when exactly. We're hoping it hasn't happened yet, and that you can prevent his death this time."

Ken Miyamoto's file opens in my head, and an image appears of a handsome guy about my age, with short black hair and bright brown eyes. He's grinning and wearing a green shirt that says, *Chemists Have All the Solutions.* Something in his expression reminds me of Trent, even though they look nothing alike, and my chest tightens at the memory of Trent's pale hand rising from the trash. I squeeze my eyes shut and try to block it out, but I can't.

This guy is going to die, just like Trent. Just like Zoe. And I already know that like before, I won't be able to stop it.

I jerk to my feet before I know what I'm doing, my body on autopilot, trying to get me as far from here as possible. My knee hits the table, making a loud *thunk* that gets everyone staring and sends shooting pain up my leg. Ow.

"Elena, are you all right?" Dr. Campbell asks, her forehead creased.

The pain brings me back to reality, and I realize I'm about to dart away like a startled bird. My heart bounces around in my chest so fast I'm surprised it doesn't jump out and run away on its own. But I'm *here*, not living in a memory, and I manage to fight back the panic.

"Yeah. Sorry." I sit back down, and the others look at me like I've lost my mind. All except Adam. He reaches under the table and sets his hand on my knee. I place my hand over his and hope he can't tell that my leg is shaking under the thick fabric of my cargo pants.

I shouldn't be this upset over some guy I've never met, but I can't escape the memories of the others I failed to save and the feeling that this is all much too familiar. Still, I can't react like this every time I'm faced with something that reminds me of the past. I need to get it together if I'm going to survive the next few hours.

Adam turns to Dr. Campbell, but his hand is steady on my knee as he speaks, grounding me in reality. "If you knew from your files that Team Echo would go missing and that one of them would die, why not warn them? Or stop them?"

Dr. Campbell's eyes slide away, in the direction of Dr. Chow and the other people in the room. "We were forbidden from telling them…by Vincent Sharp."

00:18

The three of us stare at Dr. Campbell for a heartbeat. "Why would he do that?" Chris finally asks.

"Vincent worried that if we told the team what happened to them, we might give them the idea in the first place. Instead, we sent an escort with them to make sure they stayed on track, along with two tails following them. But the team managed to abandon all of them in their first few hours here."

"How?" I ask.

"We're not sure exactly. From what we can tell, they led our people on a wild-goose chase around the city while picking up supplies, then managed to drug them and disable the trackers we had placed in their tech, allowing the team to escape without detection. As you'll see in their files, each one of them has special skills like you do."

The others go quiet, their eyes distant. Studying the information in their flexis on the other team, probably. My breathing has returned to normal, and my mind is back on the mission, thanks to Adam's calming touch. I focus on the profiles in my head, skimming each of them.

Ken Miyamoto. Only child, half-Japanese, lives with his parents. A chemistry prodigy who identified a gene that could potentially make crops less prone to damage when he was sixteen. He was arrested at eighteen for selling prescription drugs, but the charges were dropped. According to our team's mission report, we found Ken dead at Griffith Observatory, but we weren't sure if he was killed there or if his body was moved, nor did we know how he died.

I open the next files and scan the three profiles, memorizing everything inside:

Zahra Ebabi. A self-taught computer expert who runs a popular feminist video-game blog. Her parents are doctors who emigrated from Iran before she and her older brother were born, and now they all live in Beverly Hills. She was recruited after she was caught hacking into Aether's files.

Paige Hawkins. Blond, blue-eyed, and part of a wealthy family whose photos scream WASP. A potential Olympic contender in gymnastics until she was asked to leave the team after being arrested for shoplifting. Now she's a psychology major at USC.

Jeremy Sharp. Son of the CEO of Aether Corporation. Mother died in a car accident when he was thirteen. Graduated high school at fifteen. Graduated from MIT at eighteen with a double-major in physics and chemistry. Worked as Dr. Walters's assistant for a year. His file is the shortest, and yet he's the main reason we're here.

"Damn," Chris says. "Team Echo is like a bunch of Adam clones."

He's right. Every one of these people is on Adam's level. No foster kids this time. Each one of them is rich, brilliant, or both.

Dr. Campbell coughs. "After Team Delta—that was your group—Aether decided to go in a...different direction with their new recruits. Foster kids with special skills were Lynne's idea, and that didn't work out well for any of us. For the next team, we decided to recruit some of the top minds in the country, who might be more…willing to cooperate."

"You mean, you recruited a ton of geeks who would follow orders," Chris says.

Adam raises an eyebrow. "I think I should probably be offended by that statement…"

"They're not so perfect though," I say. "Most of them had problems with the law not long before they were recruited. My guess is that Aether magically made all of those problems go away."

Dr. Campbell's lips form a tight line and she doesn't answer, but that's enough of a response for me. These people may not be foster kids, but they definitely have dark spots in their past that Aether can exploit to force them to cooperate. Like us, they never really had much of a choice.

"What was their mission exactly?" Adam asks Dr. Campbell. "There's not much information on that in these files."

She hesitates a moment before answering. "They were sent to… infiltrate a Pharmateka lab and obtain a design for a machine that could create synthetic water, which we believe could potentially cure the drought and hunger problems of the world."

I remember Pharmateka from the other future, where it was a rival of Aether Corporation, although in the present it hasn't even been formed yet. "So they were supposed to break into your rival's lab and steal this design, then bring it back to the present so Aether can make it instead? That's some serious corporate espionage."

"Essentially…yes."

"No wonder Aether doesn't want us to break the confidentiality agreement," Chris says.

"Aether may resort to some…not entirely ethical means of doing things, but only with the best intentions," Dr. Campbell says. "If Team Echo brings back the synthetic water generator's design to your time period, imagine how much better the world could be in ten or twenty years. No more drought, and enough water for crops all over the world. It could end famine and water wars completely."

I'm not sure I agree with her reasoning that the ends justify the means, but whatever. It's not our mission to get the design, just to bring the original team back. If they have it, great. If not, that's their problem. I'm sure Aether will send them to the future another time to get it.

"Why not have your own people do the breaking and entering part?" Chris asks.

"It would be too risky for us. We can't let Pharmateka get even a whiff of the fact that we're involved in something like this. Or that we have the ability to travel through time."

"But if the team is successful, wouldn't this future change anyway?" Adam asks.

"Would it?" Dr. Campbell replies, raising her eyebrows. "Or would it simply create an all-new timeline parallel to this one, while we continue on and have to live with the consequences of our actions?" She shrugs. "There's no way to tell."

Time travel. What a pain in the ass.

I go through the rest of the file, trying to look for any clues as to where the other team could have gone. Like Dr. Campbell said, we didn't give Aether much info when we returned to the present with the other team. We mention that they split up, and that we stuck together and tracked them down one by one, and that's about it.

I have a sneaking suspicion I know what they're up to.

"Do you know if Team Echo ever looked up their future selves?" I ask. "In this future or any other?"

She frowns. "No, they were instructed not to, because of the potential for paradoxes, like you were. Why?"

"If we knew about their future selves, it might help us find them."

"Hmm. Good point. I'll have that information compiled and added to your flexis."

"We should go to their last known location and see if we can find anything," Chris says.

Dr. Campbell shakes her head. "We already examined the areas surrounding the Pharmateka lab and found nothing. You're welcome to investigate as well, but I suggest you don't spend much time there."

She's right. The clock is ticking, and we need to get going. I shove the last bite of my sandwich in my mouth and wipe my hands. I've never met this other team, but from their profiles, I'm starting to think I know what they were up to. "All right, let's go. We only have"—I check my mother's watch—"a little over four hours to find these people and bring them back."

Dr. Campbell rises from her chair. "We'll have someone escort you to—"

"Nope," I say. "No babysitters."

"But—"

"Look, we were sent here to help because we can find them and you obviously can't. But you need to let us do it our way, or we're not doing it at all."

She considers my words with a frown, and looks across the room to where Dr. Chow stands with some other scientists. Finally, she nods. "Very well. But in that case, I should give you something else." She waves Dr. Chow over. "Edwin, we'll need three neutralizers." He gives a sharp nod and walks away, his lab coat fluttering behind him.

"Neutralizers?" Adam asks.

"In case any member of Team Echo proves to be uncooperative," she says.

Dr. Chow returns and hands each of us something that looks like a lipstick tube. "Simply press this part"—he says, holding up one end, which is flat and red—"against the person's skin, and it will render them unconscious for about thirty minutes or so, depending on height and weight. That way, you can bring them back here and through the aperture without any problems."

"Do you think we'll need those?" I ask. Seems a bit extreme, especially since no one on Team Echo seems to be a fighter. Chris or I could take any of them down easily.

"Let's hope not," Dr. Campbell says. "But we want you to be prepared for any possibility. As far as we know, they might not *want* to come back." She gives the three of us a long look while her words sink in, and then she turns away. "There's a car on the roof you can take. Follow me."

We leave behind the stares of the other scientists and follow Dr. Campbell into the elevator. The door closes, she hits a button, and a second later it opens again on a different floor. I didn't even feel the elevator move.

She leads us down a windowless hallway with bland, gray carpeting and that just-vacuumed smell to a door that opens to the roof—and for the first time, we get a real glimpse of this future.

"Holy shit," Chris says, while Adam draws in a sharp gasp.

My jaw's hanging open too, but I'm speechless as I take it all in. Because this future is nothing like the one we went to before. Oh no. It's so much *more.*

Beyond the Aether building, the barren desert has been transformed into a sprawling corporate oasis. But the first thing I see are the cars—not on the road, but in the *air*. They're flying. Or more aptly, hovering, gliding, plowing through the air like a speedboat on a wave. Hundreds of them zip across the sky in every direction, following invisible traffic flows. They look a lot like normal cars, except they have wings that arch over them like spider's legs. The bright afternoon sun glints off their gleaming bodies as they crisscross and overlap and trail behind each other, darting between buildings that don't exist in the present. Somehow, miraculously, none of them crash.

As we watch, one lands on the other side of the roof, which has become a parking lot for Aether's corporate cars, or so I assume from the branding along the side of them. It moves into position and drops straight down, then hovers a foot above the ground so the man inside can get out. Once he's gone, the car parks itself, with tiny wheels coming out of the bottom while the insect-like wings fold up and blend into the side of the car seamlessly.

"This future..." Adam whispers, with awe in his voice. "It's so much more advanced than the other one we went to."

Dr. Campbell smiles as she leads us through the parking area. "It's all because of Project Chronos. Each trip to the future resulted in new technology brought back in time, which was then developed years before it would have been otherwise. And the effect was cumulative—after Team Echo brought back the flexi technology, it led to a dozen other innovations, so when they visited the future a second time they were able to bring back technology that was even *more* advanced."

She stops in front of a silver car, one of the few without the Aether logo on the side of it. Like the others we saw flying around, it's sleek and aerodynamic, unlike the strange egg-shaped cars we saw in the other timeline. This one is a larger model, like a van, and a wide door slides open so we can get in. A new icon of a tiny car appears in my vision.

Dr. Campbell gestures at the open door. "I've transferred the keys to your flexis. Are you positive we can't convince you to let someone go with you? Not as a babysitter, but as a guide. The technology in this time is vastly different from what you know..."

"We got it." Chris slips inside the car without another word. Adam climbs in next, and the two of them begin talking in low tones about the car and how it must fly.

Dr. Campbell gives me a hug, which is unexpected. "Good luck, Elena. Please contact us through your flexis if you need anything."

"Thanks."

I slide inside the car, and the door closes behind me. Like the self-driving cars in the other timeline, this one is like a moving lounge, with comfortable leather seats around a table in the middle. Except in this one there are seat belts that go over the shoulders and around the waist, strapping us in tightly. There's no steering wheel or other way to drive the car, and although there are some buttons along the walls and on the center table, the car is mainly controlled through our flexis.

"I've entered the address for the Pharmateka lab," Adam says, as I strap myself in beside him.

Chris scowls as he snaps his seat belt on. "We already know we're not gonna find anything there. But I guess we have no other clues, do we?"

"It doesn't matter," I say. "I already know what they're doing. They're tracking down their future selves."

"How do you know?" Adam asks.

"Because it's what *we* did."

00:34

With one quick movement, the car lifts straight off the ground and rises ten feet above the parking lot. My stomach jumps into my throat at the sudden altitude, and Adam lets out a yelp—he's afraid of heights. Chris leans forward and yells, "Hot damn!"

We each stare out the windows like little kids on a roller coaster, gripping our seat belts with our mouths hanging open and our eyes wide. The ride is smooth and confident, and the car knows what to do and where to go without us doing a single thing to control it. Dr. Campbell waves as she gets smaller and smaller below us. Then the car darts forward, straight into traffic.

We quickly pull up behind another car and merge into the "lane," or whatever this stream of cars heading in one direction is called. There's an order to it, but it's overwhelming, chaotic, and impossible for my brain to comprehend. Only a massive system of computers could control such a system, especially at these reckless speeds.

Chris gazes at the hundreds of other cars speeding by us. "We're in a flying car. Un-fucking-believable."

"Technology is so advanced now," Adam says, shaking his head.

"It's only been thirty years, and we have flying cars, computer implants, and who knows what else."

"Because of Aether and their damn time machine. They created this future, and they're getting all the benefits from it." Chris runs a hand over the leather seats almost reverently. "Although I wouldn't mind opening one of these babies up and seeing what's inside them. I'm dying to know how they fly."

Adam's voice grows distant, his eyes glassy. "It says in Aether's files that Team Echo brought back self-driving car technology on their second mission along with some hovercraft tech, which led to Aether creating these cars many years later. It's all controlled by a massive traffic network, which directs the cars and makes sure none of them crash. That makes sense—the only way that flying cars would become common like this is if computers controlled them. Otherwise, it'd be far too dangerous. Supposedly it's cut down on Los Angeles's traffic problems in a major way."

"Team Echo did all of this," I say, as I gaze out the window. "They're what we were supposed to be: smart, talented, and obedient. Our mission was the same as theirs, but we never completed it 'cause we broke Aether's one rule: to not look up our future selves."

"And you think they did the same?" Adam asks.

I nod. "These people have gone on two missions being Aether's dutiful servants, but their curiosity must have finally gotten the best of them. No matter what Aether is holding over them, the urge to know what will happen to you in thirty years is too hard to resist." We should know. We failed that test in our first couple hours in the future.

Chris leans back in his seat and scrubs a hand over his face. "This is so messed up. A few hours ago, I was kissing Shawnda good-bye and heading to my engineering class. Now we're in the future against our will, hunting down a bunch of nerds who can't keep out of trouble."

"At least we'll only be gone a few minutes in the present," Adam says.

"True." Chris's face shifts, and he gives us a devious grin. "And while we're here, we might as well do a little digging of our own, right?"

I flash him a skeptical look. "I'm not sure that's such a good idea."

He shrugs. "You two can do whatever you want, but I need to know I'm alive in this future and that my son is okay. Like you said, the temptation is just too damn strong."

He instantly takes on that glazed look that signals he's using his flexi, while Adam gazes at me like he's asking permission. If I'm honest with myself, the idea of looking up my fate has been dancing around in the back of my mind ever since I learned we were going to the future again. I tried hard to ignore it, but it's difficult to banish completely.

I want to look so bad. I want to know if I'm alive in this future.

But what if I'm not?

The thought of finding out I'm dead again renders me immobile, and my chest constricts to the point where it's hard to breathe. Memories burst through the mental barriers I've tried so hard to erect—of our original team looking ourselves up, of speaking with Future-Adam and visiting his house, of finding crime-scene photos of my friends' deaths and mine in his safe. Once again, I relive the sheer horror from when I learned I had supposedly killed the others and myself. The rush of emotions overwhelms me, and I close my eyes, straining to keep my breathing steady.

Even though I saved Chris and changed our futures, I'll never be able to forget what might have happened. And I'm not sure I can go through that all over again.

"I don't know," I manage to get out. "Last time..." The words become too difficult, and I shake my head.

But Chris seems to know what I'm getting at. His eyes refocus and meet mine. "If we hadn't looked up our fates last time, you and I would be dead right now, and Adam would be stuck working with a killer for the rest of his life."

"He's right," Adam says. "We should look. Just to be sure nothing bad is going to happen to us."

My throat is so dry it's like a lizard has died inside it. "But what if by looking at the future, we cause it to change?"

"I don't think it works that way. Last time, you had to consciously do something you knew was different to change the timeline. Otherwise, the future would have happened exactly as we'd seen it."

"True..."

"I can look for you, if you want." He rests his hand over mine, his voice sympathetic.

"No!" I jerk away from him before I can stop myself, a reflexive move I immediately regret. "I mean, thanks, but I can do it."

He looks like he wants to say something, but his lips press in a tight line and he nods. I should apologize to him for being so jumpy and for pushing him away, but I can't get the words out. I'm too scared of what I'm about to see.

"You guys..." Chris says with a laugh. "My son is a lawyer. A freaking lawyer! He went to Harvard and everything. Guess I didn't screw him up too bad, eh?"

In the other future we visited, Chris was dead and his son was in prison. Hmm. Maybe this future won't be so bad after all.

"That's great." Adam's eyes go distant. A sign he's using his flexi.

"Wait." I grip Adam's arm, suddenly hit with a new thought. "What about the cure?"

His brow furrows, and he focuses on me again. "What about it?"

"Promise me you won't look it up. Like Chris said, if you get the cure here, you'll be stealing it from your future self, not actually creating it on your own. You can't cheat fate like that."

He stares at me for a long pause, and I think he might argue with me. But then he brings my hand to his lips and kisses my knuckles one by one in a way that makes my pulse race. "I won't. I promise."

"Thank you." I slide my arm through his, leaning against his side. I don't want him to be upset with me, but this is important.

He gently takes my chin and captures my lips with his, showing me he's not mad at all. I kiss him back, my fingers tracing the stubble along his jaw, and allow myself to forget everything but this moment for a few blissful seconds.

"Okay, let's do this," I say when we finally pull back. "And if we see something bad…" I swallow hard. "Well, we know we can change the future."

"We won't see anything bad. Of that I have no doubt."

That gets a smile out of me. "So confident."

"I have faith in us." He gives me another quick kiss. "Are you ready?"

"Ready," I whisper.

But I'm not quite ready. Instead, I watch as Adam's face changes, as he gets lost in whatever is inside his flexi. After a minute, a slow smile crosses his mouth. He looks up and meets my eyes, but perhaps he senses I want to see it for myself, because he says nothing.

That's when I do it: I search for myself.

Last time I did this, I didn't get anything current on myself, not among the dozens of other Elena Martinezes of the world. Mainly because I'd been dead for thirty years. Now, I'm the first hit in all the searches. And the second, and the third...

Except my name isn't Elena Martinez anymore. It's Elena O'Neill.

Oh my God. Adam and I are married in this future.

Before I let that bombshell sink in all the way, I click on the first link. It's a Wikipedia page on me. *Me.* I have a freaking Wikipedia page.

Elena Milagro Martinez O'Neill is a Mexican-American businesswoman and philanthropist. She is the CEO and cofounder of Future Visions Industries, the founder of the Esperanza Foundation, and the wife of Nobel Prize–winner Adam O'Neill.

There's a picture of me on the side of it, older than I am now. I stare at it for a long minute, noting my wrinkles, my wavy hair, my black suit. Me, wearing a suit. I've never worn a suit in my *life*. And how did I become CEO? Is that a mistake? It has to be...right?

I scroll through the rest of the article, trying to figure out how this is my life. Each new revelation is a shock that sends me reeling.

Adam and I got married in our twenties, after I graduated from college and he finished his PhD. But instead of becoming a social worker, as I originally planned, I went to business school for some reason. Around the same time, Adam, Chris, and I formed something called Future Visions Industries together. Through it, Adam developed and distributed genicote, the cure for cancer, along with other groundbreaking medical advances over the next few years. Chris led an engineering division that revolutionized how engines work, allowing them to run cleaner and to use just about anything for fuel. And I guess I was pretty good at the business stuff, because the three of us turned our little start-up company into one that rivaled both Aether Corporation and Pharmateka.

But the Esperanza Foundation, according to a quote on the Wikipedia page, is what I considered my greatest achievement. It's an organization that helps kids in foster care find homes, assists them with college applications and scholarships, and offers job training and placement. Many of the kids in it go on to work for Future Visions Industries, which is Esperanza's number one backer, of course.

My heart swells about ten times reading this. No wonder I went into business instead of social work—I must have realized I could do more good by helping Adam and Chris form a company and using our success to help foster kids that way. And from the look of things, we really did it.

"You guys," Chris says, laughing. "We're *billionaires*!"

Adam's face is lit up with a bright smile that makes him look so handsome my heart clenches. "We must have taken the money we got from Aether and used it to start Future Visions." His face searches mine, but he doesn't mention that *other* thing, the thing I'm still processing. It hangs between us in the silence, and I look away, unable to take it any longer.

Adam and Chris talk about the company we're going to start together and all their plans for the technology they want to develop, but I tune out the science talk. Even though Chris jokingly calls Adam a nerd sometimes, he's just as big a geek when it comes to this stuff.

I wish I could be as happy as they are. And I *am*, truly. This future seems perfect. So why is it harder for me to accept that Adam and I are married than that we created a multibillion-dollar company together?

I can't look at my fate anymore. I close the page and let my mental interface go blank. Now that I know I'm alive and that my future isn't a disaster, I don't need to stress anymore.

I don't want to know anything else.

00:58

It isn't long before the car lowers to street level, although it never actually touches the ground. Instead of using wheels, it hovers a foot or so above the surface, gliding along without a single bump. We're in the middle of nowhere, with rows of warehouses and other nondescript large buildings on every block, interspersed with a fast-food restaurant now and then. The car pulls in front of an unmarked four-story building with dark windows that takes up the entire block. A burly-looking security guard is perched outside the one entrance I see.

"That must be the Pharmateka lab," Adam says.

"Not much here." Chris scans the area through the car windows. "What's the plan?"

I watch the security guard in front of the building pick at his nails. "Aether's bodyguards were found unconscious near here. Let's go ask that guard if he saw anything."

The security guard squints at us as we approach, but he doesn't whip out a gun or anything. I offer him my best impression of a friendly smile. "Hey. We're looking for some friends of ours. They came by here a couple hours ago, and we were wondering if you saw them."

He glowers at me. "How the hell should I know? Lots of people come by here."

Seriously? I glance up and down the street, which hasn't had a single other car pass by in the entire time we've been here.

"There were four of them," Adam says. "About our age. Two guys and two girls. I can show you pictures if that would help."

The guy grunts. "Yeah, I saw them."

"Any idea where they went?"

"The Asian kid and the two girls each got in separate cars. The other guy…I think maybe he went with one of them. Or maybe not." He shrugs.

Well, that was no help at all. We already knew the team split up. "Is there any security footage or something we could look at?" I ask.

He eyes me like I'm something stuck to his boot. "I can't let you see that."

"Is there anything else you remember?" Adam asks, his voice much more diplomatic than mine. "Anything at all? We really need to find them."

"Nope."

I give the guy one last scowl before we stroll across the street to the spot where our car is hovering patiently. "Dammit, we need that security footage. It probably at least has the license plate numbers of the cars, which we might be able to track down. Chris, can't you do something to get it?"

"Me? What do I look like, a hacker or some shit? I fix cars, for Christ's sake."

Adam leans against our car, his eyes thoughtful behind his glasses. "Well, we know they split up and took different cars. If we figure out what's happening with their future selves that might give us some clues to where they went."

His words spark an idea. "In Aether's report about this mission, it says we went after the other team one by one." I speak slowly, the plan forming in my head as I go. "But by the time we got to Ken, he was already dead."

Chris crosses his arms. "Yeah, and…?"

"None of that has happened yet. Which means we might be able to save him."

"How?" Adam asks.

"We split up and go after them separately. We know we stayed together when we did this before—so by splitting up we'll be purposefully changing what we do and what happens as a result."

Chris slowly nods. "Like how you purposefully changed the timeline before and stopped Lynne."

"Exactly." Last time, we seemed to be stuck in a loop where everything we did led to the same inevitable fate. But by doing something I didn't originally do—in that case, trusting Adam—I was able to break us free of the cycle. I think the same thing might work now.

Adam frowns and adjusts his glasses. "I don't like the idea of us splitting up. We're safer together. What if, by splitting up, we fail in our mission?"

"It's a risk," I admit. "But the other option is to just accept that Ken is going to die and let it happen. I can't do that. Not after what happened with Trent and Zoe. Can you?"

"Of course not, but…" Adam sighs and runs a hand through his hair. "You're right. If there's a way to save his life, we should do it."

Chris is looking at me oddly. I'm surprised he hasn't said anything so far. He uncrosses his arms and says, "I'm in. But I want to be the one to go after Ken."

"No, it should be me," I say. "It might be dangerous. We don't know how he died or who killed him, and you have a kid on the way. It's better if I go."

"I'll be careful," Chris says. I open my mouth to argue, to insist I be the one who tracks Ken down, but he fixes me with a steely gaze. "Trent and Zoe were my friends too, and it's partly my fault they're dead. Not a day goes by that I don't wish I could have done something differently, or that I could go back and change things. I survived and they didn't, and it's not fucking fair. But if I can save *this* guy..." His words trail off and he shrugs. "It won't bring them back, but it's something."

I know what he means, because it's the same reason *I* want to go after Ken. This guy isn't Trent or Zoe—but unlike them, he can still be saved. His death doesn't need to be on our hands too, not if we can help it. And maybe by saving him, we'll be redeemed in some tiny way. Maybe then the nightmares and flashbacks will stop.

"Besides," Chris adds, slapping me on the back. "You saved my life. I owe you."

"You don't owe me anything." I roll my eyes, but I can tell he won't back down from this. "Fine, you go after him, and we'll find the others. I'll take the hacker girl. Adam you can track down the ex-gymnast. Based on what the guard said, Jeremy Sharp is probably with one of them."

"Got it," Adam says.

We take a minute to research our assigned person. Aether has updated the profiles on each of them with a new section about their future selves. Future-Zahra lives in Washington, DC, works for the FBI in computer security, and is single. Her older brother is dead, and the only connection she still has in LA is her mother, who is widowed and lives alone in the house she's owned since Zahra was a kid. Guess I'll start there. If that doesn't work, I have no other leads, and with her hacking skills, Zahra could be a tough one to track down. I'm sure she's the one who disabled all of Aether's trackers.

"Bad news," Chris says. "Future-Ken died ten years ago."

"How?" Adam asks.

"He had something called Huntington's disease. Sounds like a pretty awful way to go. Shows up in your thirties or forties and really messes you up, and then you die shortly after. Says here he's buried with his parents, so I'll try the cemetery to see if he's gone there to check out his grave."

"Good idea," Adam says. "Paige Hawkins is married to a congressman and lives in Pasadena. I'll head to her house and see if she's there."

"What about this Jeremy guy?" Chris asks. "What if he isn't with the others? He's the whole reason we're here. If we don't bring him back alive, our deal with his father will be off."

Adam's eyes go vacant as he uses his flexi. "Hmm. According to the files, Future-Jeremy is divorced, has no kids, and is working as a physicist for Pharmateka, of all things—guess he left his father's company at some point to join Aether's rival."

"His house is near the cemetery where Ken is buried," Chris says. "I'll stop by there on my way and check it out."

A hunter-green car zooms down the street—or a few feet above it, anyway—and halts beside us. The windows are tinted black, but the door slides open and a familiar face peers at us from inside. "Get in!"

All I can do is stare at the guy in the car, someone I never imagined seeing again. Someone we only know from the other timeline we visited. Someone who hasn't even been born yet in the present.

"...Wombat?" I ask. "What are you doing here?"

"My boss sent me to help you."

"Who's your boss?"

He grins at me. "You are."

01:17

Wombat gestures for us to get in the car. "Come on, I'll explain everything once you're inside."

The guys are speechless as they stare at Wombat, like they've seen a ghost. "What about our car?" Chris finally asks.

"Leave it. Or tell it to head back to Aether. Whatever. You don't need it anymore."

The three of us share stunned looks, but then we slide inside. Wombat's car is smaller than the one we borrowed from Aether's and smells like fried chicken and pine. Empty food containers and other trash litter the floor, and there's a dry, crusty air freshener hanging in the center, which I guess explains the pine.

"Sorry, I should have cleaned this first," he says, shoving a fast-food bag off the seat so I have more room. "I've been really busy, but I should have made time. I mean, it's not like I didn't know you were coming, eh?"

"You knew we'd be standing outside the Pharmateka lab at exactly"—I check my watch—"5:21 p.m.?"

"You can thank yourself for that. Your memory is on point, even at almost fifty."

So I *am* alive in this timeline. And I'm his boss. Everything I saw on the Wikipedia page must be true. I don't know why I'm so surprised, but I suppose it's one thing reading about your future, and another thing having the evidence right in front of you.

As the car takes off and begins speeding in the direction of downtown Los Angeles, I study the man sitting in front of us. He's our age, with dark hair and impish brown eyes, wearing a black button-down shirt with lights along the collar that subtly shifts colors.

He's thinner than the guy I saw in the other timeline, and looks more polished and put-together. The Wombat I remember lived out of his mother's garage, was surrounded by technology both new and old, and looked like he hadn't shaved or bathed in weeks. He made us fake IDs and made puppy-dog eyes at Zoe, but we knew nothing else about him except that he was a friend of Future-Adam's.

"It's warped, seeing you guys my age," Wombat says, squinting at each of us. "You're so *young*."

"It's strange seeing you too," Adam says. "You look...different."

"Oh right, you told me you'd met me before, in another future. So rad!"

"He...I...told you about all that?" Adam asks. My question is, who says *rad*?

"Yep. The three of you came to my house two years ago, when I was sixteen. I was, like, no frickin' way, the founders of Future Visions Industries are at my house! I thought I was in trouble or something, but you offered me a job and told me this ridic story of how you time traveled and met me in another timeline and I helped you out. Have to admit, I never really believed it until I saw the three of you standing here at exactly the time you told me you would be." He lets out a low whistle. "Time travel, right? So mega. Hey, what did Aether give you? Flexis? Hand 'em over."

He thrusts his hand toward me, and I'm so overwhelmed by everything that's going on that I peel off my flexi and slap it in his hand. He presses a button next to him, and a little black trash can pops out. He throws my flexi in, and the container closes up and makes a shredding sound.

I lurch forward, but it's too late. "Wait, I need that!"

Wombat waves a dismissive hand. "Aether is tracking you on those and seeing everything you do. But don't stress. I'll set you up with some fresh gear that they won't be able to trace." The trash can finishes, and Wombat gestures for Adam and Chris to put their flexis inside. Once they do, it starts shredding again. "It turns anything you put in it into fuel. Chris designed it. Pretty spiff, eh?"

I raise an eyebrow at him, while Chris starts examining the machine he's destined to invent. Wombat couldn't take a second to clean up all his garbage, even with his own personal disposal system right there? Or was he saving it for a day he ran out of fuel and needed some emergency trash?

"What do you want? Imbeds? Flexis? Smartphones?" He rattles them off like they're drugs he's selling from the back of his car. Which is not far off, really.

"You have smartphones?" I am so done with having the Internet in my head.

"Ha-ha-ha, as if! They haven't made those in *years*."

I scowl at him. "Fine, I'll take a flexi."

"I figured you'd say that." He hands me a new flexi, and when I place it on my temple, a message pops up: *Hello, Elena O'Neill.*

"I'm very curious about imbeds, but I'll take a flexi," Adam says.

"Same," Chris says.

"It's syncing with my profile," I say. "How do I get it to stop?"

"Don't worry about it," Wombat says, while he hands the others their flexis. "Consider it a gift from your older selves. You can use their money, contacts, whatever else you need. Just don't do anything too wild, or my ass will be on the line."

So much information inside my head, waiting to be accessed. I want to know everything. I'm scared to find out too much. *Stick to the mission,* I remind myself. *Get the others. Get back alive. Then get on with your life so you can* live *this future.*

"Now what?" Chris asks, once we're all set up with our new gear.

"The car will drop me off near Future Visions, and you can take it to find the people you're looking for," Wombat says.

"That's it?" I ask. "You give us some new flexis and run?"

He shrugs. "I can't get more involved than that. Something about possibly messing up the timeline, blah-blah-blah."

"Do you know where the other team is?" Adam asks.

He shifts in his seat, clearly uncomfortable. "No. You never told me anything else."

"I don't get it," Chris says. "Wouldn't it be faster and easier for you to take us to the other team members so we can drag their asses back to Aether now?"

"Hey, I don't question what Elena tells me to do. She said to pick you up, give you this stuff, then send you on your way. I'm not supposed to do anything more than that. And I know better than to argue with her." He shoots me a quick glance as he says it, like he's worried I might yell at him.

Chris snorts. "We have no idea what we're doing, no clue in hell where to go, and we're wasting time with each minute we spend trying to figure it out. Maybe we should have a chat with Future-Elena about this."

Wombat rolls his eyes. "She won't talk to you. All of your older selves were *very* clear that there should be no contact whatsoever with them. They also said you'd be stubborn about this."

"Man, are we dicks in the future or what?" Chris asks.

"Nah, you're actually pretty mondo. Of course, you also pay my salary, so I have to say that," he adds with a grin. I assume *mondo* is a compliment, but half the stuff out of this guy's mouth is a mystery to me.

"All right," Adam says, glancing back and forth between the two of them. "We'll do this on our own, but we need two more cars. We're splitting up."

"You're…what?" Wombat's grin drops. "That's not what you told me you were going to do. Are you sure that's a smart move?"

"We're changing the plan," I say. "If you have a better idea…"

He holds up his hands like he's surrendering. "Nope. If you want more cars, I'll get you more cars."

We zoom through the skyscrapers of downtown Los Angeles in a steady stream of traffic, passing buildings I recognize and many I don't. One I know well is the tall, black granite skyscraper that's home to Aether's main headquarters, which looks identical to when we broke into it in the other timeline. Down below, I spot the distinct architecture of the Disney Concert Hall and the Central Library, while in the distance the Hollywood sign stands over the city, just as it does in the present. It's comforting to see that even in this advanced future, some things remain the same.

But some things are all new. We approach a building that reaches high in the sky with shimmering silver walls and light-green windows. As the car circles around it, I see the words *Future Visions Industries* across the top.

Are our future selves inside there, watching us arrive through the windows? I try to imagine what it would be like to go inside, to get a glimpse of what my life is like in thirty years as the CEO of a powerful corporation and the wife to a Nobel Prize winner. But my excitement and curiosity fades away when we leave the building behind and instead fly down into a nearby parking lot.

"One of you can use this car," Wombat says, as the door slides open. "I'm getting keys for two other cars now, but it'll take a minute to get them transferred over."

He hops out, and the three of us share a look. This is where we split up. I know it's the right thing to do, yet I can't shake the feeling that something is wrong with this plan. Or that it should be me going after Ken and not Chris.

"You can take this car," Adam says to Chris.

"Gee, thanks," Chris says, and kicks one of the fast-food containers across the floor toward Adam. "Give me the one that smells like the bathroom inside a KFC."

"Are you sure you want to do this?" I ask. "I still think it should be me who goes after Ken."

His eyes are determined as they meet mine. "No. I need to do this."

I nod slowly and rest my hand on his arm. "Let us know if you need help. And bring him back alive."

He gives me a quick squeeze. "I will. You two stay safe."

"Good luck," Adam says, and they clasp hands briefly.

We climb out, and the door slides shut. Chris gives us a solemn nod before the car rises into the air and shoots off, heading east. Splitting up is the only way to save Ken, but as the car disappears across the sky, I can't help but wonder if we're making a huge mistake.

01:39

"Your cars are ready," Wombat says as two cars glide in front of us, one black and one white. "I've transferred the keys to your flexis. Do you need anything else?"

"I don't think so," Adam says.

"Then I'll bounce." He shakes Adam's hand, and then mine. "It was mega to meet you both. I can't wait to tell—" He stops himself and slams his mouth shut.

"Tell who?" I ask, raising an eyebrow.

"Tell your future selves." He grins, but it's obvious that's not what he was going to say. "And hey, don't forget to track me down in twenty-eight years or so."

He gives us a little wave and then starts walking down the street toward the Future Visions Industries building, whistling a quiet tune as he goes. We both stare after him for a full minute, until he disappears from sight.

"That was strange," Adam says. "Seeing Wombat again. I didn't even recognize him at first."

"Everything about this future is strange."

"It is. But I like this future a lot better than the other one we saw."

"It's nice to not be dead for a change," I admit.

Adam wraps his arms around me with a smile. "You're alive. We started a company together. But the best part is that we're—"

"Don't," I say, slipping out of his embrace.

His smile drops. "What is it?"

"I just..." I turn away from him, my throat closing up. "I can't get used to the idea of us...you know."

"Is it that hard to believe you'd marry me?" he asks, and I can hear the frustration and pain in his voice.

"No. Hard to believe you'd want me to."

"Why? You know I care about you. *You're* the one who keeps pushing me away."

He's right, and I'm an idiot for doing it, but it's like I'm on a self-destruct sequence and can't seem to turn it off. I scrub my hands over my face. "Can we talk about this once we get back to the present? I can't think right now. When the mission is over, we can figure all this out and what it means for us."

"Yeah. Sure. Once we get back."

I can tell he's hurt, but he doesn't walk away. He doesn't get mad. He's nothing like the men I grew up with, and it surprises me every time when he doesn't react the way I expect him to. Yet I keep pushing him away, even after all we've been through. Why is it so hard for me to let him in? Or to accept that we might be together in the future?

"I'm sorry," I say, even though my throat is tight and each word is a struggle. "I care about you too. I just suck at this relationship stuff."

"It's okay. Like you said, some things can't be rushed." He gives me a slight smile. "But I'm willing to wait."

The sincerity in his voice breaks me, and I move into his arms.

He holds me against him, his body warm and solid, and I tilt my head up to his. His eyes search mine for a moment before our lips meet. Our kiss is tentative and soft, like we're both asking permission from the other. But soon my eyes flutter shut and I grip his shirt, holding on as I'm swept away to a place that only Adam has ever taken me, the one place I feel safe and loved.

He rests his forehead against mine, his eyes closed. For a long moment we stand there, our breaths moving in and out as one, and I regret this decision to split up.

"We should go," I finally say.

"Be careful."

"You too."

I give him one last kiss and then head for the black car. The digital key in my flexi unlocks the doors as I approach, and I slip inside. This one has a soft blue glow inside, like mood lighting, and reclining leather seats. Not a bad way to travel. Plus, it doesn't smell like fried chicken.

While Adam gets in the white car, I enter the address of Zahra's mother's house. I wave at him while my car takes off, and I say a silent prayer that nothing bad happens to him. My breath hitches as the car rises up, as I leave the city below me. I don't know if I'll ever get used to that feeling, or the sight of the ground disappearing at rapid speed.

Adam's car is right behind mine as we move into traffic, but it soon darts off in a different direction, heading north while I go west. As I zoom through the city, I start to notice an order to the invisible lanes. The ones high in the sky are like freeways, with the cars zipping about at top speeds and for longer distances, while closer to the ground the cars move slower and tend to take more turns or dart off to land.

The skyscrapers of downtown give way to the mix of modern and art deco buildings of Koreatown, where each shop has flashing signs in Spanish, Korean, and English. Below us, old-fashioned cars and buses drive along the street like in the present, with no wings to lift them off the ground. I run a search in my flexi and learn that flying cars are still fairly new and expensive enough that many people don't own them yet, and that public transportation in LA is still mostly grounded as well. Class inequality is still alive and well in LA, no matter how much things have changed over the years.

In only minutes, my car is speeding above the residential streets of Beverly Hills, over rows of palm trees and massive houses with pools in their backyards. There are very few cars on the ground here, and many of the roofs have been modified to include parking for flying cars on top of them.

When my car pulls up in front of Zahra's mother's house, I can tell the place has seen better days. It's bigger than any house I've lived in, but paint is peeling off the windowsills and the plants outside are overgrown. There's no parking allowed on this street, so I tell my car to fly around the area until I call it back. I ring the doorbell, then bang on the door when there's no response.

A woman with ginger hair finally opens the door. She's wearing nurse's scrubs and gives me a slow look up and down. "Yes?" she asks, her voice dripping with disdain.

"Hi. I was wondering if I can speak to Sayeh Ebabi?"

"Mrs. Ebabi does not accept visitors. Is there something I can help you with?"

"I'm a friend of Zahra's, and I'm looking for her. I was hoping to ask Mrs. Ebabi if she's seen or heard from her today. It will only take a minute."

"Mrs. Ebabi is not well, and she hasn't had any visitors today."

She starts to shut the door, but I push my hand against it. "Are you sure? Is there a way I can get a message to Zahra?"

Her eyes narrow. "If you're her friend, you should have her contact info, shouldn't you?"

"We've been out of touch for a while..." But the words have barely left my mouth before the door is slammed in my face. Well, great.

I trudge back to the street and summon my car, trying to figure out what to do next. It estimates a two-minute arrival time. What was my car doing—going on a joyride?

I head down the street, mostly to stretch my legs and help me figure out where to go next. I'm out of good ideas, and the more time I spend on this street, the more out of place I feel among the luxurious homes and cars. I wonder if Future-Adam and I live in an area like this, although it's hard for me to believe I'd ever feel comfortable here, no matter how much money I might have.

When I'm down by the corner, I notice the garage door opening back at Mrs. Ebabi's house. A sleek, black luxury car glides out with a dark-haired woman inside it—Zahra.

My car arrives right as Zahra takes off into the sky. I leap inside and quickly order my car to follow her. It bursts into traffic at full speed, and soon I'm trailing behind her with a few cars between us. There's no "tail someone without them noticing" mode on the car (kind of an oversight there really), and I can't get it to slow down much if I want to stay in this lane. I just have to pray she doesn't notice me behind her. With all the other cars and the fast speed we're moving at, I can barely even see her car, so I think I'm safe.

We head northeast, over the mountains and into Glendale, and I'm amazed at how quickly we get there. It will be tough to go back to sitting through LA traffic in a normal car once I get back to the present.

Zahra's car pulls onto a street lined with tiny shops and cafés, and stops in front of an Armenian market. I tell my car to stay a little way down the road. I don't think she's seen me, but I want to get an idea of what she's doing before I go after her. Right now, she could speed off again and lose me if I'm not careful.

She gets out of the car, glances up and down the street, and then starts walking. I ditch my car and follow her on foot at a safe distance. I'm not sure where she's going, and there was nothing in her profile that mentioned anything in Glendale. Not that it matters. As soon as she stops, I'll corner her and drag her ass back to Aether with me, with or without the neutralizer. But I have to make sure she can't bolt first. I can't afford to lose her. If I do, I doubt I'll ever find her again.

The street isn't very crowded, although a few people eat on the patio of a French-Chinese fusion restaurant. As I pass by a clothing store, it sends pop-up ads into my flexi with news about sales and suggesting clothes in my size and favorite colors. I'm not sure how they even know all this stuff, and I mentally close it all as fast as I can. But the next shop—a store selling rugs—does the same thing, along with the cosmetics store beside it. Does everyone get these ads all the time? I can't find a way to turn them off, and I'm tempted to peel off my flexi and throw it in the trash so I never have to see another of these ads in my head.

Zahra slips into a flower shop selling fall-themed bouquets with mini-pumpkins and yellow and orange flowers. The signs on the window are in English, Spanish, and Russian, and one of them says *Closed*. The store is dark inside, but the door must not have been locked because Zahra has already disappeared beyond it.

As I approach, the store reminds me with a pop-up notice that Halloween is coming up soon. I growl and push the door open. The shop is dark and smells of roses and other flowers, along with a damp, musty odor that clings to everything. I don't see Zahra anywhere, nor anyone else for that matter. Bouquets and plants cover every surface and crowd into the aisles, their branches and flowers reaching out like they're trying to grab me. I step carefully, ducking leaves and thorns, trying not to knock anything over. Something about this place feels wrong, but I can't put my finger on what it is. Everything about it appears to be normal, yet my gut tells me to be careful.

There's only one place Zahra could have gone, and that's through the back door that says *Employees Only*. I scout the place anyway, making sure I haven't missed anything, and get a notification from Adam flashing in the corner of my vision. When I focus on it, something similar to a text message or a chat window pops up. It's sent to both me and Chris.

I'm at Future-Paige's house. Paige was here, and she walked in on her husband in bed with one of his interns. She took off about thirty minutes before I got here, but I'm not sure where she went.

I focus on replying, and the words write themselves into a box at the bottom as I think them. Does her husband have any idea where she could be? I mentally hit Send, and the message pops up below his.

Not really. He's freaking out. Thinks some stalker is pretending to be a younger version of his wife. Needless to say, he's not being very helpful.

A message from Chris pops up next. Dead end for me too. I'm at Future-Jeremy's apartment, but there's no one here.

Sounds like we're all having a great time, I message back. I followed Zahra to a flower shop in Glendale, and I'm about to corner her.

Good luck, Chris says.

Thanks. Hopefully I'll be able to convince her to go with me without having to use the neutralizer, which is tucked in my pants pocket. If not, I have no problem using it on her.

I push open the door into the back area, and the musty smell grows stronger. Dim fluorescent lights buzz overhead, and crates and boxes are stacked along the walls next to bags of soil. I hear muffled voices, but can't tell from where.

Another door with a computerized lock is hanging open. Zahra must have hacked it somehow. I head through it and down a narrow flight of concrete stairs. The air grows darker and colder with each step, like I'm heading down into a crypt. I make as little noise as possible, moving slowly and keeping every sense alert. The voices grow louder, as does the unease in my gut.

I reach the bottom of the stairs and find myself in a dimly lit underground tunnel made entirely of concrete. Other tunnels lead off from it, and there's an open door up ahead. There's no sign of Zahra.

I approach the door silently and peer inside. Two guys with black hair and tan skin play cards at a table, while smoking cigarettes and chugging beer. They're speaking in a language I don't understand—Russian maybe? They both have guns strapped to their chests, and another rests on the table within reach.

I jerk back before they can see me. What has Zahra gotten herself into?

02:15

I back away from the door, my heart racing. I start a message to Chris and Adam, but then change my mind and send it to Chris alone. Adam will only freak out.

I've got a problem.

What's up? Chris asks.

I think I'm in some sort of criminal hideout. Two guys. Lots of guns. I hold my breath and check the room again, memorizing it with the briefest look, and then retreat to the stairs. Both guys have their backs to me and seem to be distracted by smoking, drinking, and playing cards, but I need to be ready to get out with a second's notice. Especially since I saw some plastic-wrapped bricks of white powder piled next to them. Maybe drugs or something too. I don't know. It's bad.

Shit. Sounds like a gang of some sort. Where's the girl?

I don't know. For the first time ever, I miss the gun I had in the other timeline. Now all I have is this puny lipstick-size neutralizer that can knock someone out *if* I manage to press it against their skin, along with my kickboxing skills. I don't like my odds against two guys with guns. And probably even more behind other doors.

But Zahra must be in here somewhere. I can't leave without her. Dammit.

You should get out of there, Chris says. I don't like this.

Me either. But I need to at least try to find her. If I can sneak past the open door, I can scope out the rest of the place. One quick look, and then I'm out of here. I don't even know this girl. I'm not getting shot because she decided to break into a place like this.

I'm not far. I can be there in five or ten.

No, I quickly send back. I won't risk anyone else's life, especially not Chris's, not with Shawnda and his unborn kid waiting for him. I've got this covered. You find Ken.

Fine, but check in as soon as you're safe, or I'm coming to get you.

Will do.

I minimize our chat and try to psych myself up enough to face possible death. *Go in five*, I tell myself. But five comes and goes, and I'm still standing there on the steps. The two guys inside are laughing over something, and although I have no clue what they're saying, they sound drunk.

I creep to the door and peer inside. Both men are focused on their game, staring at their cards with intense expressions. I sneak past them with silent footsteps, praying neither of them glances my way. I keep expecting a shout or a gunshot, but nothing comes.

Only when I'm all the way down the tunnel do I take a much-needed breath. I made it.

I flee around the corner and down the next tunnel as quietly as I can, but I feel like a rabbit about to be caught in a trap. At any moment, one of the other doors could burst open and men could rush out with guns. Being here is such a bad idea, and I have no clue where Zahra is. If I don't find her in the next minute or two, I'm out.

This underground lair seems to go on forever. The flower shop was small, but this basement seems to continue down the entire block, under all the other shops. Does this gang control all of them?

A door opens up ahead, and I jump back around a corner. A couple men emerge, speaking that unknown language, and I pray they don't head toward me. If they do, I'm screwed. But their footsteps move the opposite way, and soon their voices grow soft and then disappear. I'm surprised no alarms have sounded yet, or that no one has noticed a strange girl (or two) creeping around their hideout. Zahra must have turned off all the security—or so I hope.

When I've worked up enough courage to go forward again, softer footsteps sound around the corner. I sneak a peek and see a swish of long, black hair entering the door the men just exited from. *Zahra.*

I rush after her and manage to grab the door with my fingertips right before it shuts. She turns around as I squeeze inside, her dark eyes widening at the sight of me. The door shuts behind us with a click, closing us in a small room.

We're not alone.

"Who are you?" a man asks from behind a large mahogany desk trimmed in gold. He's older, maybe in his fifties or sixties, but his hair is thick and all black and his eyes are beady like a raven's. He's wearing a dark-blue shirt with a heavy gold chain underneath, and his hands are covered in thick, gold rings. When he rises from his desk, he's not much taller than I am, but there's a deadly air to him. It's the way he moves, like at any second he could launch forward and snap your neck with the slightest movement. "How did you get in here?"

Zahra turns away from me and faces the man. "Anton Zubarev?"

He takes her in with a silent appraisal, then does the same to me. "You shouldn't be here, ladies. You have five seconds to turn around and leave."

"I'm here to ask you about Navid Ebabi."

His face doesn't change, but there's a slight tensing in his arms and shoulders. "I don't know that name."

"I think you do." Her voice is pure menace, and she steps toward him. "And you're going to tell me what happened to him. What you *did* to him."

The man doesn't react at first, his bird eyes never leaving her face. Without warning, he reaches for something in his desk, and I spot a flash of dark metal.

"Get down!" I knock Zahra over, and we hit the floor in front of the desk. Bullets fly overhead, slamming the wall behind us with forceful thuds, not nearly as loud as they should be. His gun must have a silencer.

Zahra is frozen beneath me, probably stunned. I roll off her and to my feet in one quick movement, then kick the desk hard, sending it sliding into the man's gut. He lets out an *oof*, and the gun clatters to the floor. He rounds the desk and comes for me, anger seething off him. He grabs my arm hard, jerking me toward him, but I give him a quick jab to the face that he doesn't expect. Those kickboxing classes are finally coming in handy for more than just stress relief.

With a growl, he shoves me back against the wall. The back of my head hits it with a sharp flash of pain, while he lunges for the gun on the floor. I rush forward and knee him in the head, and then kick the gun across the room. He drops to the floor and I raise my fists, ready to throw another punch or block an attack, but he doesn't get up. My blood sings, and I hate how good it feels to be fighting again.

But I kind of love it too.

Zahra scrambles up and lunges for the man. I block her path and come this close to punching her too. But I drop my fists. "We need to get going."

She pushes past me with a sharp glare. "Get out of my way. I didn't ask for your help."

Oh, so it's going to be like that, is it? Fine. Let's ignore the fact that I just saved her from being gunned down by this guy. But I'm done being nice and saving her ass. We're getting out of here before we get killed.

As she moves to stand over the man, I grab the neutralizer from my pocket and get ready to jab it into her skin. But before I can, the guy jerks to life and seizes her leg, wrenching her off her feet. She hits the floor and then he's on her, one hand around her neck, the other holding a knife he's pulled out of his boots. Christ, he's fast.

The knife comes up, but I jump into action and stab the neutralizer into his neck, hard. He freezes, and an instant later, his body collapses on Zahra's. The knife slips from his hand, and my heart starts beating again. As I catch my breath, it's the only sound I hear.

I drag the man off Zahra and roll him over with my foot, ready to kick him hard if he moves. But he's totally out.

Zahra picks the knife up off the floor. "What'd you do?"

"Knocked him out for a while. I'm about to do the same to you if you don't come with me."

We stare at each other for a beat and I size her up, while she does the same to me. Silky black hair falls in waves around her face and matches her thick eyebrows, which frame her dark-brown eyes. She's beautiful in a stately way, with a long, thin nose and plush lips. She wears a charcoal-gray shirt with jeans, and determination radiates off her small frame.

"You're from Aether," she says, her voice as sharp as her gaze.

"No. I'm from the past. Sent to bring you back to it."

"I'm not leaving without what I came for."

Outside the door, the sound of boots pounds toward us, and someone shouts. I swear under my breath. "We're out of time."

"I only need a minute." She kneels beside the guy and grabs his wrist, almost like she's checking his pulse. I don't think I killed him, but honestly, I don't even care if he's dead at this point. I just want to get the hell out of here.

"What are you doing?" I ask.

She ignores me, and the door starts to open. I throw myself at it and slam it shut. Someone outside yells. Now what? I topple over a bookshelf next to the door, spilling its contents all over the floor with a loud clatter. Next, I move behind the heavy mahogany desk and push it against the bookshelf, wedging it in tight. The men outside bang on the door, but they can't seem to open it. Of course, we're also trapped in here, so we're basically screwed.

Zahra's still crouched beside the guy with her eyes closed. I grab the gun off the floor and check the bullets. I've taken a few shooting lessons since my last trip to the future. I'm not an expert and my aim isn't great, but I know how to not accidentally shoot my foot off at least. I was hoping to never need that training, but I had a feeling it would come in handy. Guess I was right.

The banging on the door intensifies, and the shouting gets louder. I glance back and forth between the door and Zahra, wishing she would hurry it up, trying to plan my next move and coming up blank.

"Are you done yet?" I ask. No response. Dammit. What is she doing? Why is it taking so long?

Something slams against the door hard, making it rattle. The bookshelf bounces back an inch, and I know they're going to find a way in here soon. I shove my entire weight against the desk, but I'm not sure I can hold it long against a group of determined men. Especially if they start shooting.

Another hard slam. The door opens a crack, and someone wedges the nose of a gun inside. A shot fires, slamming into the wall to my left.

"I could really use some help here!" I yell over my shoulder at Zahra, while I push against the desk, trying to get the door closed. Another bullet tears through the ceiling, sending plaster raining down on my head.

"Done," Zahra says, popping up beside me.

"About damn time. Maybe you haven't noticed, but we're in a bit of trouble here."

She pushes against the desk with me, and the door slams shut. But the relief is short, because after a second they start shooting again. And this time, they're shooting *through* the door.

02:36

We duck down and press our backs against the desk for cover. When the gunfire stops, I survey the room again. It's a small office. No windows. No other doors. We're completely trapped. I might be able to find some more weapons, but somehow I doubt Zahra and I would fare well against the men outside in a battle. The "running out with guns blazing" technique works in the movies, but not so much in real life.

"Any bright ideas, since we're trapped in here, thanks to you?" I ask.

"I didn't ask you to follow me here," she snaps.

"Fine," I growl. "New plan. I knock your ass out and see if the guys outside will let me go if I turn you in." I'm not serious, of course. Although it is pretty damn tempting.

"Do that, and you won't be able to take me back to Aether."

"Slim chance of that happening now." I debate calling someone for help. Chris or Adam. Wombat. Maybe even Aether. But I'm not sure any of them could get here in time.

"Give me a minute. I might be able to do something." She crawls across the floor, ducking down as more shots are fired through the door. She grabs the man's arm, and her eyes stare off into the distance.

"What are you doing?" I ask.

"Hacking into this building's security system through his imbed."

She can do that? How? Whatever. It doesn't matter, as long as it works. "Hurry."

More gunshots fire. I debate firing back at them, but ultimately decide to save the bullets. We might need them to get out of here.

There's a click and a hiss above me, and then water shoots down from the ceiling onto my head. At the same time, an ear-piercing siren starts going off all around us. I cover my ears and duck my head from the sudden downpour.

"What the hell?" I yell, glancing back at Zahra, whose hair and clothes are immediately plastered to her skin.

"I set off all the alarms. Fire, police, everything. And now, for my final trick…" She turns to the wall behind us, where a seam appears in the otherwise smooth surface, quickly forming a door. As I watch, it pops open.

"What the…"

"Secret escape route, known only to him as far as I can tell. Probably didn't trust his cronies." Zahra scrambles to her feet and darts toward the door. A light flickers on beyond it, illuminating more concrete steps leading up.

I crawl away from the desk. The men outside are still banging and shouting, but their voices are drowned out by the siren blaring and the water spraying down on everything. I check the man on the ground—he's still alive, and I guess I *do* care—and then slip through the door. As I do, the bookshelf is shoved forward and a hand reaches inside the room. I slam the door behind me, and it immediately disappears into the wall again.

Zahra is already heading up the steps toward another door. We have no idea what's on the other side of it, but our only choice is to go forward.

"Who were those guys?" I ask as I rush up the stairs after her.

"They're part of the Russian mafia."

"Seriously? I didn't know they had a presence in LA."

"They're a lot more powerful in this future than in our time. Now they control this whole area."

At the top of the stairs, I hold out a hand to block her from running out. "I'll go first. Stay close."

I raise the gun and slowly ease open the door, peeking out with one eye, ready to pull the door shut at the first hint we're not alone. I don't see anything, and we emerge into a dark alley behind the row of shops.

A bullet slams into the door, and we duck behind a nearby car. Bullets *thunk* against the side, but we're safe behind it. Of course, we're also trapped again.

"Any more genius plans?" I ask.

She scowls at me. "I got us out. I can't do everything around here."

"If I remember, I was the one who saved your ass back there."

"I didn't need saving! All you did was get us shot at."

I grit my teeth, but before I can respond, a guy with a knife rushes us from the side. I swing the gun toward him, but he knocks it out of my hand. He throws a punch at me, but I dodge it and disarm him with a move I learned from my kickboxing teacher, who was big on women knowing how to defend themselves. Now it's just us, without any weapons. I like those odds a lot better.

Another guy tackles me from behind, while the first guy slams his fist into my gut, making me double over in pain. They ignore

Zahra, so they must have realized I'm the threat here, not her. I struggle against the guy holding me from behind and stomp on his foot, but he doesn't let go. Another hard punch to my stomach makes the world go red. Large hands wrap around my throat, squeezing hard, cutting off my air. The man choking me says, "Die, bitch."

Suddenly the guy behind me howls and releases my arms. I throw a quick punch into the guy trying to choke me, and his hands fall away enough for me to jerk back. I suck in a huge gulp of air, coughing painfully, and my vision returns to normal. I grab the neutralizer, and when he lunges for me, I stab his arm with it. He collapses.

Behind me, Zahra has stabbed the other guy with the knife that was dropped, but he's already getting up again. He rips the knife out of his thigh and steps toward her. She looks pale, the whites of her eyes showing, and she backs up slowly. But there's nowhere for her to go.

I rush him from behind and try to touch the neutralizer to his skin, but he's more covered up than the other guy was. We wrestle, and the knife slashes my side and up my shirt, sending hot, wet pain through me. Zahra grabs the gun off the ground and bashes him over the head with it. He sinks to the ground, and I use the neutralizer on him too, just in case. Does this thing have charges? Will it run out? I have no idea. Hopefully I won't have to use it again.

"Zahra." The words come out as a croak. My throat aches, and I'm sure I'll have bruises tomorrow. I rub my neck and try again. "You okay?"

Zahra shakes herself out of whatever shock she's in and nods. "Yeah."

"Where's your car?"

"Not mine. My mom's. Gone now."

"Mine should be nearby." I open up the car app in my flexi and order it to come find us. Three minutes estimated arrival time. Not acceptable!

Zahra hands me the gun, and I aim it over the top of the car we're hiding behind. I pause and wait for more bullets to fire, but it's eerily quiet now in the alley. No signs of movement.

Police sirens sound in the distance. I gesture for Zahra to follow me, and we sneak down the alley, sticking to walls and ducking behind dumpsters and whatever else we can. Hopefully, if we get back to the main part of the street, we'll be in less danger.

Before we can turn the corner, shouts ring out behind us, along with more *plink plink plink* from silenced gunfire. We take off with a burst of adrenaline-fueled speed, but I know my car will never make it in time. One of us is going to get shot.

A huge fire truck flies through the air over us, siren blaring, lights flashing. It drops to the ground quickly, and men in fire-protective gear rush out toward the building we were in. Two police cars arrive next. I glance back, but there's no sign of the guys behind us. They must have bolted when the authorities showed up.

I wipe the fingerprints off the gun and drop it in the nearest dumpster—I don't want to get caught with it. Zahra and I keep walking, directionless, stumbling along down the main street past the clothing and rug shops. My throat burns, my head pounds, and my side throbs. Plus, my ears are still ringing like crazy from the alarm.

Zahra and I reach an Aid-Mart, a huge drugstore I remember from the other future, and stop in front of it to wait for the car. People go in and out of it in a steady stream, so I figure no one will shoot us here. Or so I hope.

While we pause outside the store to catch our breath, I send a quick message to Chris and Adam: I've got Zahra. You guys have any luck?

Adam messages back: The police arrested someone for breaking into the congressman's office. I figure it has to be Paige, so I'm on my way to the police station now.

Probably. Her profile did mention she'd been caught stealing before. Need help?

I think I've got it covered, but I'll let you know.

There's no response from Chris, so I ask, Chris, you there?

Nothing.

Maybe he's found Ken and is talking to him, Adam says. I'm sure he'll get back to us soon.

Yeah, probably. I'll head over to the cemetery to make sure he's okay. Just in case.

Stay safe.

You too.

Zahra looks up and down the street, squinting against the glare of the setting sun. "I don't think they've followed us. Is your car nearby?"

"It's coming. Care to tell me why you broke into a Russian mafia hideout and almost got both of us killed?"

"Point one, I didn't ask you to follow me in there. Point two, I had it handled until you showed up and ruined everything. Point three, it's none of your business."

"Oh, it's definitely my business since I was sent to track you down and bring you back to the present. The only question is if you go willingly or not."

She rolls her eyes. "I got what I needed from him. I'm ready to go back."

"What did you get?" I press a hand against my aching side. It's quickly covered in blood, and I'm hit with a wave of dizziness. My shirt is a tattered rag where the guy sliced at me, and the side of my pants is drenched in red. Now that the adrenaline and shock are wearing off, the pain is hitting me full force.

Zahra eyes me up and down. "You're bleeding all over the place."

"I wonder whose fault that is."

"Come on."

She heads into the store and I limp after her, clutching my side. This Aid-Mart is a lot like the one I visited in the other timeline. It's one of those big stores that sells everything from cosmetics to dog food to cleaning products. I follow Zahra while she heads down an aisle and grabs something off the shelf. People eye the blood on my clothes, but no one says anything to us. She continues back to the front, where she picks up some candy bars and bottles of water. Then she walks out of the store without stopping at a register or anything. In fact, I don't see any registers at all in the place.

"Did you just steal that?" I ask, while my car swerves over us, hovering like an eager dog waiting for a treat.

"Hardly. The store automatically charges you through your imbed when you walk out, if you're carrying something," she says while we get in the car. The door closes behind us, and we strap ourselves into the seats. I order the car to head toward the cemetery where Ken's body is buried, and it lifts off the ground.

Only once we're in the air do her words sink in. "You have an imbed?"

"Obviously. How else would I hack into that guy's head?"

I have so many questions I don't even know where to start. I can't fathom why she would get an imbed for only a few hours in the future. All I can get out is, "Why?"

"Why did I hack into him? Or why do I have an imbed?"

"Both."

She gives a casual shrug. "Flexis are too limiting. Only an imbed would let me access his memories." She tosses me one of the things she got from the store. It looks like a pen, and seeing it brings back memories of another life. Another future, where Trent stole a laser pen like this in the other timeline and later used it on Adam when he was injured. I squeeze my eyes shut, fighting back the memories.

"You use it on your cut," she says like she's explaining to a toddler.

"I know," I snap, but then I add, "Thanks." It's more sincere than sarcastic, since she was smart enough to buy this from the store for me. I pull up my shirt, which is ripped and hanging off me, and use the pen's laser along my side. It instantly seals up the skin with a slight bit of pressure and numbs the pain. The bleeding stops, and I wipe my side with the edge of my shirt, since it's already soaked with blood, along with my pants.

"How did you learn how to hack imbeds anyway?" I ask.

"When we arrived in the future, Aether showed me how so that I could hack into the security system at Pharmateka for our mission. My future self gave me even more tips once I contacted her." She gives a casual shrug. "It really wasn't that hard to learn. The hardware's changed over the years, and security has gotten a bit harder to crack, but the basic principles are still the same."

I'll have to take her word on that, since computers have always been a mystery to me. I still can't believe she'd get one in her head though. "What happens to your imbed when you get back to the present?"

"Imbeds dissolve inside your bloodstream after two years. That's how the tech companies keep people shelling out money all the time."

Two *years*? I can't help but shudder at the idea. "That's a long time to have it inside you doing God knows what."

She cocks her head and studies me. "Oh, I get it. You're one of those people who think technology is evil."

"I don't think it's evil. I'm just not a fan of having it in my head. Or my body."

She leans back and crosses her arms. "Good luck with that in thirty years."

Why is this girl so obnoxious? I saved her life, and all she's done is give me grief. I huff and sit back, staring out the window so I don't have to look at her any longer.

Now she's made me wonder—what *does* my future self think of imbeds? Does she have one, or does she still use an old-school flexi?

It doesn't matter. That's not why I'm here.

But now that I've started wondering about my future life, I can't stop.

02:58

We head southwest over rugged, dusty hills dotted with brush and thick trees, while the sun sets along the sparkling blue of the Pacific Ocean in the distance. The sky is crowded; we're right in the middle of rush-hour traffic, though it's much faster in the sky than on the ground.

Zahra still hasn't answered my question about why she nearly got us both killed. I should probably leave it alone, but her refusal to answer makes me even more determined to find out. Especially if those guys try to come after us again. I need to know what we're dealing with.

"What were you looking for in that guy's head?" I ask. She doesn't answer, so I try again. "Something related to your brother? Navid, right?"

She shoots me a fierce glance. "If you must know, that man back there killed my brother twenty-five years ago. I needed to find out how, so I can stop it when we get back."

"Are you sure that guy killed him?"

"According to my future self, yeah. Navid had a bad gambling problem and owed the Russian mafia a ton of money. My parents wouldn't help him out, because every time they gave him money, he just lost it again. When he couldn't pay up, the Russian mafia had him killed. Everyone knew they killed my brother, but there wasn't enough evidence to get a conviction and no one would rat them out. Which is why I had to hack into Anton's memories to figure out the details of my brother's death—so I can stop it from happening."

"Why couldn't your future self hack into this guy's memories for you?"

Zahra shrugs. "To her, it happened a long time ago. She's moved on, I guess. Got some fancy job with the FBI she doesn't want to mess up. Guess it's easier to have me do the dirty work and hope it changes the timeline."

How strange to think that our future selves could be so different from us now and have completely different goals, but I suppose it makes sense. It's inevitable we would change over the thirty years and have new priorities.

Would I even recognize my future self, if I ran into her? Or would she be a complete stranger to me? I can't even imagine what she's gone through these past thirty years, and from what I read, she sounds like a different person entirely. I'm so tempted to try to find her. Zahra talked to her future self…why couldn't I?

I look up Future-Elena's home address in my flexi's contacts out of curiosity, or so I tell myself. The location pops up on a map, and before I know what I'm doing, I tell the car to make a stop. My clothes are all messed up. I can't walk around with blood all over me and my shirt in tatters, right? I'll just pop in, grab a change of clothes, and leave. That's it. And if I happen to learn a little bit about my future life with Adam…well, what's the harm in that?

"Where are we going?" Zahra asks, as the car changes direction.

"To the cemetery where Ken is buried to look for him and Jeremy, although we're making a quick stop first. Do you know where the rest of your team went?"

"No clue. All I know is that they took off together in the same car."

Together? Maybe Chris will find both of them. "Do you have any way of contacting them?"

"Yeah, but I've sent messages and neither of them have responded."

"Neither of them?"

"Nope. Strange." Her eyes stare at nothing, and the left one twitches. Doing something with her imbed, I assume.

We lapse into silence, and I watch the houses below us get bigger and bigger through the window. I think I know where we're going. I've been there before.

When the car hovers over a mansion with topiaries out front—including a unicorn and a T. rex—I can no longer deny it: Adam and I are living in the same house he owned in the other timeline. But...why? Wouldn't it bring back memories of that other, horrible future?

As the car circles down, I get a message in my flexi welcoming me home. It says the house's security defenses have been disabled and we're cleared to land. Security defenses? Is that really needed?

The car lands and the door opens, but I hesitate. As soon as I go in there, the memories of Trent and Zoe might overwhelm me again. Maybe it's not such a good idea to find out *my* fate either.

"Who lives here?" Zahra asks. "It's huge."

"I do, it seems."

"Nice place. I don't blame you for checking it out. But once you go in there, there's no going back."

I swallow, but my throat is as dry as sand. "I have to know. Not everything, but…something."

I'm not sure why this is so important to me, but it's like I can't do anything else until I see for myself that my future is real. Otherwise, I won't be able to believe it. A part of me still thinks I'm supposed to be lying on the beach with a gunshot wound to the head, like those photos I saw in the other timeline. Maybe because I can never quite scrub those images from my relentless memory. But if I see that my future has changed, maybe I can convince myself that things will get better, and I'll be able to move on from the other memories that continue to haunt me.

"Whatever," Zahra says, lying down across the seat and closing her eyes. I guess the two of us aren't going to be best buddies. God, I miss Zoe. She was quiet too, but she never made me want to slam my fist into her face. Her life was cut way too short, and I think if she hadn't died, we might have become friends.

Zahra and me? Probably not.

I force myself to get out of the car and make my way to the front door, admiring the house's grand arches and columns, and landscaping that is so perfect and green it doesn't look real.

The front door opens for me with the lightest touch of my hand, probably checking my DNA or fingerprint or something. As soon as I step inside, two dogs rush toward me, tails wagging. One is big and friendly, a golden retriever with a happy smile and a shiny coat. The other is a little terrier mix of some sort with scruffy hair and a crooked grin with one snaggletooth sticking out. I love the little dog instantly, and judging by the way it bounces in front of me, I get the feeling this one is mine and the other is Adam's. Makes sense. He's the purebred dog. I'm the mutt.

I gaze past the dogs, taking in the polished wooden floors and thick, soft rugs at the entryway. Damn, I forgot how massive this house is. I slowly move through it and lights turn on overhead, while the dogs bounce around me, tails wagging madly. No one else seems to be home.

Even though this house is the same as the one Adam owned in the other timeline, the decor here is completely different. The giant living room is still there, but instead of the antique furniture that looked like it would break if you sat on it, this one is filled with plush gray couches that seem perfect to curl up on with a book. A wooden coffee table rests in front of them, but there are old scratches on the surface and the telltale ring from when someone forgot to use a coaster. A ratty tennis ball lies in the middle of the room, and the golden retriever grabs it as we walk by.

The other Future-Adam's house was like a ghost town, as if he only stopped by to change his clothes now and then. This is a *home*, with memories stored between the walls and in the cracks of the floor and the fibers of the carpets. I can feel its history with every step I take.

I pause in front of a large framed photo on the wall. It's of me and Adam on the beach, with the sun setting behind us over the waves. I'm wearing a long, white wedding dress and jeweled sandals, while Adam wears a tux and flip-flops. We're a few years older than we are now, and the photographer has caught me laughing, probably at something Adam said, based on the grin on his face and the amusement in his eyes. It's a perfect, happy moment between us, one I never imagined we would share. Especially not on a beach, not after what happened the last time I visited one.

I touch the frame to assure myself the photo is real. Proof that Adam and I are really together in this future, and that I was able to move on from the past.

There's a camera app in my flexi, and I use it to snap a picture to show Adam later. Of course, that would require me confessing to him that I came here. I'm not sure I'm ready to admit that, or to face what this means for us.

I enter the kitchen, where Trent once made us French toast using whatever he could scrape together in Future-Adam's barren cabinets and fridge. The kitchen in this timeline is not the dark, cold one we visited before; this one is all warm beige, swirling gold, and brown granite countertops. When I open the fridge, there's tons of food inside. A pop-up in my head tells me we're out of milk and asks if I want to reorder it, but I ignore it.

I grab an apple off the shelf and pause at the sight of a container of strawberries. Adam is allergic to them, and I can't stand the taste because when I was a kid, I once ate three entire containers at once and had red vomit all night. Maybe I'll be over that in the next thirty years and will like them again.

The dogs get excited as I approach one side of the kitchen, jumping and circling me with doggy grins and happy tails. There's a little plastic container on the counter with dog paws on it and treats inside—they must know this is where their goodies are.

"All right, all right." I make them sit and then hand them each a treat. The golden retriever darts off to another room with it, but the terrier scarfs it down and then gives me another hopeful look. I bend down and give the dog some love, and then check the collar. "Taco?" I ask, wrinkling my nose. "What was I thinking when I named you *that*?"

"You didn't name him," a female voice says behind me. A voice I recognize, even though it sounds wrong to my ears.

I slowly stand and turn around—and come face-to-face with myself.

03:14

"What are you doing here?" she asks. Not in a friendly way.

"I…" The words die on my tongue. Every answer seems inadequate when faced with the blazing eyes of my future self. All I can do is gape at her, at the familiar way she stands, at the annoyed expression on her face that I've never actually seen before but somehow recognize. She's staring me down, hands on her hips, wearing black slacks with a coral silk shirt that probably cost a fortune. Her face is dusted with fine lines and her hair is shorter than mine, making it curl around her neck.

She's me…but also *not* me.

"And what happened to your clothes?" she asks, giving me a long once-over with a frown. From her tone, I can't help but feel like she's disappointed with me, like I've let her down somehow.

"I got stabbed by someone in the Russian mafia," I manage to say. She should know what happened without my explanation. She rescued Zahra too, after all.

"You *what*?" Her eyebrows pinch together, and the frown deepens. "No, that's not right. That's not how it happened. I didn't get injured; Chris did. And I never came here, to this house. What have you *done*?"

I shift my weight, my cheeks burning. I'm hit with the feeling that my mother is scolding me for doing something wrong, which is ridiculous because this is *me*. She's thirty years older, but she's not my mother—even if she looks a lot like her. "We... we split up."

"You split up. You changed something purposefully." Her tone shifts, and there's more than anger in her eyes now—there's fear too. "Oh God. What were you thinking?"

"We were trying to save Ken's life. We thought if we split up, we might have a better chance."

"At what cost? Your own future?"

"What do you mean? Do you know something about his death?"

"Nothing more than you do, really. But splitting up is dangerous." She gives my shirt a pointed look. "Obviously."

I cross my arms to cover it. "Hey, I'm fine. And maybe you were okay with letting Ken die, but I'm not. We're going to save him this time."

She presses her palm against her forehead. "This is a disaster. God knows how much you've changed in the timeline already. You need to get out of here before you make anything worse."

"Why? What could go so wrong?"

She gestures around her, at her gleaming kitchen and her excitable dogs. "Do you see all this? I've worked hard for this future. Adam has too. And we're *happy*. It took a long time to get here, but we made it work, and life is pretty damn good now. For me, for Adam, and for Chris and his family too. But what you've done could jeopardize *everything*."

Damn, am I always this intense? And bossy? Or will I get worse with age? "All we're doing is trying to save one guy's life. Nothing else is changing."

"How do you know? By coming here and seeing a glimpse of your future, you might make different choices than I did, which will change the course of your entire life." She shakes her head. "I have to get you out of here and back on track as quickly as possible and hope the damage to the timeline is minimal."

"Fine, whatever," I say, checking my watch. Less than two hours left before we have to get back to the aperture. Time for me to go anyway.

"I'll get you some new clothes. Wait here." She points a finger at me. "Don't move even one step. Not. One. Step!"

She exits the kitchen with a brisk pace. The dogs look back and forth between us, like they're unsure who to stay with, before finally deciding to follow her. I scowl and lean against the counter and wait for her.

After about five seconds, I get bored of standing around and decide I have to pee. I find the guest bathroom near the front of the house, the one I visited in the first future, where I found a code inside the origami unicorn Future-Adam made for me. This bathroom doesn't look as formal or pretentious as the other one, although it's still just as big and unnecessary. And there, on the windowsill, glinting under the light, is a crumpled and slightly dusty silver origami unicorn. Mine is sitting next to my bed at home. This must be the same one, with thirty years added to it.

When I'm done, I find my future self waiting for me outside the door, looking pissed.

"I told you not to move," she snaps.

"I had to pee," I say in exactly the same voice.

She narrows her eyes and thrusts the clothes at my chest. "You have no idea. No clue what your future holds and how fragile it all is. But I do."

"So tell me then. Tell me why it's so important I don't change anything."

"I can't. The more you know, the more likely you are to do something differently." She plays with her wedding band as she speaks, making it go round and round on her finger. "I went into my future totally blind, armed with only the knowledge that Adam and I would make it work somehow. That's all you need to know. Anything else is too dangerous."

I scowl at her, irritated that she didn't give me anything useful. "I won't look into anything else. All I want is to get the others and head back to the present."

Her shoulders relax an inch. "Good. Get changed and get out of here. You need to join Adam and Chris as soon as you can and make sure you're all back to the aperture in time."

"Working on it. Zahra's outside and Adam's tracked down Paige, but we still have to find Jeremy and Ken. And I don't know what's going on with Chris."

She frowns. "What do you mean, you don't know?"

"He went to find Ken at the cemetery, but he hasn't checked in for a while."

"Find him. Find the others. Stop wasting time here."

"You could help me out and save me a lot of time by telling me where the others are."

Her lips press in a tight line, but she finally relents. "Fine. Jeremy is in Cedars-Sinai Medical Center."

"See, that wasn't so hard, was it?" I send a message to Chris and Adam telling them to meet me at the hospital. "Why is he there? Is he injured?"

"Yes, he was injured. I can't believe I have to tell you any of this. You should have found this out by now, but instead you were off playing hero and getting stabbed."

"Hey, maybe if Wombat told us where to go, we could have done it all in fifteen minutes and been back at Aether by now."

"That wasn't an option. It might—"

I hold up a hand to interrupt her. "Yeah, yeah, it might mess up the timeline, I know. Just tell me what you know about Ken, at least. Do you know what happened to him?"

"Only that we found his body at Griffith Observatory, but we had no idea how he died. We assumed he was murdered, but we could never figure out who killed him or why."

"Damn. I hope Chris has found him."

"Me too."

I slip back into the bathroom to change into the clothes she gave me—a black tank top and olive-colored pants, nearly identical to my current clothes. While I'm in there, Adam sends a message: Paige is in the police station, but I got the charges dropped. We'll head to the hospital when we're done here.

Good, I send back.

Still nothing from Chris. He should have checked in by now. He's a tough guy and he can handle himself, but I'm still worried. Maybe Future-Elena is right and splitting up was a bad idea—not that I'd admit it to her.

When I'm ready, she walks me to the front door, but we both pause in front of it. Like me, she's probably trying to figure out how to end this awkward moment. Should we hug? Shake hands? Or walk away with a quick "bye" like we're strangers?

I offer her my hand. "Thanks for the new clothes and for the tip about Jeremy."

She eyes my hand, then sighs and pulls me in for a tight hug. It's strange, being hugged by myself…but oddly comforting too.

"Go find the others, and when you get back to the present, try to forget the past and focus on the future. I know that's impossible, but just…try. And remember that Adam loves you."

My throat closes up, and all I can do is nod. Now I really feel like my mom is talking to me. But it's nice. I haven't been mothered much in my life.

I'm reluctant to pull away, but I finally step back. There are so many things I want to ask her about my future, about her life, about what she's seen and done and experienced. I want to know what Future-Adam is like in this timeline, and about the company they created together, and a million other things. But all I know is that they're together and they're happy. I guess that will have to be enough.

"I hope, for your sake, that the timeline hasn't been disturbed too much." She sighs and opens the door, but when I walk out, she grabs my arm. "Just promise me one thing. Whatever happens, make sure you go with Adam to Cabo San Lucas for his thirtieth birthday."

"Um. Sure." I don't understand why some vacation is such a big deal, but I guess I'll find out in about twelve years.

"This is really important," she says, pleading with her voice and her eyes. "Please, promise me you'll do it."

"I promise."

She releases my arm and nods. "Good luck."

"Thanks." I step through the door but turn back one last time. "I guess I'll see you in thirty years."

"No," she says with a knowing smile. "You'll *be* me in thirty years."

03:27

Adam and Paige arrive at the hospital at about the same time Zahra and I do, and we meet in the parking lot. Relief slams me in the gut at the sight of Adam getting out of the white car, and I practically throw myself into his arms. He lets out a surprised sound as I kiss him hard, with thoughts of our future still fresh in my mind. Our house, our dogs, our wedding picture. Our life together.

He studies my face. "You okay?"

I debate telling him I met my future self and about everything I saw, but maybe it's safer if Adam doesn't know what our future holds. Future-Elena's dire warnings about changing the timeline have made me wary, so I simply nod. "I'm just relieved to see you. And there's still no word from Chris. I'm getting worried."

"Me too. If he doesn't check in soon, we'll go find him."

A short girl with long, blond hair pops out of Adam's car and bounces over to us with a giant smile. "Hi, I'm Paige!" she says, and throws her arms around me. They're muscular and strong, especially for such a tiny girl. Must be from the gymnastics she used to do.

"Elena," I say, patting her back and feeling awkward.

"Ooh, you're Adam's girlfriend. It's so good to meet you. He told me so much about you, I already feel like I know you!" She glances at him with shining blue eyes. "Isn't he the best?"

He holds up his hands in surrender. "I barely said anything."

"He's so modest. I just love him," she says, swatting at his arm. My eyebrows shoot up at her familiar touch, but she flings herself at Zahra next, grabbing her in a tight hug. "How did it go? Did you get what you needed? Are you okay?"

Zahra cracks a tiny smile. The first one I've seen from her. "I got it."

"Oh, yay!" Paige grabs her in a second hug, but Zahra doesn't seem to mind. "I was so worried about you."

"I'm fine. What about you? You got arrested?" She genuinely sounds concerned, all her sarcasm gone. The two of them seem to be close, which surprises me 'cause they seem so different. Then again, opposites attract. Adam and I are proof of that.

"Yes! What an ordeal. Thank goodness for Adam, or I would still be in prison." She gives him another beaming look, but I don't think she's hitting on him or anything. That seems to be how she is with everyone.

"How *did* you get her out?" I ask Adam.

"I had to convince Paige's husband that Future Visions will back his next congressional campaign in exchange for him dropping the charges. I'll have to send our future selves an apology for that." Adam sighs, his face exhausted. I don't blame him. I am too after five seconds with Paige.

"What happened exactly?" Zahra asks Paige.

"First I went to my house, which was seriously amazing, but then I caught Brad in bed with a girl my age! Like, my age *now*, not my age in the future, ugh. He said he thought I was going to be out all day, and then he freaked 'cause I looked so young, although really I think I look pretty damn good in my late forties too, if I do say so myself." The girl talks a mile a minute and bounces on her heels, like she has to be doing something physical or will die. Like a shark who can't stop swimming. "Then I got really mad, 'cause how dare he cheat on me! What about our marriage? So I found his office and broke in and stole something, which is how I got arrested. But the police didn't search my underwear, so I still have it."

"That asshole," Zahra spits out. "I'm going to hack into his accounts and wipe them clean. Both now and in the past."

"Please don't," Adam says, pinching the bridge of his nose. "It was hard enough getting Paige out of trouble."

"Please. Like they'd be able to trace it back to me."

We step into the hospital, and Adam heads to information to find out where Jeremy is, while the three of us hang back and wait in the lobby.

"What did you steal?" I ask Paige.

"Some papers from thirty years ago. I knew Brad would keep them because he's obsessed with organizing things and never throws anything away, even at twenty-one. They prove he hired people to write his essays in college and that he paid for test answers. As soon as we get back, I'm using them to get him kicked out of USC. After I dump his sorry ass, of course."

"You're already dating him? In the present?"

"Yes, sadly." She collapses dramatically on the bench in the lobby, her skirt flaring as she sits. "I met him a few months ago and thought he was the *one.* So hot and rich and charming. I was seriously in love, and then I saw him today with that…that…" She sighs. "No, I can't call her anything bad. For all I know she's a perfectly nice girl who got sucked in by his smooth talk and good looks and had no idea he was married. Well, okay, she probably knew he was married. There were pictures of us all over our bedroom. But she's so young, and maybe she's going through a really rough time right now and he took advantage of that, you know? He's the jerk, not her."

I have to hand it to Paige. She's not anything like what I expected when I read her bio. I'm torn between liking her and wanting to give her a mild sedative.

"I'm sorry Brad turned out to be a dick," Zahra says, sinking onto the bench beside Paige.

"Thanks." Paige rests her head on Zahra's shoulder and sniffs. "Now tell me everything that happened to you today."

Zahra gives Paige a quick rundown of our encounter with the Russian mafia, although she leaves out some of the parts about how we almost got killed along the way. I try to contact Chris again, but still get no response. As soon as we get Jeremy out of the hospital, we're going after Chris next.

Adam returns a few minutes later, and we follow him up an elevator and to a numbered room. We slip inside and shut the door behind us quietly. There's one bed in the room, and a young man I recognize as Jeremy is in it, his eyes closed. He's covered by a blanket and wears a hospital gown, but a heavy bandage peeks out from under it on his upper chest and shoulder. There are no IVs connected to him, and no monitors showing his heart rate or anything else. He doesn't respond to our presence at all, but his body moves with each breath he takes, so I know he's alive.

"Jeremy?" Paige asks softly, approaching the bed.

He doesn't stir. The curtains are open, giving us a view of the cars flying through the dark sky, their bright flashes reflecting off the side of his face. He's handsome in that boy next door kind of way, with thick auburn hair and a strong, masculine jaw. He looks more like a jock who should be out playing football than a genius on par with Adam. There are only hints of his father in his face, mainly in the shape of his nose and mouth. I'm guessing he takes after his mother more.

"What happened to him?" I ask.

"According to the nurse, he was shot in the shoulder," Adam says.

"He's unconscious," Zahra adds. "That must be why his flexi couldn't pick him up."

Could that be why Chris's isn't working either? I send Wombat a message asking him to look into Chris's whereabouts, and he replies that he will. The car should be trackable, if nothing else.

"Poor Jeremy," Paige says, brushing hair off his face.

I check my watch. "We need to get him out of here. We only have about ninety minutes before the aperture opens."

"Can he be moved safely?" Paige asks.

"He's coming with us one way or another," I say. "Any ideas, Adam?"

He glances around the room with a frown. "I don't see his chart or any other information."

"It's all computerized now," Zahra says. "The doctors and nurses have access to all the files in their imbeds so they can monitor the patients from anywhere. Give me a second, and I'll have access too."

Her eyes go distant, just as Jeremy's flutter open. He blinks slowly, then focuses on Paige. "Hello," he says, his voice hoarse. "Where am I?"

"You're in the hospital," she says. "Do you remember being shot?"

He closes his eyes and takes a few breaths before opening

them again. Still drowsy, maybe from something they gave him. "Yes, I remember."

"Can you tell us what happened?" Adam asks.

Jeremy's gaze travels to Adam and then to me. "Who are you?"

"They're from Team Delta," Zahra says.

"You know who we are?" I ask, surprised.

"Obviously. One of the first things I did when they recruited me was find out what happened to the previous time travelers. I recognized you immediately."

I scowl at her. "You could have mentioned that before."

She shrugs and goes back to whatever she is doing with her imbed.

Adam gestures at us. "I'm Adam, and this is Elena. We were sent by your father to bring your team back to the present."

"I'm surprised he cares that much," Jeremy says, his hands tightening on the sheet.

Paige rests her hand over his. "Of course he cares. He's your father."

"He only cares because Aether's stock prices would plummet if word got out that his son went missing." He stares out the window, his jaw clenched.

I roll my eyes. "He cared enough to drug us and lock us in the aperture to make sure we brought you back."

"He did *what*?" Paige asks with a gasp.

"That does sound like something he'd do." Jeremy picks at a loose string on his sheet and sighs. "He never wanted me to be part of Team Echo. He didn't think I could handle it. I can already picture his face when I return and he finds out he was right." He lets out a harsh laugh. "The best part is that I got shot because of him."

"How?" Adam asks.

"After our team split up, I went back to Pharmateka to complete our mission on my own. Since my future self works for them, it was easy to get into the lab, and then all I had to do was find the design for the synthetic water generator. But on my way out, a security guard stopped me. He didn't believe I was Future-Jeremy, and when I tried to escape, he shot me. Next thing I knew, I woke up here."

"We all agreed to abandon that mission," Paige says. "Why would you do it on your own?"

"I know we decided it was too dangerous, but it seemed so easy with me pretending to be my future self. And I thought if I brought the formula back, then my dad would be impressed or something." He picks at the yellow hospital wristband on his arm and shakes his head. "Stupid, really."

"Do you know where Ken is?" I ask. "Did he go with you?"

"No…he hasn't checked in?"

"Not for a few hours," Paige says.

"His flexi doesn't seem to be connected either," Zahra adds.

"What do you mean?" Jeremy asks, sitting up straighter and cringing. "What happened to him?"

"We're not sure…" I trail off and glance at Adam. The others don't know about Ken's final fate.

Adam nods. "We should tell them."

"Tell us what?" Paige asks, her eyes wide.

"Ken is going to die," Adam says. "Unless we can stop it."

03:40

Paige gasps and covers her mouth. Zahra just stares at us. Jeremy sits up even straighter, his face pale. "How do you know?" he asks.

"Dr. Campbell told us," I say. "They knew all along and never told you."

"Those assholes," Zahra says, her thick brows pinching together. "How is he supposed to die?"

"We were told that he would be found dead at Griffith Observatory," Adam explains. "But our future selves weren't sure if he was killed there or somewhere else. They didn't know how or why he was killed either."

"This can't be true," Paige says, shaking her head. "Why would anyone kill Ken?"

"Does he have any enemies?" I ask.

"No, of course not. He's the sweetest guy I know."

"His file said he was arrested for drug possession before Aether recruited him," I say.

The three of them exchange a look. They clearly know something.

"Ken's mother is really sick," Jeremy says. "He was trying to come up with a cure, or with something that would help slow her symptoms at least. He got hold of a large quantity of prescription drugs to study, but the police caught him in his car and he had enough on him that they could charge him with possession and intent to sell. But Aether got them to drop all charges."

I raise an eyebrow. "In return for him working for them?"

"That's how they got most of us," Zahra says. "Except Jeremy, of course. He just has daddy issues."

"What can we do?" Paige asks. "We have to save Ken!"

"The last member of our team, Chris, was trying to track him down, but we haven't heard from him either," Adam says. "Jeremy, did you see him at all?" He gives a brief description of Chris, but Jeremy shakes his head.

"Zahra said you and Ken took a car somewhere?" I ask.

Jeremy nods. "I went with Ken to visit his grave. I didn't want him to face his death alone. But he told me he needed some time by himself, so I left. I haven't seen him since then."

Dammit. No sign of Chris or Ken and no hint as to where they've gone. At this point, all we know is that they were both at the cemetery—but what happened next?

"And after that you went back to Pharmateka?" Adam asks.

"Not right away. First I visited my future self's house. Found out that he hadn't spoken to my father in ten years, since before he left Aether to join Pharmateka. That's when I decided to try to complete the mission on my own. I don't want to end up like Future-Jeremy, passed out in a puddle of vomit on the floor of a one-bedroom apartment."

Yikes. I feel bad for the guy. I know what it's like to see a future you don't want, yet feel powerless to stop. Makes sense he would do whatever he could to try to change it, even if it meant trying to patch things up with his dad.

"I've got access to Jeremy's medical files," Zahra says. "Says here he had a gunshot wound to the shoulder, but it didn't hit anything major. They patched him up using something like those laser pens except on a bigger scale, then they pumped him with drugs to ease the lingering pain and help his body recover from the blood loss and trauma. They wanted to keep him overnight for observation, but I changed that in the system. He's free to go now."

I rub my thumb over the face of my watch. "Good. We're running short on time, and we still need to find Chris and Ken before the aperture opens."

"But where will we go?" Paige asks.

"Our best option is to go to Griffith Observatory, where Ken is supposed to be found dead," Adam says. "Maybe if we go now, we can still prevent it. And Chris might be there too."

I try to think of anything else we could do, but come up blank. Everything about this is wrong, but I'm not going back to the present without Chris. "We need to hurry."

"Can you walk?" Adam asks Jeremy.

"I don't know." He eases his legs off the bed but stumbles as soon as he puts weight on them. Paige catches him and helps him sit back down on the edge of the bed. "Guess not."

"We'll get you a wheelchair," Adam says.

"Some clothes would be good too," he says, looking down at his pale-blue hospital gown. He touches the bandage at his shoulder, then takes the end of it and peels it off. Underneath, the skin is perfectly smooth, no trace of any injury except for some lingering redness. Amazing.

We find his jeans and shoes in the room, but no shirt. It must have been covered in blood after he was shot. Adam brings us a wheelchair, and while we help Jeremy into it, Paige slips off to find

Jeremy some clothes. She returns a few minutes later with a soft, faded LA Marathon shirt.

"Where did you get that?" I ask.

"I found it in the staff locker room."

"Found it or stole it?"

She gives a quick shrug. "No one was using it."

"Great, I'm probably walking off with some doctor's favorite old shirt," Jeremy mumbles, but he tugs it over his head anyway.

Paige wheels Jeremy out the door and down the hall, but a nurse stops us before we can reach the elevator.

"Where are you going?" she asks. "He's supposed to stay overnight for observation."

"The doctor told us he can go now," Zahra says.

The nurse's eyes go distant and she frowns. "That's not right. He shouldn't be released yet. I need to speak to the doctor before I can let you go."

Adam gives her a warm smile. "Of course. Maybe you can help me with something too while we wait. My name is Dr. Adam O'Neill, and I'm from Future Visions Industries. I want to ask you about the genicote in this hospital."

Her mouth falls open, and her cheeks flush. "Oh my gosh. You're *the* Dr. Adam O'Neill? I'm so sorry, I didn't recognize you. You look so young in person."

He chuckles. "I get that a lot."

"How can I help you?"

"I want to make sure the genicote is stored properly. We've been having some troubles with that lately, and as I'm sure you know, it can be dangerous if used improperly. Is there someone I can talk to about that?" He leads her away from us, and unease settles in my stomach. He said he wouldn't go after the cure for cancer, but I'm not sure I believe he could resist taking it if it were in front of him.

But the distraction works, and we get Jeremy in the elevator without a problem. Jeremy rubs his shoulder, his face twisting up. "Hang on, that guy is *the* Adam O'Neill who created the cure for cancer?"

"Yeah, he is," I say.

"Wow. What's he doing on Team Delta?"

"It's a long story."

We make it out of the hospital and into the parking lot, and a minute later Adam runs to catch up with us.

"Any problems?" I hope from the tone of my voice he knows what I'm really asking—if he got the cure or not.

"Nope. She told me I had to speak to a hospital administrator, so I told her I'd come back another day."

My shoulders relax. "Good."

"Did you get the cure?" Jeremy asks. "I mean, you probably could, right? Since you created it and all."

"Um. No, I didn't get it."

"Too bad. Imagine what we could do with it if you brought it back."

Adam coughs and gives me a quick look. "That's not what we're here for."

We head for the pickup zone, where both cars are already waiting for us. A girl with long dark hair leans against my car with her arms crossed. She's wearing black jeans and a black tank top with glowing green fractal patterns swirling and shifting on it. As we approach, her head swivels toward us. I see her face—and gasp.

I recognize her, even though I've never met her before in my life. Some sort of primal instinct takes root deep inside me, one I've never felt before. It makes me want to wrap my arms around this girl and protect her to my last breath, even though I don't know her at all.

Beside me, Adam comes to a halt, sucking in a sharp breath. The others keep going toward the cars, but the two of us can't take another step and can only stare at the girl. Piece by piece, her features come together in my mind. Thick, wavy hair the same shade as Adam's. Flawless brown skin, not quite as dark as mine. Intelligent eyes that don't seem to miss a thing.

It's like looking into a mirror...and not at all.

She pushes off the car and heads toward us with the hint of a grin on her lips. I take a step back, unsure if I can face this, but she keeps coming, becoming more and more real. Adam rests a hand against my lower back, but I'm not sure if it's a gesture of support or because he needs me to steady him.

"Who are you?" I ask, even though I know the answer deep in my soul and in every strand of my DNA.

"I'm Ava," the girl says. "Your daughter."

03:51

I'm hit by a rush of emotions so strong I can't breathe. I want to cover my face with a pillow and scream. I want to run away as fast as I can and never look back. I want to grab this girl in a hug and never let her go.

I have a daughter.

"No," I whisper. "Impossible."

I see it though. She's about the same age as me and looks like she could be my sister, but she has traces of Adam in her too. The slant of her nose, the shape of her eyes, the color of her hair. I can't quite put my finger on it, but I can see both of us in her, somehow.

"You're..." Adam starts, but his voice is as uneven as mine. "You're our daughter? Mine and Elena's?"

"Yeah." She looks back and forth between us with a grin, but there's something hesitant on her face too. It's an expression that reminds me so much of Adam it makes my heart clench. "You both look so *young*. It's so warped."

"Is everything okay?" Paige asks, glancing back and forth between us and Ava.

"Yeah, just...give us a minute," Adam says.

Paige nods, and she and the others get into the white car. They close the doors, giving us some privacy.

"Ava..." I can't seem to form any other words except her name. My daughter's name. I say the word again, letting it roll off my tongue. Did I name her, or did Adam?

She studies me with wide, brown eyes. My eyes. "Damn, everyone told me I look like you when you were younger, but I had no idea, Mom. We could seriously be sisters."

Mom. She called me *mom*. I'm going to throw up. I can't have a daughter. I'm too young, I'm not ready for this, I can't I can't I *can't*.

Adam adjusts his glasses, like he's not sure of what he is seeing. "How old are you?"

"Eighteen." She brushes back a lock of her dark hair, and I spot Mamá's watch on her wrist. *My* watch. She catches me staring at it, and touches it with a gesture that's all too familiar. "You gave it to me for my birthday."

I look down at my own wrist, at the same exact watch. Proof that Ava really is my daughter, and that this is actually happening. "Sorry, this is just..." I shake my head, unsure of the right word. Overwhelming. Confusing. Amazing.

I never imagined myself as a mother. Never thought I would have kids. Hell, a few months ago I didn't think I'd make it past eighteen. Now I'm standing in front of my own flesh and blood, this perfect combination of me and Adam, and I don't know how to react.

I want to know everything about her. What does she like to do for fun? What's her favorite color? Does she eat strawberries, and is that why Future-Elena has them in the fridge? Does she get along with her parents—with *me*?

But the question that comes out is, "Did you name our dog 'Taco'?"

She laughs, and it's the most beautiful sound I've ever heard.

"Yeah, I did. Hey, I was nine. Give me a break. I named Cookie too."

Adams glances at me. "Taco? Cookie?"

"Our dogs," Ava says.

I wonder if this moment happened in the timeline Future-Elena went to. When she was my age, did she meet her daughter too? Or is this encounter a result of us changing things?

"How did you know we'd be here?" I ask.

"I got home, and Mom was cleaning up bloody clothes but wouldn't tell me what was going on. I checked the house's security records and saw that it had logged two instances of her in the house at the same time, and I realized today was *the day*. From there, it was easy to track down the car, since it's owned by Future Visions."

Our daughter is as smart as Adam and as stubborn and strong-willed as I am. I'm oddly…proud. And very sympathetic to my future self. Ava must be a handful.

Adam's staring at me with a frown, and he must have realized there's a lot I didn't tell him. But he turns back to Ava and asks, "So you knew about time travel already?"

"Yeah, I overheard you two talking about it when I was fifteen, and I made you tell me everything. For the longest time I thought you were making it up, but sometimes you would know things…" Her eyes dart to the watch on my wrist, and she smiles. "Now I see you were telling the truth all along."

I open my mouth to ask her one of the millions of questions running through my head, but another car pulls up beside us. The door slides open and Wombat jumps out. "What are you doing here?" he asks Ava. "Your parents gave you strict orders not to get involved with this."

She plants her hands on her hips. "Are you kidding me? I wouldn't miss this for anything. Why should you have all the fun?"

"You shouldn't be here." Wombat rubs his forehead and groans. "Elena is going to *kill* me."

"I'll tell her it was all my fault. She'll be mad at me for five minutes, and then she'll get over it." She moves close to Wombat and takes his hand. "Don't worry. You won't get fired. I promise." She gives him a kiss, and I swear my eyes almost bulge out of their sockets.

"Are you two *together*?" I ask.

They break apart and jump back, like they've been caught with their hands in the cookie jar. "Um, yes," Wombat says, his face going bright red. "Please don't be mad."

I'm in motion before I know what I'm doing. I grab hold of his shirt and slam him back against the car, hard. "If you hurt my daughter, I will tear you apart limb by limb."

Wombat takes one look at my face and then bursts into laughter. Beside me, Ava rolls her eyes and says, "Oh my God, Mom. Please stop."

"What's so funny?" I ask.

"The other Elena had the exact same reaction when she found out Ava and I were dating," Wombat says.

I release his shirt and step back, looking down at my hands. Damn, that protective instinct was so strong it was hard to control. I want to lock her up in our house and never let her outside. And have armed guards posted at every window and door. How does my future self deal with it all the time? And with Ava *dating*?

I scowl at Adam. "How can you be so calm about this?"

He lets out a strained laugh. "I'm not calm, not even close. But if Ava is going to date someone...well, she could do a lot worse than Wombat."

Wombat grins. "And that's exactly what the other Adam said too."

I suppose Adam is right. Our future selves seem to trust

Wombat, at least. I don't like it, but I'm not actually her mom. *Yet*.

"Sorry, Wombat."

"It's okay. I know this must be a lot to take in."

No kidding. I went from having no idea I would ever had kids to being the mother of an eighteen-year-old girl. My emotions are shifting so fast it's giving me whiplash.

Ava leans close to Wombat and asks, "Why do they call you Wombat?"

"I don't know," he says. "Warped, right?"

"You don't go by that name?" Adam asks.

"Nope. But you can keep calling me that if it makes you feel better."

"What's your real name?" I ask.

"It's Jesse. Jesse McIntosh."

"Huh," I say. He doesn't look like a Jesse somehow. He'll probably be stuck in my head as Wombat forever.

Ava rubs her hands together. "So what's the plan? Where are we going?"

"The plan is, you go home, while I help your parents," Wombat says.

"We both know that's not going to happen. I'm here to help."

"I'm not sure that's such a good idea," Adam says. "It could be dangerous."

"But Dad—"

"He's right," I interrupt. "There's no way you are coming with us. We're almost out of time anyway. Wombat—I mean, Jesse—do you know where Ken or Chris are?"

"No. The tracking system in Chris's car was disabled, and all the records had been wiped clean. I'm sorry."

"Damn." This is bad. Really bad. We're nearly out of time, and we have no idea what happened to either of them and no clue where to go next. I'm starting to suspect we won't find Ken in time. Or at least, not alive.

"Are you sure we can't help?" Ava asks.

"We have to do this on our own," Adam says. "But...I'm really glad we met."

"Me too, Dad." She grabs Adam in a hug, and he stiffens for a second, then hugs her back. She throws her arms around me next and I hold her tight, memorizing everything I can about her. The strength in her arms. The jasmine scent of her hair. The difference in our heights. I don't want to let go. Now that I've found her, how can I walk away from her?

She steps back and smiles at me. "Take care, Mom."

"Good-bye, Ava," I say, with an ache in my throat.

Adam shakes Wombat's hand. "Take good care of her. We'll see you both in a few years."

We return to the black car and get inside, but both stare out the window as we take off. Below us, Ava leans against Wombat, and he wraps an arm around her. The two of them wave at us as we fly behind the others in the white car. I never take my eyes off her, trying to savor every last second in her presence. Only when we can no longer see them do we sit back in our seats.

"That was..." Adam's voice trails off, and he removes his glasses and wipes at his eyes.

"I know." I rest my hand over his. "I didn't want to say good-bye to her."

He entwines his fingers with mine. "Me either. But we'll see her again in oh...twelve years."

"That's a long time to wait."

"It'll be worth it."

I can't help but smile. "Yeah. It will."

04:03

Our cars head toward the mountains in the north where the Hollywood sign sits watch over the city. Even though the sun has set completely, we can see it clearly—its giant letters are lit up and shift color every few seconds. That's definitely new.

We fly over the rugged, untamed hills until we come to a building that looks sort of like the White House, except with two large domes on either end and another huge one in the center. It sits right on the edge of the mountain, overlooking the rest of the city.

Griffith Observatory.

Construction equipment—some familiar, and some high-tech and unrecognizable—is scattered about the grounds. Scaffolding and lights are set up along the outside of the building, and in front of it there's a huge trench going deep into the earth with a giant mound of dirt next to it. No one seems to be working this late. The place appears to be empty, and the building is dark.

The car stops and hovers in place, while a notification pops up in our flexis that we're entering an off-limits area. It warns us of risks and hazards and asks if we're sure we want to enter. We bypass it, accepting the terms and conditions, but the car still refuses to descend.

We land a short distance down the hill, outside the construction zone, next to a silver car. Jeremy, Paige, and Zahra burst out of their own car and rush toward the silver one, while Adam and I follow them.

"What is it?" Adam asks.

"This is the car Ken took," Paige says, while Jeremy throws open the door.

"Ken?" he asks, poking his head inside the car. Then he yells into the dark trees around us, "Ken! Where are you?"

His voice echoes through the canyons, but the only response is the soft chirp of crickets in the nearby brush. The air smells of dirt and metal, of wild nature and cool starlit skies. I shiver and take a deep breath, sucking in eucalyptus and oak and other things I can't identify. Things I rarely smell in Los Angeles, especially in this future one.

Jeremy limps around the area, calling Ken's name while clutching his shoulder. Paige and Adam join him, but Zahra slips inside the silver car. I sit beside her, scanning the interior for any hints of what Ken has been up to all this time.

"Let's see where he's been," Zahra says, as she turns on the car's navigation. She flips through the GPS records, but there's not much there. Ken went to the cemetery, then stopped by a nearby Aid-Mart, and then he came here.

Adam pokes his head inside the car. "There are tracks leading up to the observatory. He must have gone up there."

"Any sign of Chris?" I ask.

"Not that I can tell."

I slide out of the car and survey the area, but it's so dark I can't see anything beyond our ring of lights. "Why would Ken come here, of all places?"

Jeremy leans against the car, holding his shoulder, his face tight. "Ken loves the Griffith Observatory. He comes here all the time in the present to hang out because it's free and near his house."

"How do you know?" Adam asks.

He shrugs. "Ken's my best friend. I came here once with him."

My eyebrows shoot up. "Your best friend? You haven't known him that long."

"Maybe not, but we've been through a lot together."

Paige nods and wipes at her eyes. "We've all grown really close. I can't imagine not having them in my life. And Ken..."

Zahra throws an arm around her. "We'll find him."

I don't know why it surprises me that they're all such good friends. They've been going on missions to the future for months now; it makes sense they would have developed a bond after all they'd experienced together. Especially if they all became united against Aether over time. I wish I'd had the chance to develop that kind of friendship with Zoe and Trent. Adam, Chris, and I have gotten pretty close, but the pain of our past mistakes still keeps us apart. Although now I wonder if it's me who keeps them at a distance.

"I just don't understand who could want to kill Ken," Paige says, sniffing. "Or why. He's the nicest guy in the world!"

"We don't know if he's dead yet," Adam says. "There's still time to find him."

"We should split up," Zahra suggests. "We can cover more ground faster that way."

I check my watch. We have less than an hour left in the future. "We need to hurry."

"Let's go," Jeremy says, pushing off from the car. But with the first step up the hill, his face twists and he stumbles, clearly in pain.

Paige rests her hand on his arm. "Maybe you should wait here."

"No, I can do this. I want to help find him."

"Please, Jeremy. Don't hurt yourself."

"Someone should wait at the car," Adam says. "In case Ken heard you and is on his way back."

Jeremy frowns, rubbing his shoulder, but finally he sighs and nods. "All right. But let me know as soon as you find something."

"We will," Zahra says.

He gets into the car, and we hike up the hill through the darkness. With every step, my nerves pull tighter and tighter, like a rubber band ready to snap. Each branch that breaks under my feet and every brush of leaves against my arms makes me jump. I don't know what we will find once we reach the observatory, but at this point there's no way it can be good.

We're silent as we pass an obelisk in the middle of the lawn and approach the large, white building, majestic in its grandeur even while being remodeled. Plastic covers blow in the wind and the scaffolding creaks, but there's no other movement or sound around us. There's no hint that anyone has been here for hours, or even days.

We climb over a barrier to get inside the building and go around a huge round pit with some sort of science exhibit inside it. We have no lights, and our footsteps echo loudly across the pitch-black halls. The dust is heavy, making us cough, and many of the entrances and stairwells heading downstairs are blocked off.

We split up to search, with Adam and me taking the left wing and Zahra and Paige taking the right. Adam finds some construction lights and flicks them on, illuminating the large domed room in a murky glow. The air is full of sawdust and paint fumes, and but there's no sign of Ken or Chris inside.

I've only been to the Griffith Observatory once on a school field trip in the fifth grade, but memories flicker through my head.

Standing on the observation deck and gazing across the city, realizing for the first time how truly huge Los Angeles was. Running after a boy who stole my hair clip past a long wall with stars all over it. Sitting in awe during one of the planetarium shows inside the giant dome, staring up at the constellations and distant galaxies.

We make our way carefully around the equipment to the door leading outside and climb the stairs to the roof where the observation deck is. Once there, I take a deep breath of clean air and stare across the city, taking in the impressive view. Behind us, the mountains disappear into the darkness, but in every other direction, the sky is lit up with flying cars and buildings stretching far into the distance. It's so bright that when I look up, I can't see any stars, even though the night sky is clear. The sight fills me with emptiness and dread, like all that vast, dark space above is pressing down on me.

We walk slowly around the smooth, white concrete deck to one of the domes where the high-powered telescopes are kept. Adam checks the door to the dome, but it's locked and we continue on. There's nothing here but a few telescopes along the balcony, and I'm starting to think that we'll never find Chris or Ken.

We continue around the dome, and then I see it.

A hand on the ground.

I stop, clutching my stomach, waves of revulsion and fear slamming into me. The hand is attached to an arm, to a shoulder, to a chest and a head with black hair and an entire body. But I can't process any of that. All I can see is the hand, pale and stiff, fingers outstretched, like they're reaching for something but were unable to grasp it in time to save them.

"Adam," I whisper, grabbing his arm. My throat closes up like someone is squeezing it tight, suffocating me. My gut aches like someone's just kicked it hard. I want to throw up. I want to run away. I want to do anything except move forward.

"It's okay," he says, but his voice trembles. He rests his hand over mine, and my fingers dig into his skin as we creep forward.

I've never met Ken before, but I recognize him as we get closer. In life, he was handsome, with a friendly face and smart eyes and a kind smile. But in death, he looks like a wax copy of himself. There's a gunshot wound in his chest, and blood covers his clothes and pools below him, staining the white concrete red. It looks so much like Zoe's blood dripping down the white tile that it's all I can do to not let out a scream. I cover my mouth, afraid the sound might escape me anyway.

He's dead.

We're too late.

We've failed. *Again*.

"We have to tell the others," Adam says, as he kneels beside the body to inspect a gun near Ken's outstretched hand. Small and black, a dark shape in the night. Like the gun Lynne used to kill Trent and Zoe. Like the gun I killed her with.

I wrap my arms around myself, my skin clammy despite my racing pulse. Cold sweat drips down the back of my shirt, and my hands tremble uncontrollably. I turn away from the body, hoping the familiar sight of the city will help me get hold of myself.

"Oh no," Adam says with a sharp intake of breath. I turn back, but he's not looking at Ken. He's staring across the deck around the dome, at something in the shadows.

I'm scared—no, *terrified*—to follow his gaze, to see whatever is making Adam mutter, "No, no, no," over and over. But I look.

Of course I look.

Another body. One I recognize instantly, even in the darkness.

Chris.

04:32

My knees give out and I sink to the ground, but even the hard jolt of concrete can't stop the flashbacks from overtaking me. Trent, dead in a dumpster, his hand pale and cold and reaching for me. Zoe, dead in a bathtub, her blood mixing with the water. Lynne, dead on the beach, with the smell of gunpowder and ocean air.

And now Chris, dead on the concrete, his dark eyes staring up at the starless night.

Memories hit me of Chris's body from the future that almost was, that I only glimpsed in photographs. Lying on the floor of the auto shop he worked at with a gunshot wound to the chest. It's so similar to the reality in front of me now that my brain flips back and forth between them. I prevented one, but not the other. And the blood…oh God, the blood.

I can't breathe. Can't get enough oxygen. I'm hyperventilating, choking on the very thing I need to survive. My head pounds so hard I think it might explode. My vision is blurry, with tears or from the pain and dizziness, I don't know. Chris can't be dead. He *can't* be. He has a son about to be born. A girl he loves and wants to have a future with.

Dammit, it was supposed to be *me* who went after Ken. Not him. Why didn't I argue with him more? Why didn't I do *something*?

Adam wraps an arm around me and says my name over and over, but he's shaking and his voice is high-pitched and strained. He buries his face in my shoulder, and I cling to him too. He's the only thing keeping me from falling apart completely, although he's not doing much better.

A scream rings out, and Paige rushes over to Ken and drops to her knees beside him. Zahra moves beside her, speaking to her in a low voice. But Paige won't hear it and grabs Ken's body, pulling it onto her lap while she rocks back and forth, letting out a soft wail. Zahra stands beside her friend stoically, her hand on her shoulder, while tears stream down her face.

I don't want to look again, but I can't help but stare at Chris, at his ashen skin and too-still body, at the blood on his chest. More flashbacks take over: Chris showing us the ultrasound. The pictures of his son's room. How excited he was to be a dad.

I have to pull it together. For Chris and his son. For Ken and his team. For Adam. I have to do something. But…what? What is there to do? Chris is dead, and there's nothing I can do to change it.

I drag myself off the floor and make my way to Chris, fighting back the urge to vomit. Every breath is agony, but that's nothing compared to what Chris has gone through, and I swallow the pain and nausea. I push all my emotions to the back of my brain, locking them in a box for now so I can focus on the facts. I'll fall apart later when I'm alone, but right now I need to memorize as much as possible of this scene.

Chris has been shot in the chest, most likely with the same gun that shot Ken. It's unclear if Ken shot Chris and then shot himself, or if someone else shot both of them. I suck up every detail and then move on to Ken's body before taking in the entire area. But there's not much to find. There's no explanation. No rhyme or reason for these deaths. No clues to find or motives to uncover.

"We need to find out who did this," Adam says.

"What's the point?" Zahra says. "It's too late to stop it."

I can't argue with that, no matter how much I want to. We're running out of time, and there's nothing we can do here. All we're doing is wasting our few moments left in the future looking for ghosts.

I check my watch. "We need to go."

"We can't just leave them here!" Paige says.

"We have to. We can't take them with us. And the aperture opens in twenty minutes."

"I'll alert the police when we leave," Zahra says. "It's the best we can do."

Paige bites her lip and looks like she wants to say more, but Zahra leads her away. With one last look at the two bodies on the ground, I silently say good-bye. Adam takes my hand, and we turn our backs on Ken and Chris.

We have no choice.

We leave them behind.

04:49

I don't know how we make it back to Aether. Thank God the car can drive itself and knows where to go, because we're all a mess. Paige weeps loudly during the entire ride while holding on to Zahra, who tries to comfort her but keeps wiping at her eyes too. Jeremy seems to be in shock. He holds his head in his hands, muttering to himself over and over about how it isn't possible. On the other side of the car, I cling to Adam, my face buried in his shirt, focusing on each breath he takes to remind myself I haven't lost everything. He holds me tight and sits in silence, but he shudders slightly. Trying to be strong for me, but barely holding it together himself.

Dr. Campbell is waiting for us on the roof of Aether's building in the desert, her brows pinched together, her face tight with worry. Her eyes pass over each of us when we get out, like she's mentally tallying us up in her head. Seven of us went out into the world of this future. Only five of us returned.

"Ken?" she asks, even though she must know the answer.

"We couldn't save him," Adam says.

Her frown deepens. "And Chris?"

Adam shakes his head, looking away sharply.

"Murdered," I manage to get out.

"Oh no. Not Chris too. Do you know who did it? Or why?"

"No," Adam says. "We didn't see anything."

"We'll try to find out what happened," Dr. Campbell says. "We'll do everything we can to bring the killer to justice."

"What good will that do?" I ask. "What are we supposed to tell their families back in the present?"

She sighs. "I don't know. I'm so sorry."

She leads us into the elevator and down to the basement. Another large team of scientists is waiting for us, but the space where the aperture will open is clear. The floor is marked off with a red circle—so no one accidentally stands in it, I suppose. What would happen if they did?

Dr. Chow scans all of us again and takes all of our flexis, neutralizers, and everything else we've picked up while in the future. Jeremy shows him the design for the synthetic water generator from Pharmateka, and the man nods.

While the others are busy with Dr. Chow, I turn to Dr. Campbell, who stands with Adam. "Has anyone ever tried to go to the past through the aperture?" I ask, grasping for something. Anything. Even the tiniest shred of hope that we might be able to change what happened.

She shakes her head. "No, it's impossible. Only people who are sent to the future can return to their time through it. For anyone else, it does nothing."

"Are you sure?" Adam asks.

"I tried it myself," she says, her voice quieting. "I wanted to go back and stop my husband from going to the store to pick up champagne on our five-year wedding anniversary. But it didn't work."

"What happened to him?" I ask.

"He was mugged in the parking lot. He bled to death before anyone found him."

"I'm sorry," Adam says, while my heart twists. So much death, and it always seems to be inevitable.

"Thank you. It was a long time ago." She puts on a smile, though I can tell it's strained. But then her smile drops and her head tilts. "Hang on. There might be a way to save them after all..."

"How?" I ask.

"If you set the accelerator to take you a few minutes after the moment when you arrived in the future, you could try to save them."

"Won't our other selves be here already?" Adam asks.

"Yes." Dr. Campbell frowns, tapping her fingers to her lips. "There is a high chance of a paradox if you meet with the other instances of yourself, the ones that are also traveling through time. That's why we never send you to the same day, or even the same week. Too risky."

"It's worth the risk to try to save them," I say.

"Is there any other way?" Adam asks her.

"No. Not that I can think of."

"Then that's what we have to do." I swallow hard. "Come back to the future and do it all over again."

"The aperture will open in five seconds," a loud mechanical voice says, echoing through the basement. The scientists turn toward the center, to the red circle on the floor, and the room seems to collectively inhale.

Golden light blinks into existence from out of nowhere. The bright dust reflects off the equipment around us, casting sparkles across the room. It's beautiful and otherworldly, but I'm weighed down by sadness and guilt and can't move.

"Go," Dr. Campbell says, pushing me forward gently. "You only have sixty seconds."

Every step toward the aperture is slow. I don't want to go back to the present, because when I do, I'll be faced with the truth of what's happened and the impossible task before me. But I can't stay in this future either, with this terrible fate for Ken and Chris. If there's a way to save them, we have to do it. No matter what the risk.

Zahra and Paige go first, stepping forward until the golden dust settles on their shoulders. They instantly disappear, fading away into nothing. Jeremy limps into the circle next, one hand pressed to his shoulder but able to walk on his own. Adam waits for me beside the light, gazing at me with worry etched on his face.

I step forward and stand with him, but stop to take one last look back at Dr. Campbell. She gives me a stoic nod, her face grim, and then Adam and I move into the light.

It blinds us. Overwhelms us. Surrounds us and reaches deep inside, filling us with burning white light. I'm torn apart and put back together.

And then I'm reborn in the present.

PART III
THE PRESENT

FRIDAY

As the golden light disappears, it's replaced by swirling white tendrils and the sound of a loud, piercing alarm. Smoke creeps up my nose and around my body, filling my eyes with fog and making the room murky. I try to suck in a breath, but that's a mistake. Big, racking coughs overtake me, and I can barely make out the dim figures of my friends through the smoke.

We're huddled together inside the dome, all of us coughing as we stumble toward the exit. The metal door is thrown open with a thud, and shouts echo across the walls. People rush inside the accelerator, faceless figures in the gray murk, and hands grasp my arms and tug me forward. I stumble through the door and into the wide expanse of the basement, where the smoke thins enough for me to see better. Scientists rush around, while lights flash on the machine and smoke billows out of it. The alarm is incessant, a harsh warning sound that only makes my heart race faster.

"Get them out of here!" Dr. Campbell yells. I blink at her for a second, my mind struggling to accept this younger version of her again. I'd gotten used to the older one, and now this version, the *real* version, seems off somehow.

"Is something wrong with the accelerator?" I ask her, while someone else tries to nudge me forward.

"I don't know." Then she's gone, darting toward the machine through the smoke.

"Please come with me," Dr. Kapur says, and leads us away from the chaos by the accelerator. I don't know what's happened to it, but it doesn't look good. Before they trapped me inside it and sent me to the future, I would have been thrilled that it was malfunctioning. Now I need it to save Chris.

We're pressed into the elevator, still coughing, still dazed, and get out on the third floor. Dr. Kapur takes us into the medical labs, and we're instructed to sit while nurses start taking our vitals.

Vincent Sharp bursts through the door, making it bang against the wall. When he spots us, he lets out a long exhale. "You did it." He moves to his son and clasps a hand on his shoulder. "Thank goodness you're safe, Jeremy. Once the doctors finish their evaluation, you can go home and we can put this all behind us."

Jeremy shoves him back with a glare. "Jesus. Two people are *dead*, Dad!"

Red-hot anger shoots through me. All Vincent cares about is his son. Did he even notice we're short two people? "You bastard," I spit out. "Thanks to you, our friend is dead. And so is Ken."

He frowns, taking in our group. "I'm sorry. Losing Ken and Chris is a great loss. But I'm thankful the rest of you returned unharmed and brought my son back to me. Don't worry, I will still honor our agreement, and I'll make sure their families are compensated."

I yank my arm away from a nurse who is trying to check my blood pressure and stand up. "I don't care about that. I want you to send us back to the future."

Vincent blinks at me. "I'm sorry?"

Everyone else stares at me now too, including the stunned nurses. "Go *back*?" Zahra asks, while Paige starts crying again into her hands.

"The Dr. Campbell of the future said it would work," Adam explains. "If the accelerator sends us a few minutes after we originally arrived, we might be able to change what happened and save Chris and Ken."

Jeremy sits up a little straighter. "Hmm, I suppose it *is* possible, although it might cause a paradox. It could be dangerous."

Paige wipes at her eyes. "But if there's a chance we can save them…"

Vincent shakes his head. "No. I can't risk sending any of you to the future again. Once Dr. Kapur finishes his tests, all of you are going home."

"Oh, *now* you're worried about risk?" I ask, my hands clenching into fists. "What about when you locked us in the accelerator and forced us to go to the future?"

"I take full responsibility for what I've done, and I would do it again. But that doesn't mean I need to put you in even more danger now." He fixes me with a level stare. "Besides, I thought you didn't want anything to do with Aether anymore."

"That was before my friend was killed," I growl.

While the nurses watch from the side of the room with wide eyes, Dr. Kapur steps toward me. "We need to examine all of you before you go anywhere."

"No, we don't have time. We need to get back—"

"Elena," Vincent says, placing his hands on my arms. I instantly shrug him off and step back. He should know better than to touch me. He frowns and starts again. "Elena, you all need to rest. You've been through a lot, and each of you needs some time to recover. And *we* need time to find out what is wrong with the accelerator."

"But—"

"He's right," Adam says with a sigh. "We'll have a better chance of saving Chris if we're rested. We need to be at the top of our game when we go back."

"I have to agree," Jeremy says. "I want to return to the future and save them as much as you do. But it won't matter if we wait five minutes or a day or even a year. They can send us to that moment in the future whenever we're ready."

I scowl at him. "It *does* matter, because Chris's son is about to be born. What am I going to tell his girlfriend about his disappearance?"

Paige bites her lip and nods. "Ken's parents will be worried too. We have to rescue them right away."

"First, the exam," Dr. Kapur says, his beady eyes staring us down.

"Give us time to check out the accelerator," Vincent says. "We can't do anything 'til we figure out what went wrong with it. In the meantime, Dr. Kapur will check you out, and then we'll debrief you on what happened in the future. After that…I'll *consider* sending you back to the future."

I hate admitting he's right. Hate accepting that there is nothing I can do at this very minute except wait. I don't want to wait. I want to fix this, *now*. I let out a frustrated growl, but then say, "Fine. Let's get these stupid tests over with."

* * *

We're checked out quickly by the nurses and by Dr. Kapur, who makes us undergo all sorts of tests to be sure we're not suffering from future shock or from any other injuries or side effects. Both Jeremy and I are completely healed from our wounds, thanks to the medical technology of the future. Honestly, that's what Aether should have had them bring back. Too late now. They'll have to find another team of teens to send to the future for their dirty work next time.

Once Dr. Kapur deems us healthy, Vincent Sharp calls us in for a meeting. We sit around a conference table with him at the head of it and Dr. Campbell next to him. Her head is bowed, and she won't meet any of our eyes.

"First, I want to thank both of your teams for your help," Vincent says, folding his hands on the table. "Dr. Kapur says you're all healthy, but before we do anything else, I need to know—did you bring anything back with you from the future?"

Jeremy reaches into the back of his pants and pulls out a small notebook, then throws it on the table in front of his father. "Here. This is what we risked our lives getting for you. The design for a machine that makes synthetic water. Hope you're happy."

His voice is like acid, but I don't blame him. He got shot getting the design because he wanted to impress his father, and now his friend is dead as a result.

Vincent flips through it quickly, his eyes scanning what's inside, and a slow smile spreads across his face. "Yes, this will do. A very good find."

"Jeremy got that for you on his own," Zahra says. "He should get all the credit for it."

Vincent eyes his son for a long moment, but then turns back to Paige and Zahra. "And what were the rest of you doing? Why did you miss your aperture?"

Paige opens her mouth to respond, but Zahra stops her with the shake of her head. "We don't have to tell you anything," she says. "We're done being your test subjects. Once we get Chris and Ken, we're through."

I'm not sure when they decided this, but Zahra seems firm on the subject and Paige nods beside her. Jeremy seems less certain, but he doesn't contradict her. It's a good move—they need to get out now, before they're trapped doing Aether's dirty work any longer. All it leads to is death.

"I'm terribly sorry about what happened to Ken and Chris," Vincent says. "I know they were your friends, and I regret that their lives were lost on this mission. We will be donating a large sum of money to both of their families in retribution."

I cross my arms. "You don't need to do that. We're going to bring them back alive this time."

"Ah yes, about that..." He turns to Dr. Campbell.

Dr. Campbell frowns, but finally looks up. "The accelerator is broken. We can't send you back."

"*What*?" I ask.

"Broken?" Jeremy asks. "How?"

She glances at Vincent and shakes her head. "We're not sure."

"Can you fix it?" Zahra asks.

"I-I don't know."

"You don't *know*?" My hands shake, and my heart is in my throat. I can't believe this is happening. They have to be lying. There must be *something* they can do. I refuse to accept that this is the end.

Dr. Campbell stares at the table. "I've done everything I can think of, but I haven't been able to fix the accelerator. I'm not sure it *can* be fixed, honestly."

"How do we know Aether didn't sabotage the machine on purpose?" Zahra asks.

"We have no reason to sabotage it," Vincent says. "We've spent millions of dollars on the accelerator and need it to send more teams to the future. It's more likely one of you did it when you stepped inside the accelerator so it would be your last trip to the future. You, Zahra, with your computer skills? Paige, perhaps you stole a part from inside it? Or Jeremy? You used to assist Dr. Walters with his research. You know how the accelerator works almost as well as Dr. Campbell does."

Each of them looks horrified, but Vincent makes a good point. The most likely explanation is that one of them tampered with the machine. Except…it let us go to the future after them. So why would it break when we returned?

"I don't believe it was sabotage," Dr. Campbell says. "Most likely it's a malfunction caused by stress to the machine from being used so frequently in a short period of time."

I jump to my feet and slam my hands on the table. "I don't believe you. You're just saying all of this so you don't have to send us back."

"I swear to you that the accelerator is broken. I'm very sorry." Her eyes meet mine, and I detect sincerity in them—and sadness.

"There must be another way," Adam says.

Dr. Campbell sneaks a glance at Vincent and says, "The one person who might be able to fix it would be Dr. Walters, since he invented the accelerator in the first place. But even that seems like a very slim possibility."

"Then we need to get Dr. Walters," I say.

"That might be difficult," Vincent says. "Dr. Walters didn't exactly leave Aether on good terms. I can't imagine he would want to come back and fix the machine he once tried to destroy."

"We'll talk to him," Adam says. "He'll listen to me and Elena. And in return, you'll send us to the future again when it's fixed."

Vincent drums his fingers on the table for a long moment before answering. "Very well. *If* you can convince him to come back and *if* he manages to fix the accelerator, you can return to the future to find your friends. Otherwise, I'll honor our agreement and Aether will stay out of your lives from now on—and I'll expect you to do the same with us."

I know he's using us to get his precious time machine fixed, and that's the only reason we're getting another shot to return to the future. But I'll take it, even if I'd love to leave the accelerator broken. We have no other choice.

* * *

While Adam drives us to Dr. Walters's place in Silver Lake, I stare out the window at the setting sun, fighting back the grief that threatens to consume me and the memories that try to force their way to the front of my mind. *Not yet*, I tell myself. Later, I can fall apart. Right now, I need to get this done. Nothing is more important than convincing Dr. Walters to help us.

It takes forever to find a parking space. That's one thing I miss from the future—you never needed to find parking when your car could fly around. Even if it had a tendency to get stuck in traffic on its way back.

Adam shuts the car off but lingers with his hands on the steering wheel. "Elena, about what we saw in the future..."

My throat tightens up. "Don't."

His eyes never leave my face. "I know you don't want to talk about it, but I have to know what you saw. You went to our house, didn't you?"

I shake my head. "I can't have this conversation right now. Once we save Chris, we can discuss it. Until then..." I can't even think about my future with Adam when Chris's has been wiped out completely. Especially since it should have been *me* instead.

"Please, just...give me something," Adam says, his voice

breaking along with my heart. "Some hint as to what our life is like. It's tearing me up inside not knowing."

I sigh and stare at my hands, folded in my lap. "Our house was the same as the one you owned in the first future, but it was different. Warmer, somehow. Happier. We had two dogs."

"Taco and Cookie?"

"Yeah. And I saw pictures of our wedding. We got married on the beach in sandals. The silver origami unicorn your future self gave me was there too. But that's all I saw, really. Future-Elena didn't let me look around too much. She was worried I might change things if I knew too much about my future."

He sits up a little straighter. "You met her? What was she like?"

"Intense."

The hint of a smile touches his face. "That sounds about right. What else did she say?"

"Not much. Just that whatever happened in the future, I had to make sure we went to Cabo San Lucas for your thirtieth birthday."

"My thirtieth..." He inhales sharply. "I bet that's when you're going to get pregnant with Ava."

"Must be. That explains why Future-Elena was so secretive. She wanted to make sure we didn't do something that would wipe our daughter out of existence. She never met her future self or learned about Ava, but I did...and that worried her."

"We'll be careful," he says, taking my hand in his. "I won't let anything happen to jeopardize our future together."

Our eyes meet and emotions stir within me, things I can't put into words. I care so much for Adam, but everything's changed now that we know the future. How can we go on living a normal life once we've seen our fate? Will we spend every day wondering if we're accidentally changing things, never knowing if we're still on the same path?

I don't know if I can live that way without going mad.

Later, I remind myself. First, we need to save Chris and Ken. I'll worry about my future with Adam once this new mission is a success.

I pull my hand from his and open the car door. "We should get going."

Dr. Walters lives in a gray house with a huge tree that has sprinkled his lawn with brown leaves, making a crunchy blanket for us to walk over to get to his door. Adam rings the bell, and I check my watch. By the time Aether let us leave, it was late in the afternoon, our entire day wasted. By now, Shawnda must be wondering where Chris is. I pray she hasn't gone into labor yet.

The door opens, and a Latino man stands behind it. He's younger than Dr. Walters but not by much, maybe in his forties or so, and ridiculously good-looking with shapely cheekbones, a strong jaw, bronze skin, and a hint of curl to his dark hair. "Yes?" he asks with the faintest trace of an accent.

"We're looking for Dr.—I mean, Bill Walters," Adam says. "Is this the wrong house?"

The man leans against the door and studies us both. "Who are you?"

"We're..." Adam trails off and looks at me helplessly. I know what he means. We can't exactly tell a stranger we're time travelers who went to the future in a machine Dr. Walters invented.

"We met him when he was working at Aether," I say. "We need his help."

"Who is it, Armando?" Dr. Walters calls from inside, and footsteps sound as he gets closer.

"Some people want to talk to you. They say they met you at Aether."

Dr. Walters moves to the doorway. He's an older man with a head of gray hair, his face wrinkled but kind, and he's wearing a pale-blue polo shirt and jeans with a hole in the knee. His eyes widen when he sees us. "You…I never expected to see you two again. Did Aether send you?"

"Not exactly," I say. "Can we come in?"

He glances at Armando. "We were about to have dinner, but I suppose you can join us."

"We'll be quick," Adam says, as the smell of roasted garlic wafts over to us, making my stomach growl. We haven't eaten since we had that sandwich in the future. "We don't want to bother you."

"It's no bother," Armando says. "If you are friends of Bill's, then you are friends of both of ours. And my husband always makes tons of food."

We step right into the living room, a small and cozy space with dark-gray furniture and wood accents. Books are shelved on every wall, ranging from mystery novels to science textbooks to music journals. I'd love to spend time here perusing their collection, but now's not the time for that.

"I'll finish up," Armando says, resting a hand on Dr. Walters's arm. "You spend time with our guests." He turns to the two of us and flashes a dazzling smile. "Can I get you something to drink?"

"Just water, thanks," I say, and Adam nods.

"I didn't know you were married," Adam says to Dr. Walters, after Armando disappears into the kitchen.

"I try to keep my work and private life separate. And we didn't exactly get a chance to know each other, did we?"

"No, I suppose not."

I know what Adam is getting at. In the first future we went to, Dr. Walters lived alone in a nursing home. I wonder if Armando had passed away by then, or if they'd split up. It's a grim thought either way.

Dr. Walters heads into the attached dining room and sets out two more plates on his long wooden table. "How have you been these last few months?"

"We've been...okay," Adam says. "It's been tough to move on from what happened."

"I'm sure. What you two went through..." He shakes his head. "Going to the future is stressful enough on the mind and body, and then what Lynne did...Well, it's amazing you're not falling apart completely."

I let out a short, bitter laugh before I can help myself, and both of them focus on me. I look away but can't hide the scowl on my face. Who says we're not falling apart?

He gestures for us to sit down, and we take our seats around the table. "Why are you here?"

"We need your help," I say.

Adam launches into a quick recap of everything that happened over the last day, covering Aether locking us in the accelerator, Chris and Ken's deaths, and the malfunction when we got back. Armando walks in during the middle of the story and serves us roasted chicken with potatoes and green beans that all smell delicious, then joins us at the table. Adam pauses, but Dr. Walters gestures for him to keep going, and he continues his tale while we eat.

Dr. Walters doesn't touch his food the entire time Adam speaks. "How awful," he finally says. "It horrifies me knowing the technology I created is being used to send people to their deaths. Especially against their will." He stares at his food, his face pale. "I didn't realize just how far Aether would go to get what it wants."

"I can't believe they could do this," Armando says, his voice thick with emotion. "Sending so many teenagers to the future, so recklessly. That can't be legal."

"It is," Dr. Walters says. "They're very careful to make sure of that. But I had no idea they were sending another group of teens to the future. I knew they wanted to, but I argued against extending the project after what happened to your team. When they wouldn't listen, I tried to destroy the accelerator, but all that did was get me fired." He slams his fist down, and the table shakes, rattling the dishes. "Dammit, I should have tried harder to destroy the accelerator before any of this could happen."

Armando rests a hand over his. "You didn't know it would come to this."

"I should have known. I should have considered all the consequences."

"There's nothing you can do to change the past," I say. "But you can still help us now."

"How?" Dr. Walters asks.

"We need you to fix the accelerator," Adam says.

Dr. Walters's mouth drops open. "Why would you want to do that? I assumed you'd both be thankful the accelerator is broken."

"We would be, except that we need to return to the future to rescue our friends," I say.

"Rescue them?" His thick gray brow furrows. "You want to go back to the same five hours?"

I nod. "We're going to rewrite the future and prevent their deaths."

"No, it's too dangerous. You'd have to be very careful to not run into the other version of you already time traveling."

"Yeah, yeah, we know. It could cause a paradox, right? You told us the same thing about meeting our future selves before, and that didn't happen."

"This is different. There will be two versions of you out of sync with time. If both versions interact, it could be catastrophic, possibly even resetting the entire timeline. In fact, the other versions of you shouldn't even know you're in the future with them. You'll have to stagger when you arrive and leave to make sure you don't overlap."

"I promise we won't interact with our other selves at all," Adam says. "They'll never know we are there."

"Even then..." Dr. Walters frowns and traces the paisley print on the tablecloth with his finger. "I can't fix it. It might lead to more of your deaths."

"But if you fix it, we can use it to *save* lives," I say.

"You can't guarantee that. And who knows what Aether will do with it once it's fixed? No, it's better to leave it broken so they can't cause any more chaos."

"Give us one chance," I plead. "One chance to save our friends."

Dr. Walters doesn't move, his face set. I worry he is never going to agree to this, and then what will we do? He's our only hope for saving them. But Armando turns to him and says, "Bill, you must help them. Otherwise you will never forgive yourself."

He stares at Armando for a moment, and then his shoulders slump. "Very well. I'll try to fix the accelerator. But after you bring back your friends, I'm going to destroy it."

"We'll help you," I say. "We'll make sure Aether never sends people to the future again."

* * *

After dinner, Adam and I return to my apartment. Dr. Walters said he would go to Aether's facility right away, but there's no way to know how long it will take him to fix the accelerator. My fingers itch with impatience, with the desire to do something, *anything*. I hate feeling so helpless, but there's nothing we can do right now except wait.

I pause outside my door, hesitating to open it. Last time we were in my apartment, we talked about going to the zoo and I foolishly believed everything might get better in my life. It's only been hours since then, but it feels like an eternity.

"We're going to bring Chris back," Adam says.

"What if we can't?" I ask. "What are we going to tell Shawnda?"

He sighs and runs a hand through his hair. "I don't know. I have to believe it won't come to that, and that his fate is only a temporary one."

I wish I could believe that, but with each minute that passes, my confidence shrinks. What if we go back to the future and can't save him? What if we only get more people killed?

I unlock my door with shaking hands, but linger in front of it. I know Adam wants to come inside so we can take comfort in each other, but I can't right now. All I can think about is how Shawnda is alone tonight because of me. Adam doesn't understand. He never could. He hasn't carried the weight of the others' deaths on his shoulders like I have—and he doesn't bear the guilt of Chris's death now. But I do.

"Do you want me to stay?" Adam asks.

I hesitate, but then shake my head. "I'll be fine."

"Are you sure? The nightmares..."

"I just want to be alone tonight."

His face falls, and it hits me that maybe *he* doesn't want to be alone. He's hurting too, after all. But I'm one step from breaking into a million pieces, and I can't let him see that.

"I'm sorry," I say, and slide my arms around him. He embraces me tightly, his face pressed into my hair, like he might fall apart himself if he lets me go. He takes a long, steady breath that shakes us both, and then we step back from each other. He pauses like he's waiting for me to change my mind, and I stare at the floor in silence. With one last heartbreaking look, he walks away.

As soon as I slip inside my apartment, the emptiness surrounds me. Grief wells up inside my chest, a big black pit that sucks me into it. Tears fill my eyes and I let them come, but once they start, they don't stop. Big, choking, gasping tears, the kind that make it hard to breathe. My knees gives out and I slide to the floor, hands pressed against the wood for support while my body shudders with each sob.

Chris is gone. He's dead. And it's all my fault. *Again.*

It should have been *me* who went after Ken. I should have fought Chris harder. Should have reminded him that he has a son on the way who needs him. What will happen to that son now? Will he end up in prison again, like he did in the other timeline? And what about Shawnda? I can't let her become a single mom because of me.

I lie on the floor, sobbing harder than I have since I was a kid. I can't stop, and the flashbacks and memories overwhelm me. So much death. So much blood. So many futures cut short because I failed.

The tears eventually dry up. When my eyes are raw and red, burning like they've been rubbed with sandpaper, I stand up and stumble to bed. I'm exhausted, but I don't know how I will ever sleep again.

I pass out in minutes, and then the dream comes for me.

Trent in the trash bin.

Zoe in the bathtub.

But this time, instead of Lynne in the ocean, Chris is there on the observatory deck.

"It should have been *you*," he says.

SATURDAY

I wake with a start, Chris's words from the dream echoing through my mind. My face is wet with tears I must have cried during my sleep. My throat aches like I've been yelling for hours. The relentless sorrow washes over me like a tidal wave, carrying me back under. I curl up in my bed, pulling the covers over my head, and scream.

And scream.

And scream.

When my voice is completely gone, the despair shifts to rage. I'm so angry that my limbs shake. At myself. At the other team for getting lost in the first place. At the scientists involved in the time-travel project. And above all else, at Vincent Sharp. My hands squeeze into fists, and I want nothing more than to slam them into his face over and over.

I force myself out of bed and head to my gym, where I spend the next hour working through my anger, guilt, and grief with a punching bag. It feels good to get it all out, to let my body give in to those urges in a way that doesn't actually hurt anyone. When I'm done, I'm sweating hard, but I can think clearly again for the first time in hours.

I head back to my apartment to take a quick shower, and then sit down with a piece of paper and a pen and get to work. Going back to the future isn't enough. I have to figure out who killed Chris and Ken so that I can stop it.

I close my eyes, take a long breath, and then sort through my memories of my five hours in the future. I go over the crime scene again first, picking apart what I saw and trying to make sense of it. In retrospect, there wasn't much blood around the bodies. It seemed like a lot at the time, but it's actually much less than I would expect if the two of them were shot there. Then again, it *was* pretty dark and I'm no expert on this stuff. All of my forensic knowledge comes from watching TV. But it makes me wonder if they were killed somewhere else and then dumped there.

And what about the gun that killed them? It hits me now that it was the same kind of gun as the one the Russian mafia used, that I'd held in my hand earlier that day as Zahra and I escaped. But I don't know if that's a clue or just a coincidence. That gun could be really common in the future, for all I know. But Chris did say he wanted to come help when I was facing off with the Russian mafia. I thought I'd convinced him not to do that, but it's possible he ignored me. If he showed up there after we left, he might have gotten himself in trouble and then somehow dragged Ken into it too.

Chris and Ken were both shot by the same gun, which means they were either killed by someone else who staged the bodies, or Ken killed Chris and then shot himself. But why would he do that? He didn't even know Chris before today. Was Chris trying to stop him from doing something?

I rack my brain for any other clues, going over what Chris and Ken both did during their time in the future. Chris checked in last after going to Jeremy's house and heading to the cemetery where

Future-Ken's body was buried. We heard nothing from him after that. We know Ken left the cemetery at some point and then went to Aid-Mart for some reason before going to the observatory. Did Chris go with him? Is that why Wombat found nothing in his car's GPS after that?

There's one other thing I need to consider. Future-Elena said she didn't know how Ken was killed, and Future-Chris was still alive in that future. Aether's notes said that Ken's body didn't have any visible injuries on it. Which means in the original timeline, before we split up and changed it all, Ken died from something *other* than a gunshot wound. But from what?

My phone rings and I jump, coming out of my trancelike state. I don't recognize the number. "Hello?"

"Elena? It's Dr. Walters."

My fingers tighten around the phone. "Did you fix it?"

"Yes." His voice is resigned. "It's fixed."

"I'll be right there."

It's 3:14 p.m. I get dressed quickly and drive over to the facility without contacting anyone else. I'm going to do this on my own. I won't risk anyone else's lives.

I still have no solid leads on who killed Chris or Ken. I'm exhausted, both physically and emotionally. My head pounds, my limbs are sore, and my eyes are dry and scratchy from crying all day. But I have a few ideas for where I can start looking in the future, and that will have to be good enough.

I make the long drive to the Aether facility, but after I park, I stare at the building, while a war rages between my instinct to run away and my need to go inside. I never imagined I would come back to this place of my own free will. Yet here I am, doing the one thing I swore I'd never do—return to the future again—to save my friend.

* * *

Dr. Campbell meets me in the lobby, and there are dark circles under her eyes. I imagine she didn't get much sleep either. She gives me a quick nod and leads me into the elevator. When the door shuts, she asks, "Are you sure you want to do this again so soon? You can take another day off, or even a week. Get some rest."

"I won't be able to rest until I bring them back. Alive."

She shakes her head but doesn't try to convince me not to go through with it, which I appreciate. When we exit the elevator, I take a long breath and stare at the accelerator, the metal dome with thick tubes and flashing computer screens and the door I never want to enter again. The machine that has twisted and shaped my fate for the past six months, that I seem to be inexplicably bound to no matter what I do.

Dr. Walters stands beside it, along with Dr. Kapur and some other scientists. But they're not alone. Adam, Paige, and Zahra are all waiting too. The only one who is missing is Jeremy.

"What are you all doing here?" I ask. Dammit, they weren't supposed to be here.

"Adam called us," Paige says. "We're going to the future, of course."

"No, you're not." I focus on Adam when I say it. Even if the others come, I won't risk his life again.

Zahra crosses her arms and fixes me with a steely gaze. "Ken was our friend, not yours. You better believe we care more about saving his life than you do. We're coming."

Paige nods. "This is our mission too."

I can tell they won't be persuaded on this. They have as much a right to go to the future to save their friend as I do. Even if I don't like it. "Fine, you two can come. But Adam stays."

"You're not going to the future without me," he says. There's no room in his voice for argument, but I can't let him do this. He has to stay alive, no matter what happens to the rest of us, to create the cancer cure—and because I can't imagine a life worth living without him. Death seems to sit on my shoulders, reaching his tendrils into everyone I touch, striking down everyone I care about. The only one I have left is Adam, and I won't let him be next—even if it means I have to push him away.

"The three of us can handle it," I say. "The fewer people who go, the lower the chance of another of us getting killed. And your life is too important."

He shoots the other girls a quick look, and then takes my arm and moves us to a corner where we can speak in private. "Chris was my friend too. I'm not going to sit around here while everyone else goes to rescue him. And I won't let you risk your life without me there to protect you."

"I don't need you to protect me. If anything, I'll have to spend my entire time making sure *you* don't get killed too."

Hurt flashes through his blue eyes but is quickly replaced by anger. "Is that what you think of me? Wow. I had no idea you found me so…pathetic."

It kills me that he thinks this, that he doesn't know he's the most incredible man I've ever met, but I don't correct him. Instead, I push harder. "What exactly do you think you can do? You're a scientist, Adam. There's no way you can help with this mission. You'll only get in our way."

His lips press in a tight line. "Maybe I am just a scientist, but I'm going to the future to help in whatever way I can." His voice is full of quiet rage that's somehow worse than him yelling at me. "And if you care about me at all, you won't try to stop me."

I've never seen Adam this mad before, and never directed at me. I immediately regret everything I said and want to take it all back. "Adam, wait. Of course I care about you."

"Do you?" He gives me a cold look that rends my heart in two and walks over to Dr. Walters, leaving me behind.

Dr. Walters begins relaying instructions to the other scientists, who move into position around the machine. As it starts up, the metal tubes around the dome begin to hum, and the cement under us starts to vibrate. Anxiety curls itself around my stomach, and I can't decide if I'm sicker over my fight with Adam or the fact that I'm going into the future for the third time.

I'm still in the corner alone when a nearby door opens and Jeremy walks out, with his father a step behind him. "You can't do this," Vincent says. "You can't go to the future again. Especially after the injury you suffered."

"I'm not injured anymore," Jeremy snaps. "Dr. Kapur said I was fine."

They don't seem to notice my presence, and we're far enough away from the others that I doubt anyone can hear what they're saying except me.

Vincent grabs his son's arm and pulls him around to face him. "You're my son, and I demand you stay behind."

Jeremy jerks away from his father. "Ken's my best friend, and he's dead because of us. Because of *you* and your damn time machine. There is nothing you can do, not a *single* thing, that will prevent me from going to the future to get him."

"I'll stop you. You have no idea what I could do."

"What? Drug me? Lock me up like you did to the other team?" Jeremy lets out a bitter laugh and shakes his head. "You're disgusting."

"I did it for *you*. To make sure you got back alive."

"I'm doing this, Dad. If you try to stop me, I'll cut you out of my life completely, like I should have after Mom died."

"That wasn't my fault. You can't blame me for what happened to her."

"She got in that car because of you!"

Vincent doesn't answer, and the two of them stare each other down. Finally, Vincent turns on his heel and walks back through that door without another word. Jeremy lets out a long breath and notices me standing there. There's an awkward pause, heavy with the knowledge that I've heard everything that just passed between them.

"My father's an asshole too," I say.

"Family, right?" Jeremy sighs, and the tension between us eases a little. "I read your file. I'm sorry about your mother."

"Sounds like it's something else we have in common."

"Sort of." He leans against the wall, and I move beside him while he continues talking. "My mom used to work for Aether Corp. That's how she met my dad all those years ago. When I was thirteen, he shut down the project she was working on—a machine she hoped would be able to create synthetic water. He said it would never work, and they were wasting money by continuing with the experiments, but she disagreed with him. They had a huge fight, and then she got in a car during a bad thunderstorm and crashed into a tree." He turns toward me, his eyes cold. "My dad may not have murdered her, but he was definitely responsible for it."

"I'm sorry," I say. "What happened to her project?"

"Nothing. He buried it." He shakes his head. "Probably why the Vincent Sharp of the future wanted us to steal the synthetic water generator design from Pharmateka. And why I was dumb enough to get it."

"I'm surprised you gave it to him."

"Actually, I gave him a fake. If anyone is going to continue my mom's life work, it will be me."

He gives me one last pointed look before pushing off the wall and joining the others. I linger in the shadows, thinking about what he said, wondering if any of us will ever be free from our pasts.

"We're ready," Dr. Walters calls out.

Our team clusters around the accelerator door, but Adam and I stand as far away from each other as possible. I try to think of any last-minute way to stop him from going, but come up blank.

"We're setting the aperture to open an hour after you originally arrived," Dr. Campbell says. "Your other selves should be gone from this building by then, thus reducing the risk of overlap. The aperture will also open an hour earlier for your return, so make sure you're back in time."

Only three hours? That doesn't seem like enough time. But I guess it has to be.

Dr. Campbell opens the accelerator's door, and we set our watches. They're letting us keep our own clothes this time, I notice. As we shuffle inside, Dr. Walters frowns at us, his wrinkles more prominent today.

"Thank you," Adam says to him. "We won't waste this opportunity."

Dr. Walters nods, but he stops me on my way in. "I fixed the machine because you asked me to," he says. "I only hope I don't come to regret it."

"You won't."

I'm the last one inside and then Dr. Campbell closes the door, locking us in. We space out around the room, preparing for what's to come, and the countdown begins.

"Sequence initiated," the now-familiar robotic voice says. "Five."

As the walls begin to vibrate, my first instinct is to go to Adam, to grab his hand so we can go through this together as we always have. Our eyes meet, but neither one of us moves, and I look away.

I'm on my own this time.

"Four."

It's just as terrifying going into the future for the third time as it was the first. Maybe even more, actually. A million worries rush through my head. Will the accelerator malfunction again? Will it be able to send us to the future—and if it does, will it be able to bring us back? And if everything works perfectly, will we be able to save our friends?

"Three."

The ground shakes under us, but I'm expecting it and manage to hold my ground. Paige bounces on her feet, Jeremy broods on his own with his arms crossed, and Zahra has her eyes closed, her lips moving in what I guess is prayer.

"Two."

"Elena," Adam says, as the noise quiets around us. I open my eyes, and he reaches for my hand. I let him take it, surprised he wants anything to do with me after our fight. No matter how much I push him away, he always comes back.

The bright specks of light appear right just as the voice says, "One."

As the golden glow surrounds us, I squeeze Adam's hand and inhale. Here we go again.

PART IV
THE SECOND FUTURE

00:00

When the light fades, we're in Aether's basement and the older Dr. Campbell stands in front of us, wearing the same clothes as she did in the other future. I blink the stars from my eyes, and the room slowly comes into focus. Something about it feels different, but I can't put my finger on what.

"Hello again," she says. One of the screens behind her has that same ridiculous picture of a dog and a cat dressed up as witches with the date and time. It's the same day we visited before, but fifty-six minutes later than when we first arrived.

The accelerator worked. We're back.

"Have the other versions of us left already?" Adam asks, while I reset my watch to the correct time. Jeremy does the same with his own brushed-silver watch.

"Yes, they're gone," Dr. Campbell says. "It's safe now."

"We only have three hours," I say. "We need to hurry."

She nods. "Please come with me."

As we follow Dr. Campbell across the basement, I start to notice things that don't match my memory of this future. There are fewer scientists working here, for one thing. If that was the only change, I wouldn't have been worried, since some might have gone on break in the last hour, but there are other minor differences too. There are fewer computer screens around the room. The walls are a different color, a drab light gray instead of a soft beige. The conference table we sat at before is made of dark wood now, while it was slick, silver metal before. They're such minor details I doubt anyone else would notice them, but with my memory, they stand out.

There's one other difference. "Where's Dr. Chow?" I ask.

"Who?" Dr. Campbell says.

"He did a medical scan on us when we got here before," Adam says.

"I'm sorry, I don't know who you're talking about."

Adam and I exchange a wary look. What else might have changed in this future? I check the others' expressions, but none of them seem fazed by these differences. Then again, they've visited this same year multiple times in the last few months. They're probably used to it constantly shifting in small ways.

Dr. Campbell equips us with flexis and neutralizers again, and then we're taken up to the roof. This time she doesn't need to explain anything. She gives us each a quick nod and says, "Good luck."

Before I know it, we've gotten in another flying car the size of a minivan and are taking off. We rise into the sky, and I don't notice any other significant differences from the previous future, except that there seem to be fewer flying cars dotting the sky. Perhaps the changes between this timeline and the last are centered around Aether Corporation.

"What's the plan?" Zahra asks.

I've already worked the entire thing out. "We're going to head straight to the cemetery and see if we can find Ken at his future self's grave. If not, Chris should be arriving there soon."

"Jeremy, didn't you say you went to the cemetery too?" Adam asks. "Would the other you still be there now?"

Jeremy checks his watch. "No, I think my other self has left by now. I can stay in the car until we're sure though."

Paige tugs over and over on her seat-belt strap. "I hope we can get there in time. Can we go any faster?"

"The speed limit is programmed into the car, but I can try to disable it," Zahra says. "Along with Aether's tracking system, of course."

"Why disable the tracking?" Adam asks. "Surely it's better if they know where we are, in case we find any trouble."

"Only if they're not the ones responsible for the murders in the first place. Otherwise we could be leading them to us to finish the job."

"You think Aether killed Ken and Chris?" I've considered so many possibilities, but that one never occurred to me. I suppose it should have, but I can't think of a single reason why Aether would murder two of their time travelers. What's in it for Aether if they're dead?

"Ken wouldn't kill your friend," Paige says. "He's the sweetest guy in the world. I don't think he even knows how to use a gun!"

"Exactly," Zahra says. "He has no motive either. But if it's not Ken, then who else could it be? It has to be Aether."

"But why would Aether kill them?" Adam asks.

"Because it's *Aether*," Jeremy says, as if that explains everything. "I'm sure my father has some sort of diabolical plan we haven't figured out yet. He always plays the long game, and when you add time travel to the mix..."

After what Jeremy told me about his dad, I believe it. But they don't know one piece of the story—that Chris might have followed me to the Russian mafia hideout and could have gotten himself in trouble. I pray that isn't what happened.

I check the time again, rubbing my thumb over the face of my watch. My other self should be arriving at Zahra's mother's house about now. If we don't find Ken or Chris at the cemetery, then I'll tell the team my suspicions about where Chris might go next.

As the sight of downtown comes into view in the distance, I spot something odd—some sort of massive, semi-transparent dome covering the skyscrapers and buildings there. Under it, everything appears to be normal except that there are a lot fewer flying cars inside. Most other cars seem to go all the way around the dome to avoid it, even though that must make their commute much longer.

"What is that?" I ask.

Jeremy leans forward, his nose almost pressed to the glass. "It looks like some kind of force field around downtown."

"Force field…for what?" Paige asks.

Adam adjusts his glasses as he peers outside. "Some kind of security system maybe?"

"Most cars are going around it," Zahra says. "Maybe it's to manage the traffic downtown?"

"Maybe. But there are some cars inside it." Paige points at a car in the distance. "Look, that one just went in!"

"It could be that they need some kind of special clearance to get inside," Adam says.

"I'm looking it up," Zahra says, her eyes distant. "Says here it was put in three years ago to reduce sky traffic in certain areas of LA. To get in, you need a special permit, which costs a lot of money. Everyone else has to drive on the ground to get into the area. And after the downtown one went up, other ones popped up in different places in the city…"

"Let me guess," I say. "The domes cover the richer areas in the city, like Beverly Hills."

Zahra points at me. "*Ding ding ding*, we have a winner. This is just a new form of class segregation."

"There seem to be a lot fewer flying cars in this future too," Paige says.

"Probably because they're expensive," Adam says, his gaze vacant as he uses his flexi. "All the news headlines say things like 'California Unemployment at an All-Time High' and 'Stock Prices Continue to Decline,' and 'Worst Recession since the 2000s.' People can't afford flying cars like they could in the previous future."

Jeremy rubs his chin as he considers. "Hmm, that's definitely a big shift from the other timelines we've been to. All of those futures seemed to be in a golden age, not a recession."

None of them are asking the question that's been gnawing away at me since we arrived in this future. "What's causing all these changes?" I ask.

"Things are always different when we return to the future," Zahra says with a light shrug.

"But that was because you brought stuff back with you on your earlier trips for Aether."

"Jeremy gave the plans for the synthetic water generator to his father," Adam says. "Could that have changed all this?"

Jeremy clears his throat. "Actually, I gave my father a fake schematic. I decided he didn't deserve the real one."

"Really?" Paige asks, her eyebrows shooting up.

"Good," Zahra says. "He's never appreciated any of us, or what we've done for his company."

"And he appreciated Jeremy least of all," Paige adds.

"Looks like Pharmateka still developed the synthetic water

generator," Adam says, while using his flexi. "Nothing's changed there."

"Then what caused all of this?" I ask.

Adam frowns. "Chris's death might have changed some things."

I didn't even consider that. If Chris is dead, what happened to his son in the future? And to our company, Future Visions?

"Could it be because of me and Zahra?" Paige asks, while picking at her nails in a nervous way. "We both had plans to change things in our lives based on what we saw in the other future..."

Paige was going to break up with her boyfriend and expose his plagiarism in college, while Zahra planned to try to stop her brother's murder by the Russian mafia. I can't imagine that either of those things would have sweeping effects on the city like this, but you never know.

"There's an easy way to find out," Zahra says. "We look ourselves up."

We're close to downtown, but I can't see the Future Visions building from this angle. I need to know more, but after Future-Elena's warnings about changing the timeline, I'm terrified of what I might find. But maybe it's better to know so I can go back and try to fix the future somehow. Unless knowing my fate only leads to me making it worse. There's no way to tell.

I look up Chris's son first, but the news isn't good. Like in the very first future we visited, Chris's son grew up without a father in this timeline and is in prison now. And Shawnda? She's currently in rehab.

I can't let this become their fate. It's not only Chris's life hanging in the balance, but those of his entire family. I have to save Chris, no matter what else happens in this timeline. No matter what I see in my own future.

"Did you look at your future yet?" I ask Adam quietly, after the others have zoned out on their flexis.

"No. Did you?"

I shake my head. Our argument is still fresh in my head, and the lingering emotions haven't faded away yet. Even though we're sitting next to each other in the car, I feel the distance between us like a huge chasm.

He draws in a long breath. "Let's do it together."

"Okay."

I search for myself, but there's no Wikipedia page for me this time. Instead, I'm just a footnote on Adam's page, where it says we were married.

Right next to the date of our divorce.

00:23

I let out something between a gasp and a cry. Is Ava alive? Was she born before we got the divorce? I frantically scroll through Adam's page with my breath held. *Yes*, thank God, there she is: Ava Esperanza O'Neill, born November 9. The relief is overwhelming, and I have to close my eyes and sit with it for a minute. Adam and I are divorced, but at least she still exists.

"She's okay," I tell Adam. I know he will understand who I mean.

He nods, but his face is pinched. He must have seen what has become of our relationship. I'm sure it's my fault. We were fine in the other future, but I must have messed things up in that short time we were in the present. It may not have been much, but perhaps it planted seeds that grew over the years until Adam and I couldn't take it anymore. It doesn't surprise me. Everyone I love goes away in the end. Why would Adam be any different?

"What happened to us?" he asks, his voice barely above a whisper. "You said we were happily married in the other timeline."

"We were." My throat tightens up. "Something must have changed."

"It's Chris," he says. "It has to be. His death altered everything between us. And without Chris, we never started Future Visions."

We're flying parallel to the dome now, past the spot where the Future Visions building should be, but it's not there. I check Future-Adam's bio, and it says he developed the cure for cancer on his own, using grants and sponsorships, and now teaches biochemistry at UCLA. We never started our own company. My nonprofit foundation that helps foster kids doesn't exist either. And when I do a little more digging, I find myself listed in an article about Adam, but it says I'm a social worker. I gaze out the window toward the direction of our house. If we go there now, who will be living there? One of us? Or a family of strangers?

Chris's death destroyed our future along with his. I suppose it was inevitable, really. Being around Adam only reminds me of the tragedies we've shared and the future I could have prevented. I can't imagine enjoying my life with Adam knowing that I got Chris killed, that it's my fault his future was snuffed out. But I also can't imagine my life without Adam either, not after I've seen what we could have together. Which means Future-Adam must have left *me*.

"Ugh!" Paige says, snapping me out of my thoughts. "I'm still married to that jerk."

Jeremy's head snaps up. "Seriously?"

"Yep. And he's still a congressman, although now he's a corrupt one!"

Jeremy frowns, while using his flexi. "Hmm. It says he's under investigation right now for accepting bribes that led to him voting for the bill that created the force field around certain areas of the city. Sounds like a lot of people were not in favor of them."

"At least in the other future he was a good politician, even if he was a terrible husband." Paige's head falls into her hands, and she lets out a dramatic sigh. "I made it *worse* by turning him in, not better."

"My fate hasn't improved either," Jeremy says. "I still work for Pharmateka and hate my dad. Guess that's never going to change."

Zahra has been quiet this entire time, her head turned away from us. As I watch, a single tear escapes her eye and slides down her cheek. She quickly brushes it away with the back of her hand like she's scratching at an itch.

"You okay?" I ask her.

She shoots me a look that could melt plastic, but her tough-girl act won't work on me. I know all about that shit, and I'm starting to realize Zahra is a lot like me. She puts on a bitchy front to keep people away from her for protection. God knows I can relate.

When I don't back down from her gaze she huffs, but then her body completely deflates. "My brother is still dead. Nothing I did fixed anything."

"I'm sorry," I say.

"Oh no." Paige entwines her arm with Zahra's, and the two of them rest their heads against each other's. "They killed him?"

"Yeah." She leans close to Paige, and her voice drops to barely above a whisper. "He died even younger now. Because of the money."

"What money?" I ask, even though I obviously wasn't meant to hear that last bit.

Jeremy shakes his head at them. "Don't."

Paige bites her lip, but Zahra straightens up. "It didn't make anything better," she tells him. "If anything, it made it worse."

"What did?" Adam asks.

Zahra pulls out a small, thin slip of yellow-and-orange paper. A lotto ticket. "This has winning numbers for next Wednesday's lottery, back in our time. I looked the numbers up in the previous future, and when we returned to the present, I bought the ticket. We were all going to split the money between us."

Before I can tell her what a bad idea that is, and how they've probably changed the timeline considerably thanks to their actions, she rips it into tiny pieces.

"Stop!" Jeremy says, reaching for her. "What are you doing?"

Paige blocks him, scooting forward so he can't get to her friend. "Zahra is right. This is for the best. All the money did was make things worse for all of our futures."

He watches helplessly as Zahra throws the paper in the trash compactor, which sucks it up and makes horrible shredding noises. As far as I can tell, the bin doesn't convert the trash to energy, probably because Chris wasn't around to invent that technology in this future. But the lotto ticket is still gone for good.

The three of them purposefully planned to make different choices in their lives, even going so far as to buy a lotto ticket, and yet their futures seem to have fallen into the same patterns as before. While Adam and I *didn't* try to change our futures, but our lives are completely different in this timeline.

Fate must have a wicked sense of humor.

00:29

We arrive in the cemetery as the sun hangs low in the sky, just above the horizon. A chill runs through the autumn air, making me shiver when I exit the car. I glance around, rubbing my arms, while the others get out after me.

"Where's Ken's grave?" I ask Jeremy.

"This way."

We follow him over neatly trimmed grass, past stark, gray headstones. In the fading light, they remind me of a row of dominoes waiting for someone to knock one over and start a chain reaction that can only lead to ruin. Our lives are no different. No matter what we do, our choices inevitably lead to death and misery. And the more we scramble to change the future, the worse we make it all.

"It's here," Jeremy says, coming to a stop in front of Ken Miyamoto's headstone. "But it's changed."

"How so?" Adam asks.

"In the other future, Ken died when he was thirty-eight. Now it says he died when he was eighteen."

"Because he never came back with us," Zahra says.

"Is Ken here now?" I ask. His grave is next to what I assume are his parents' ones, from the names. His mother died at forty-three. I remember Chris saying Ken and his mother both had the same disease.

"Maybe he left already," Paige says, her blond hair swishing as she looks back and forth. The cemetery is empty as far as I can see, except for some people placing flowers at a nearby grave.

I check the time on my watch. "We must have just missed him. Which means he's heading to Griffith Observatory soon."

"Chris is probably on his way here now," Adam says.

It's time I told them my suspicions. "Actually, he might be on his way to Glendale instead."

"Why would he go there?" Jeremy asks.

"I messaged him when I was following Zahra into the Russian mafia's underground headquarters and told him what I was up against. He wanted to come and help me, but I told him not to."

"You asked Chris for help?" Adam asks, his eyes narrowing. "But not me?"

I shift my weight in the grass, considering my answer. "I didn't want you to worry."

"No, you didn't think I could help you."

I press my lips into a tight line instead of answering, because what can I say? Yes, Chris was a better choice for helping me against a hideout full of guys with guns. But I can't explain that to Adam, not now.

Jeremy looks back and forth between us, his expression wary. "Was that the last time you heard from him?"

"Yeah," I say.

"That does make some horrible sense," Zahra says, her head tilted. "The Russian mafia had guns like the one we found at the observatory. It's possible they're the ones who killed Chris and Ken."

"But why Ken?" Paige asks.

Zahra shrugs. "Wrong place at the wrong time, maybe?"

"Maybe we should split up and try to track them down separately," Jeremy says.

Splitting up makes me nervous after what happened in the other future, but we have three places to be and time is quickly running out. There's no other choice.

"We know Chris is supposed to come here, so one of us can stay here and wait for him," I say. "Two people can go to the Griffith Observatory and wait for Ken to show up. The rest can go to the Russian mafia hideout and see if Chris is there."

"I'll wait here," Jeremy says. "My future self already was here and gone, so there won't be any overlap."

Paige nods and rests a hand on his arm. "Probably a good idea, since you're still recovering from your injuries."

"I'm fine," he says, but she just gives him a pitying smile.

"Zahra and Elena can't go to Glendale or they might run into themselves, so Paige and I will look for Chris there," Adam says.

That leaves me and Zahra to head to the observatory. It's the obvious answer, but my gut isn't sure that's what I should do. I'm hesitant to leave the cemetery when Chris is probably coming here next, especially since Jeremy doesn't know him. But there shouldn't be any danger here, while Paige and Adam are walking into a fight with the Russian mafia without anyone to protect them. Neither one of them is a fighter. It's bad enough that Adam is here in this future; I can't let him put himself in danger.

"I'm going to Glendale too," I say. "Zahra can go to the Griffith Observatory on her own. Or one of you can go with her."

"You can't come with us," Adam says. "We can't risk you running into yourself."

"I'm not letting you go into the Russian mafia hideout without me. It's too dangerous."

"What about causing a paradox?" Paige asks.

"Scientists are always throwing that word around, but it hasn't happened yet, despite all their warnings. It'll be fine."

"This doesn't seem like the time to test that hypothesis," Adam says, his voice angry again. Every time I think we might be on the track to reconciling, I start another fight with him. But it's worth it to keep him alive.

"I'm not letting you go without me," I say, crossing my arms. I refuse to budge on this, no matter how much he argues with me. I'll use the damn neutralizer on him if I have to.

He stares at me for a long time and then throws up his hands. "Fine. But you're going to stay away from your other self, and if there's a problem or even a *hint* that a paradox is starting, you have to leave. Immediately."

"Deal."

Adam scowls at me, then turns and walks back to the car, his movements stiff. Whatever. He can be mad at me, but at least I'll be there to keep him alive. Paige shoots me a worried glance before bouncing after him.

"Well, that was awkward," Zahra says. "Guess I'll head to Griffith Observatory now."

"Can you get another car?" I ask.

"I've already ordered one to come and pick me up."

"Good. You know what to do?"

She shrugs. "Sit around by myself at a construction site. It's not exactly a tough assignment. I'll be bored out of my mind within five minutes."

"Just let us know if you see anything."

She rolls her eyes. "Obviously."

I ignore her and turn to Jeremy, who has settled in the grass beside Ken's grave. "You know what Chris looks like?"

"Yeah, Aether put his profile in our new flexis."

"Let us know right away if he shows up."

"I will. Be safe out there."

"You too."

I turn toward the car and start to walk away, but Zahra's voice makes me stop. "Try not to get yourself killed, Elena."

"Hey, don't go all sappy on me now."

She flips me off, but I think I see a hint of fondness in her eyes. Dammit, I might actually be starting to like her—and the rest of Team Echo too.

00:56

In the car, Adam won't look at me, but I'm getting used to that. I sit next to Paige, whose bright star seems to have been dimmed by everything that's happened. All that's left is her flickering energy, keeping her restless and constantly moving. She plays with her hair. She bites her nails. She taps her foot. I'm tempted to hit her with the neutralizer to get her to stop.

While the car flies us to Glendale, I give them a rundown of everything that happened to me and Zahra in the other timeline. Since we don't want to interfere with any of that and possibly alter what our other selves do or run into them, we decide to stay outside the flower shop and watch for Chris's arrival. Hopefully that will keep the three of us out of danger too.

We stop at a Middle Eastern café across the street from the flower shop, which I remember being a French-Chinese fusion restaurant in the other timeline. It has a small patio where we can sit outside and keep an eye on things. The waitress, an older woman with a dark bob, seats us at a round table on the patio and hands us menus. Behind us, a young couple sneaks pieces of kabob to their golden retriever. It's so normal that it's hard to believe there's an entire organized crime operation only a few feet below us.

We're in place, Adam messages to the others.

I just got to Griffith Observatory, Zahra sends back. There's no one here yet.

All quiet over here too, Jeremy says from the cemetery.

The waitress sets down some water for us right as Zahra—the one from the other future—gets out of her car and heads into the flower shop. She charges forward without a care for her own safety, and from this angle I can clearly see the determined look in her eyes.

I check the time, rubbing the face of my watch. Any moment now, my other self will follow Zahra inside, and there will be nothing to do but wait and see if Chris shows up.

Adam sits beside me, surveying his menu. A piece of dark hair has fallen forward over his left eye, just behind his glasses, making him look effortlessly handsome in his own geeky way. A surge of tenderness rises in me for him, and my fingers itch to push the hair back, to touch him and reassure myself we're going to be okay. I reach toward him before I realize what I'm doing, but when he looks my way, I quickly pull my hand back.

"There she is," Paige says.

My other self comes into view and we all duck down, hiding behind menus and a potted plant. I doubt it matters—that Elena is so focused on following Zahra that we could probably jump up and down and she wouldn't notice.

I can't tear my eyes off her. I'm captivated by the way she moves, the shine in her hair, the fire in her eyes. I met my older self yesterday, but this is different because she's me *now*, or at least the me from yesterday. This is the one chance in my life to see myself the way other people do.

That Elena has no idea what is coming, what memories will be burned into her brain in only a few hours. I'm tempted to go to this clueless girl and tell her everything that will happen in the next day, to warn her somehow and try to save Chris, but I can't. If I interfere, I might change the timeline and make it worse again. This way, I know exactly what she will be doing and when.

The other Elena is almost to the flower shop now, only a few feet away from me, and for a split second she looks in my direction. Sharp pain shoots through my head. My vision goes dark. The world rips apart.

I'm falling.

Breaking.

Lost.

I'm on the street, following in Zahra's footsteps.

I'm talking to the security guard at Pharmateka.

I'm getting into a flying car for the first time.

I'm being scanned by Dr. Chow while Dr. Campbell looks on.

I'm—

"Elena!"

Adam's voice hooks into me and reels me in from the darkness. I gasp and blink and claw my way back through the fog. The real world comes into focus again.

"What happened?" I manage to get out. The pain in my skull sears me, making it hard to concentrate. It feels like my brain's been torn in half, like my memories were about to consume me. I press my palms to my forehead, willing the throbbing to stop.

I'm still at the table on the patio, and the other Elena is gone. Adam has his arms around me, keeping me upright, while Paige hovers in front of my face, her eyes worried. "It was like you blacked out for a second," she says.

"Here," Adam says, handing me a glass of water. "Drink this."

I take a small sip. The water is cool, and the ice brushes against my lips. I press the glass to my forehead, searching for some kind of relief. After a few moments, the pain dims enough for me to think clearly again.

"When she looked in our direction, I..." The dizziness picks up again, and I lean against Adam for support. "I don't know. My head started to hurt and the world got dark, and then I had all these flashbacks of the other future. But they weren't flashbacks, not like the normal ones I get sometimes. They were more real than that. It was almost like I was *reliving* that timeline. And if you hadn't pulled me back..."

"Are you okay now?" Adam asks, his brows pinched with concern.

"I think so."

Paige chews on one of her nails. "We need to get her out of here."

"I'm fine," I say, but another wave of blurred vision and sharp pain sweeps over me, and I groan.

Adam shakes his head. "Paige is right. This must be caused by your proximity to your other self. A paradox created by two time-traveling versions of you being in the same place. If you had actually interacted, who knows what would have happened to the timeline...or to you."

"I'll call the car," Paige says, standing up and looking toward the street.

"No!" I reach for her, trying to tug her back.

Adam loops his arm with mine and helps me stand. "I'm getting you as far away from the other Elena as possible. I won't let you suffer like this. Or cause a paradox."

"No, we can't go now. We have to wait for Chris."

"The deal was that if anything happened, you would leave immediately. You agreed to that."

"I'll be okay on my own," Paige says with a bright smile. "It's totally safe here."

A war goes on inside me, with too many choices and decisions to make and none of them good. Someone has to wait here for Chris, but the pain rattling in my brain is making it crystal clear it can't be me. I'm no use to Adam or Paige if I'm like this anyway. But we can't leave Paige on her own either.

I pull away from Adam and stand on my own, finding my balance again. "I'll take the car and meet up with Zahra. You two wait and see if Chris shows up."

Adam studies me, his blue eyes seeing everything, even the things I don't say. He touches my cheek softly, and I cover his hand with mine, pressing it against my face. "Are you sure you'll be okay?"

"Yeah. Don't get into any trouble while I'm gone."

"I should be the one telling you that." He pulls me close and presses his lips against mine. I wasn't expecting it, wasn't sure he'd want to kiss me after our fights, or after what he's seen of our new future. But his warm mouth and gentle hands ease the pain away, both in my head and in my heart, and a spark of hope flares in me again. Maybe we're not doomed to the current future. Maybe our relationship can be salvaged. Maybe we can still fix things between us. All we have to do is save Chris, and everything will be right again.

01:24

I leave Adam and Paige at the café, and when I'm about a mile away, the blurred vision and dizziness disappear. Maybe those scientists do know what they're talking about now and then. I still have a massive headache, and I consider stopping at an Aid-Mart to see if I can find some Tylenol, or whatever painkillers the future has.

Aid-Mart. Ken went there on his way to Griffith Observatory. If I hurry, I might make it in time to meet him there. Thank God for my eidetic memory, or I wouldn't remember the address.

The car veers left once it's on its new course, and I tell it to go at top speed. I stare out the window as if I can make it faster by wishing really hard, even though I know how silly that is. It helps keep my mind off the way I left Paige and Adam behind and unprotected, and how we still don't know where Chris is, and how our window in this future is closing rapidly. If I let those thoughts take over, I might as well just give up, and I'm not ready to do that.

The car lets me out in front of this Aid-Mart, a different one than Zahra and I visited in the other timeline, yet it looks almost identical. I head inside, looking in every direction for Ken, walking up and down a few aisles, back and forth for a few minutes. The store's not very crowded, but I don't see him anywhere. Dammit, I must have just missed him. I'll have to try to catch him on the way to Griffith Observatory.

I step outside and wait for my car, but before I get in, I see a guy standing on the corner with short black hair, looking up at the sky. I can't get a good look at his face, but my instincts tell me to get a closer glimpse. I ditch my car and dart toward him.

It's definitely Ken. I've only seen him either dead or in photos, but I recognize him anyway. Straight black hair, cut close around his head. Handsome face with smooth skin and bright brown eyes. He's wearing the same clothes from the other future, the ones I saw dotted with blood after a bullet had torn through them.

"Ken," I yell, trying to wave him down. His head snaps toward me, but he takes one look at me and then turns away again. Maybe he didn't know if I was calling to him or to someone else. He has no idea who I am, after all.

I stop right in front of him, where he can't ignore me. "Ken, I need you to come with me."

This time he really looks at me, blinking quickly. "Who are you?"

"I'm from the present. I've come to bring you back."

He takes a step back. "You're *what*?"

"I'm like you," I say, hoping he knows what I mean. I don't want to say too much out in public like this. Once we're in the car, I can explain everything. "I'm here to help you get back."

His face darkens, and I only have a second's warning before he takes off running. I unleash a long string of obscenities and start after him, while grabbing the neutralizer from my pocket. I've spent too long looking for this guy. There's no way I'm losing him now.

He darts across the street, narrowly avoiding traffic. I chase after him, and the air fills with the sound of cars honking. One screeches to a halt only inches from me, just before I reach the sidewalk. "Sorry!" I yell.

Ken hurries around a corner, and I try to keep up. He's about my size, but faster than me. I'm not sure how long I can chase him like this. Why the hell is he running from me anyway? Does he think I'm going to hurt him?

He pauses at the next intersection, where the cars are moving faster. That brief moment of hesitation is enough for me to catch up to him. I slam into him and grab on to whatever I can, gripping his shirt hard. Once I've got him, I raise the neutralizer so he can see it.

"Stop running," I growl, while mentally ordering my car to come get us.

He struggles and tries to fight me off—without any real skill, but enough to be annoying. I consider using the neutralizer, but I want to be able to talk to him, to ask him where Chris is. Instead I give him a quick jab to the chin, not hard enough to really injure him, but enough to knock some sense into his stupid head.

He lets out a cry and stumbles back, clutching his face. The car lands next to us before he recovers, and I shove him inside, then climb in after him. Once the door shuts and the car takes off, I fix him with a steely gaze. "What was that about?"

He eyes me warily and rubs his face where I hit him, but doesn't speak. His hair is messy and his brow shines with a touch of sweat, but he isn't out of breath. My head is pounding harder than ever now, and I pop open the fridge on the side and grab a drink from it to press to my forehead. I strongly regret not buying any pain pills from Aid-Mart when I had a chance.

"Sorry about that," I say, gesturing to his face. "It was either that or knock you out with a neutralizer." Still no response. "Look,

I'm from Team Delta, the group who went to the future before you. Aether sent us to bring your team back after you didn't return through the aperture."

"You don't understand," he finally says. "I don't *want* to go back."

01:48

I stare at Ken, failing to comprehend what he's saying. How could he not want to go back? Why would he want to be stuck in this crappy future?

"What are you talking about?" I ask. "Why not?"

"There's nothing for me in the present except pain and death."

"And that's not true here?"

"It's true everywhere." He leans back against his seat and closes his eyes. "I was going to kill myself, okay?"

Oh. I open and close my mouth a few times, trying to figure out a good way to respond. When I tried to put together the clues surrounding his death, I never imagined suicide could be a factor. All I can manage is, "You were?"

Ken digs into his pocket and pulls out a handful of different bottles of pills. "I was going to take all these. The combination would have made me pass out before it stopped my heart."

That would explain why Future-Elena said she didn't know how Ken had died. An autopsy would show the cause of death, but otherwise there would probably be no visible evidence of what happened to Ken. Of course, that doesn't explain the gunshot wound. "But why?"

"My mom has Huntington's disease. She's dying right now, and there's nothing I can do to save her, or even ease her suffering. Trust me. I've tried." He gazes out across the city, his face grim. "The disease is genetic so there was a fifty-fifty chance I'd have it too. I refused to get tested because I didn't want to spend every day of my life dreading my fate, but when I came to the future, I found out I was going to die of the disease too. Which means in about twenty years or so, I'll go through what my mom is going through now. Pain. Memory loss. Dementia. And then...death. It's not a pleasant way to go."

"So you thought you'd take the easy way out now?"

"Nothing easy about it. But it's a lot faster and less painful, that's for sure." He tosses the pill bottles on the nearby table, and they rattle and roll across it. "When I saw my grave, I figured it was inevitable. Fate. Destiny. All that crap. There was no point in waiting 'til I got back to do it. If something happens to me during a mission, Aether has to compensate my family, so I figured it was better to end it now in the future. At least that way my parents would be taken care of for the next few years."

"But what about your life? Twenty years is better than none at all. And you have so much more you could accomplish. Maybe even find a cure."

"I've tried. I'm sure my future self tried too. He worked for Pharmateka for years." He sighs. "They can cure cancer in this future, but not Huntington's, and it's so rare it's never going to get the funding for scientists to even try."

"One of the other people here with me, Adam O'Neill, he's the one who will create the cancer cure. Maybe the two of you could figure out a cure for Huntington's together."

"Yeah, sure. Whatever." He rests his head against the window. "You don't even know me. Why do you care what happens to me?"

"I care because you're a human being. Because you're eighteen and have your life ahead of you and it isn't your time yet. Because, like me, you're stuck in this shit situation thanks to Aether." I look down at my hands, spread across my lap. "And because you remind me of someone I couldn't save."

He's gone silent again, and I worry that I've already lost him. He's dead set on ending it all, if not now, then later. He feels like his fate is inevitable, and the only way out is to take control before it's too late. I know all too well what it's like to feel that way.

I rub the face of Mamá's watch, seeking comfort in the familiar feel of it. I hate talking about the past, hate reliving it again and again, but it might be the only way to get through to Ken. "When I went to the future the first time with Team Delta, I saw something that seemed inevitable too. Something I couldn't live with."

His head slowly turns toward me. "What was it?"

"I saw that I was going to murder the rest of my team and kill myself. I had the gun and everything. I believed it was true because of my past, because my father was a murderer, and because all evidence pointed to that fate. I debated staying in the future to protect them, or even killing myself to stop what would happen."

"Why didn't you?"

"Because someone else believed in me, and that was enough to give me hope." I trace the origami unicorn tattoo with my finger. It's healed enough by now that it doesn't hurt, just itches a little. "When I got back to the present, I found out I *wasn't* a killer. I was being set up. My inevitable fate? It was a lie. I was able to change it. And you can change yours too."

He turns back to the window, watching the bright cars zip past us through the dark sky. "What if I can't?"

I can't promise him that his future will change, or that a cure will be discovered, or that everything will turn out fine. I can't promise that for anyone, least of all those of us who move through time like ghosts. But even now, even with all the death I've seen, I still have hope. I found Ken and stopped him from killing himself. I saved Chris's life once and I'll do it again, no matter how many times I have to come back to the future to do it.

"As much as I hate this time-travel crap and everything that Aether has done to us, we've been given a gift," I say. "We've seen a glimpse into our futures. We've been given a second chance. Or even a third or fourth. And there's one thing I know for sure: we make our own fate."

I pick up the pill bottles off the table and toss them in a trash compactor. Ken doesn't protest, but he turns to the side and closes his eyes, and I get the feeling he's done talking.

I got Ken, I tell the others. He's alive.

Thank goodness, Paige says.

Any sign of Chris? I ask.

Not yet, Adam replies.

Nothing here either, Jeremy says.

I'm bored as can be at the Griffith Observatory, Zahra says.

We'll be there soon, I tell her.

It worries me that Chris hasn't arrived in either location yet. If he's not looking for Ken at the cemetery or chasing after my other self, where is he?

"Have you seen my friend Chris?" I ask Ken.

"Who?"

"Black guy with a shaved head. Tall and muscular. Tattooed arms. He was the third person on my team, and he went looking for you. Now we can't find him."

"No, sorry."

Dammit. I try to think of where else Chris could be, but can't come up with anything other than one of the three places we have covered already.

A new message comes in from Adam. We're in trouble. Send help.

01:57

I'm suddenly alert, my heart rate spiking in an instant. I knew leaving them was a bad idea. I'm coming, I tell them.

Me too, Zahra says.

No, you need to wait there for Chris. I've got it covered.

I tell the car to head back to Glendale, and it takes a sharp right. Ken sits up, looking around. "Where are we going?"

"Change of plans. Paige and Adam need our help."

Ken's eyes widen. "What do you mean? Is Paige in danger?"

"I don't know any details. Just that they're in trouble." I was hoping they'd send more info, but if they're in trouble, they might not be able to at the moment. I tell the car to go as fast as it can, but even with Zahra's hacks, it won't go too much over the speed limit.

What's going on? I ask them. But they still won't respond.

Oh God, what if I'm too late?

What if they've met the same fate as Chris?

"Tell me what's happening," Ken says. "Where's Paige?" He's more intent now than I've seen him. I suppose he cares more about his friends being in danger than his own life. I get that.

I'm too anxious to talk and just shake my head, watching the front window for signs that we're getting closer, urging the car to go faster and faster. But he won't stop staring at me, and finally I give in and tell him everything that happened to us over the last few days in short, clipped sentences. I soon find that talking about it helps me keep my mind off the fact that Adam is in danger and the car can't get there fast enough.

"I missed so much," Ken says, when I'm finished. "I turned my flexi off because I didn't want my team to know where I was or what I was doing. I was…ashamed, I guess." His head falls. "But I had no idea they would end up in trouble, or I never would have done it."

"We've all made mistakes," I say. "Now's the time to fix them."

I send Paige and Adam a message letting them know we're nearby. Adam replies with a location and I send it to my car's app, while secretly wanting to jump up and cheer. He's still alive. He's going to be okay.

The car lowers itself to the street, and Paige and Adam run out of a sporting goods store a few seconds later. Ken throws open the car door, and they jump inside. I'm so relieved to see them both that I think my heart might burst, but before I can grab Adam in a hug, one of the car's windows shatters with a loud bang.

Paige screams and we duck down, glass raining around us. I tell the car to get the hell out of here, while more bullets slam into the side of it. As it lifts up, the gunfire stops, and I sneak a peek outside. Two black-haired guys follow in another car, aiming guns at us. One of them is the Russian guy Zahra stole memories from. As soon as he sees me, he fires off another shot in our direction.

Our car leaps forward and into the sky, but the other car is right behind us. This is bad. Really bad.

"What happened?" I ask.

Adam stares out the window as the car gets closer and closer. "The other Elena and Zahra ran out, and some guys were chasing them. We thought we could help them escape, but all we did was get the attention of the guys with the guns. We ran into the sporting goods store and thought we'd lost them, but I guess not."

"Can we lose them?" Ken asks.

I send a message to Zahra through our group chat. Your Russian friend is after us. Can you get the car to go any faster?

I knew I should have killed him when I had the chance.

Too late for that now, Adam says. What do we do?

Hang on. I'll figure something out.

Another round of gunfire rips through the side of the car, plinking off the metal. We flinch and plaster ourselves to the carpeted floor, but so far the walls are holding up.

When exactly? I ask. 'Cause we're getting shot at.

Turn on your flexi cameras so I can see what's happening.

We switch them on, and Zahra instructs us to try to get a shot of the other car's license plate number. It's tricky without putting ourselves in the line of fire, but Adam manages to get a clear view.

I have a plan, Zahra says. Head for downtown. Specifically into the dome.

Can we go in there? Paige asks.

Aether's cars have clearance. These other guys do too, but I'm working on that. If all goes well, they'll be trapped outside, and you'll be able to fly in without a problem.

God, I hope this works. If not, there's nothing we can do without a gun or some backup. I could try calling the police, or ask for help from Aether, but would any of them get to us in time?

Can you turn off the automatic driving and let us fly manually? Adam asks.

I might be able to, if I was there, Zahra says. But you made me go to an empty construction site all on my own. Thanks again for that, by the way.

At least you're not being shot at, I reply. Man, I wish Chris were here. He's such an expert at cars that I know he'd figure out what to do.

The black car pulls up alongside us, and more bullets pierce the car. Our windows are gone now. Glass is scattered all over inside the car. Ken is bleeding from a cut on his forehead. Paige has blood on her shirt, although I don't know what it's from. But the dome is approaching. I pray we make it in time.

It's going to work, Zahra says.

I hope you're right, I say.

Hey, this is me we're talking about here. Of course I'm right.

A message pops up in our flexis. Access to the Downtown Low Traffic Zone approved. We head straight into the dome, and the world changes colors for a second as we pass through, giving everything a silvery sheen.

We all swivel around to look behind us, as the other car slams to a halt in front of the dome. The car hovers there, unable to enter. One of the men tries to shoot us anyway, but their bullets bounce off the surface of the dome harmlessly.

Zahra did it.

We're inside, Adam says. And we're safe.

Told you it would work, Zahra says.

I'll never doubt you again, I message back.

Adam orders the car to head into the main part of downtown, where the other car should lose sight of us among the tall buildings. We brush glass off the car's seats and collapse into them with relief.

"Ken, I'm so happy you're okay," Paige says and grabs him in a tight hug. He buries his face in her long, blond hair.

Adam wraps an arm around me and leans his head against mine. I grip his shirt, digging my fingers into it, like if I hold on tight enough, I won't risk losing him again.

"I was so worried about you," I whisper.

He tucks my hair behind my ear. "I'm here. You saved us."

I nestle myself in close to him, breathing in his familiar scent, his warmth, his solid presence. "Zahra saved us. I just brought the car."

"You knew exactly what to do. As for me..." He draws in a long, shaky breath. "I almost got us all killed, and I was just as useless as you said I'd be in a fight. Perhaps I should have stayed in the present after all."

"I'm glad you're here with me."

"You are?" he asks, searching my face like he doesn't believe me.

I nod and his face looks relieved. He gives me a light kiss, and we relax against each other and watch the others.

"Paige, you're bleeding," Ken says. "Are you okay?"

She looks down at her blood-spotted shirt. "Oh, it's nothing. A tiny cut on my arm."

"Here, let me help. I got one of those laser pens from Aid-Mart." He pulls one out of his pocket and inspects her skin, then runs the object over the injury. She smiles at him the entire time, and when he looks up and meets her eyes, he flushes.

"You're bleeding too." She touches his forehead, which makes him jump. "Sorry. Does it hurt?"

His face gets even redder, and he looks away. "No, it's okay."

"My turn." She takes the pen from him and brushes his hair back to inspect the small gash on his face. He watches her with pure adoration in his eyes the entire time she heals him. It's amazing that she doesn't see it.

I wish they'd just make out already, Zahra says. She must still be watching us through our flexis. I smirk, but then I notice she sent the message to me alone. It's such a small thing, but it makes me feel like the two of us are having a private joke. Like we might become friends. I can't believe how much I want that. And from her, of all people.

Are they always like this? I ask her.

Yep. And neither one has a clue the other feels the same way.

They'd be good for each other. Ken could use something to live for, and it sounds like Paige needs to find a decent guy.

As soon as we get out of this mess, we'll make a plan to bring them together.

Deal.

We circle around downtown for a few minutes until we're sure no one is following us. I keep looking for the Future Visions building near the Aether one, but of course it's not there. And we still have no idea where Chris is.

Jeremy, has Chris shown up yet? I ask.

No response.

Jeremy? Paige asks.

Why isn't he answering? What now?

His flexi is off-line, Zahra says to all of us. He was last tracked at the cemetery twenty minutes ago. He's probably still there.

We immediately change course and head back to the cemetery, and all I can think is, *Please don't let us lose another one.*

02:26

As soon as we reach the cemetery, the car swoops down and we spot Jeremy lying in the grass beside Ken's grave. He's not moving. Oh God, why is he not moving?

I don't know who's out of the car first, but Ken's the one who kneels beside Jeremy and checks his pulse. "He's alive," he says.

Paige presses a hand to her heart. "Oh, thank goodness."

The relief is staggering, and my knees feel weak. I thought for sure we'd lost him too. But he's alive. Thank God he's alive.

Adam kneels beside Ken to examine Jeremy, since he has some medical training. I grip his shoulder to steady myself and study the scene in front of us. Jeremy is out cold, his body limp, his face pale. Like the guys I hit with the neutralizer. At least he's still breathing.

"He's been knocked out," Ken says.

Adam nods. "That's my guess too."

"Someone used a neutralizer on him," I say.

"Who would do such a thing?" Paige asks, tugging on her long hair.

"I don't know." I survey the rest of the cemetery, but it's completely empty except for us. "And where the hell is Chris?"

Zahra is watching it all through our cameras and sends us a message: Neutralizers are not all that common or easy to come by in this future.

What are you saying? I ask.

It must be someone working for Aether. They're the ones who created neutralizers. Or it could be Chris.

Chris wouldn't do this, Adam replies.

And if he did, he wouldn't have left Jeremy here, I add.

"Let's get him into the car," Ken says. He and Adam heft up Jeremy by the shoulders and drag him to the car, while Paige and I help get his legs. While they arrange him in the seat, his head flops to the side and he mutters, "Wha…?"

"He'll wake up soon," Adam says.

"Good, he can tell us what happened then," I say.

While we wait for Jeremy to fully regain consciousness, I wander the grounds, looking for any evidence that Chris was here. I find nothing and don't see his car anywhere either. The sun has completely set now, casting the graves in twilight. Our time is running out, and we're still nowhere closer to finding Chris than we were hours ago.

When I get back, Jeremy and Ken are hugging and thumping each other on the back. "I'm so glad you're okay," Jeremy says. "What happened to you anyway?"

Ken gives him a weak smile. "I'll tell you about it later. Right now it's your turn."

Jeremy lets out a long breath and bows his head. "I lost him."

"What do you mean?" Adam asks.

"Chris was here. Or I thought it was him anyway. I only saw him from a distance, getting out of a car. I called his name and he started walking toward me, but then a car flew down out of nowhere and a bunch of guys in ski masks jumped out. They hit him with a neutralizer and threw him in the car. I guess they got me next, 'cause I don't remember anything after that. I'm really sorry. I tried, but…"

Paige rests her hand on his arm. "It's not your fault. You did the best you could."

I told you it was Aether, Zahra says.

It's starting to look that way—who else would do this? But why would they take Chris and leave Jeremy? The only explanation is because Jeremy is Vincent's son, and they were under instructions not to harm him. My mind jumps to all sorts of conspiracy theories about what Aether is doing, about their real purpose for sending us to this future, about what sort of nefarious things they might be doing to Chris, but there's no proof that any of that might be the truth.

"Did you get the license plate number or anything else?" Ken asks Jeremy.

"No." Jeremy tugs on the hospital wristband on his arm. He must have forgotten to take it off after the previous future. "It all happened really fast. Sorry."

"What color was the car?" Paige asks.

"I think it was black."

"We need to get to Griffith Observatory," Adam says. "Based on what happened in the other future, they're probably heading there next."

Oh God. That means Chris could already be dead—and Zahra might be in danger too.

"Let's go," I say, jumping in the car. We don't have a second to waste, and if we're fast enough, we might be able to catch up with the people who took Chris. It's a long shot, but it's the only hope we have of saving him.

We head north through the night sky, which faintly hums with the sound of other flying cars. I'm so anxious I can't sit still. But we've barely been in the car for five minutes, when Zahra sends us a message.

Someone is here.

Her camera flips on, giving all of us a view of her surroundings. She's overlooking the observatory's grounds from the rooftop deck where we found Ken and Chris's bodies. The observatory is still under construction, like in the other future, but it seems like even less progress has been made. The giant trench is only halfway dug. There's less scaffolding on the side of the building.

As we watch, a large, silver flying car suddenly drops down to the deck from the sky.

We're too late.

Hide, I tell Zahra, while I grip Adam's hand so hard I'm surprised he doesn't yelp.

"We have to go faster!" Paige says. "Zahra is in danger!"

"We can't," Jeremy says, his voice quiet.

Her camera image gets blurry as she moves quickly, ducking out of sight, I presume. It's hard to tell what is happening, and all we can do in the car is sit and watch as it all unfolds. It's like a horror movie—we all know something terrible is coming, but we can't look away.

We're seeing through Zahra's eyes, overlooking a corner of the deck beside one of the telescope domes. She leans out to get a better view. Headlights cast bright beams through the night, illuminating the area around the car. The doors open, and two men in black ski masks get out. They grab a limp body from another guy inside and heft it out, dumping it on the rooftop.

Paige gasps and covers her mouth, while Ken whispers, "Is that Chris?"

We can't see the body clearly in the darkness, but we all know it's him. We're too late. Again.

He might still be alive, Zahra says. I'm going in.

No! I send to her. Paige and the others all send her similar messages, telling her to stop, to hide, to do anything but this, but she doesn't listen. She steps out of the corner, moving through the shadows, heading toward the car. From the shaky camera, we see her glance down at her hand, where she's clutching a neutralizer.

"What is she doing?" I ask.

When Zahra's almost to them, one of the guys pulls out a gun, the weapon's silhouette clearly visible in the bright headlights. She lets out a slight yelp in surprise. All three men turn toward her.

"Oh no, please no," Paige whispers, burying her face in Ken's shoulder.

The headlights brighten, lighting Zahra up, making her blind for a second. She pulls up a hand to cover her eyes, blocking our view of what's happening. "I've called the police!" she yells.

There's a loud bang and we all scream, unable to do anything except watch as Zahra's world tilts. The view shifts to the ground, goes sideways, and then fades to black.

She's gone.

02:41

By the time we arrive at the observatory, all that's left are the bodies and the gun.

Chris's body is in exactly the same spot as it was in the other future, and his gunshot wound is identical. Nothing has changed about his death. None of our attempts to save him did a single fucking thing.

Zahra's body is a few feet away, a soft heap on the white concrete. She's on her side, her eyes staring wide open like she wanted us to see every last second of her life. Thick, dark blood seeps out of her chest, a black pool that sinks into the cracks and crevices around her. The gun lies beside her, inches from her outstretched hand.

"Is she…?" Ken asks, but then he covers his mouth with his hands, shaking his head like he can't believe it. I don't blame him. I've seen more bodies than anyone should at my age, and yet it never gets easier.

"They shot her," Jeremy says, his face pale. "They really fucking shot her."

Paige sinks down onto Zahra's body, and loud sobs escape her.

"This can't be real. It can't be," she keeps saying, over and over. "Zahra, wake up. Wake up!"

I can barely see through the tears filling my eyes. My mind keeps flipping between Zahra's body lying before me and Zoe's body in the bathtub. Two friends bleeding from gunshot wounds. Two friends whose deaths will haunt me for the rest of my life. Two friends I couldn't save.

Panic crushes my chest like an avalanche, and I turn away from the bodies, trying to suppress the memories and find a way to breathe. How has it come to this again? We manage to save one person, but lose another? Why won't death ever give us a break?

Adam tries to hold me, but I shake my head and turn away, toward the darkness. I don't want his comfort. I don't deserve it.

"We can still fix this," he says.

"Can we?" I ask, choking on the words.

"What other choice do we have?" He wipes at his eyes from behind his glasses. "We'll keep trying until we can save them."

"Or until we're *all* dead," I whisper.

We stay as long as we can, but soon we have to get back in the car and return to Aether. Another tear-filled journey where no one talks. Not when Dr. Campbell shuffles us down to the basement. Not when we wait for the aperture to open and take us home. Not when the golden light appears.

What is there to say?

We're out of time.

We failed.

And we have to do it all over again until we get it right.

PART V
THE PRESENT

SATURDAY

The golden light fades, and in its place, reality comes crashing in. We're back. The five of us are inside the accelerator. And Zahra and Chris are still dead.

As soon as the door opens, I barge through it, pushing past Dr. Campbell. "Send us back."

My demand is met with stunned silence from the people outside the accelerator. Vincent steps forward and asks, "Pardon?"

"We need to go to the future again," I say, while the others join me, stumbling out of the machine. I'm a bit light-headed myself, but I refuse to even think about that. All I can focus on is saving my friends.

Vincent's eyes flicker over the rest of the group. "Welcome back, Ken. I'm pleased to see you've returned safely this time. But… where's Zahra?"

Paige begins to cry again, hiding her face in her hands. "She's gone."

"And Chris?" Dr. Campbell asks.

"We couldn't save them," Jeremy says quietly.

Dr. Walters shakes his head, his face grim. "I knew this was a bad idea."

"For once, I agree with you," Vincent says. "And it's not happening again. Project Chronos is officially done."

I step forward, hands clenched. "No, you need to send us back!"

"Send you back? Each time you've gone to the future you've lost two members of the team. Whatever is happening there is obviously far too dangerous. I'm not risking any more lives—especially my own son's."

"But we can fix it," I plead. "We can save them this time. We just need one more chance to make it right."

"I already gave you a second chance to save them. I won't do it again."

"Please," Adam says. "We can do this."

Vincent considers Adam for a moment. "Maybe if you told me what was happening in the future..."

Ken shakes his head, and we all exchange wary looks, remembering Zahra's words about how Aether could be behind all of this. It *has* to be them, even if we don't know why or how.

"You're the one killing them, aren't you?" Paige cries.

Vincent blinks at her. "I don't know what you're talking about."

"What are you doing to them?" she asks, her shoulders shaking. "Why?"

Adam touches her arm lightly. "Paige, he probably doesn't know anything. All of that is in the future. It hasn't happened yet."

"I wouldn't put it past my father," Jeremy says. "He probably has it all planned out already. Like I said, he plays the long game."

Vincent's calculating eyes assess us, but he doesn't show any emotion. "I need to ask all of you to leave the building."

"What?" Ken asks.

"No, you can't do this!" I say. "We can still help them!"

Vincent raises his hand and gestures for someone behind us to come forward. "Aether will honor our previous agreements with all of you, but from this moment forward, Project Chronos is shut down. For good."

Security guards seem to appear out of nowhere, surrounding us. Jeremy's head jerks back and forth between them, before settling on Vincent again. "Dad, please. Don't do this."

"Sir, I'd like to examine them before they go," Dr. Kapur says, although he sounds bored by it all.

"We should get statements from each of them about what happened in the future too," Dr. Campbell says.

"I'm sure they're all perfectly healthy," Vincent says, his voice cold. "And they didn't tell us anything last time. I doubt they'll tell us anything now. I want them out of the building before they get anyone else killed. Now."

The guards move closer, herding us toward the elevator with stern looks. I consider trying to fight them, but I don't want to put the others in danger.

"Please," I say, as we pass Dr. Campbell. "Please help us."

She bows her head. "I can't. I'm sorry."

I turn to Dr. Walters next, but his arms are crossed. I can see he's already made up his mind not to help us again. I debate making a break for it and locking myself back in the machine. But then what? I don't know how it works. If the scientists won't help us, we're screwed.

"You're just going to leave them dead," Jeremy says to his father, his voice laced with pure hatred.

Vincent shakes his head. "I'm sorry. I really am. But I can't send more of you to die."

"*You* sent them to die!" I yell, moving toward him.

The security guards grab my arms and I flinch, but I've learned how to deal with that move in the last six months, between Adam's help and my kickboxing classes. Even so, I struggle halfheartedly against the security guards as they shove me into the elevator, followed by the rest of the team. I can't believe it will end like this, not now. Not like this.

Once we're outside the building, they let us go. "Get out of here," one of them says, before they all head back inside. We stand in the middle of the parking lot, each of us looking lost and bewildered. Paige covers her face with her hands and weeps. Jeremy paces back and forth with angry steps, and Ken hangs his head. Adam stares at me, but I don't have any more answers than he does.

"Now what?" he finally asks.

Jeremy sighs. "I'll try to talk to my dad and get him to change his mind, but I don't think it will work."

"That's it?" I ask.

"You got a better idea?"

I turn away, kicking at a rock on the ground, so frustrated I could scream. We have to do something. We can't give up this easily. But what?

This is all my fault. I'm the one who let Chris go off alone, and I'm the one who sent Zahra there to wait for Chris. And I'm the one who has to fix it. I just wish I knew how.

"There must be some way," Ken says.

"There's nothing we can do," Paige says, sniffing. "This is the end."

We argue for a few minutes more, throwing out ideas like breaking into the building or trying to convince Dr. Walters to help us again, but we know none of them would work. We're just reaching for any shred of hope at this point.

Dr. Campbell exits the building, clutching her keys like she's going to her car. When she nears us, she quickly glances in every direction, biting her lip. "I can help you."

"How?" Adam asks.

Her voice is low, barely loud enough for us to hear her. "I'll get you inside tonight after everyone is gone."

"Even if you get us in, the accelerator needs at least two people to start it," Jeremy says.

"Dr. Walters will help us too, on one condition: we blow up the machine as soon as we're done."

"That only gives us one chance to succeed," Ken says.

"One chance is better than none," Paige says.

"Why are you helping us?" Adam asks. "You're only putting yourself at risk. You could lose your job."

"What Aether is doing is wrong," Dr. Campbell says. "We sent Chris and Zahra to their deaths, and we should do everything in our power to save them."

I consider Dr. Campbell for a long moment. In the future, she seemed to believe in what Aether was doing, and for all we know, she could be in on Vincent's plans. "How do we know we can trust you?"

"I..." She shoves her hands in her lab coat pocket and nervously looks out at the desert, then at the sky. "I was the one who sabotaged the accelerator."

"You?" Jeremy asks. "Why?"

"So you *didn't* want us to save Ken and Chris?" Adam asks.

"No, of course I did. I sabotaged it while you were all in the future, but I had no idea you'd come back missing two people." She sighs, her voice tired. "I just wanted the project to be over, so Aether would let you live your lives in peace. What they did—coercing Team Echo into joining the project, trapping Team Delta in the time machine—it horrified me. I didn't sign up for that, and I couldn't let it continue. Not if I wanted to live with myself. I thought I was protecting you, but then you needed to return to the future and it was too late, so I needed Dr. Walters's help to fix the machine."

"What do you think?" Adam asks me.

I fix her with a level stare. "You still work for Aether thirty years from now. If you disagree with everything they do, why would you stay?"

"I can't know that for sure, but I imagine I stayed because I thought I could help all of you. Maybe that's the only way I can make up for my past mistakes, or maybe even change the course of the future. When you go back, you should ask my future self."

"Well, I trust her," Paige says.

Jeremy rolls his eyes. "Of course you do. But I'll admit, I think this is the only way we can do this. And we *have* to go back."

I glance at Adam, and he gives me a short nod. "All right," I say. "How do we break into this place?"

Dr. Campbell gives me an amused look. "No need to break in. I can get us in with my access code. Meet me here at three a.m. Dr. Walters and I will make sure the building is empty and the security system is off-line."

Sounds easy. Almost *too* easy. I pray it's not a setup. But even if it's not, I'm sure the rest of the mission won't be that easy.

We all split up and head to our cars, planning to meet again early in the morning. Between all the hours I've been awake, the heaviness of grief, and the stress of time dilation, I'm so exhausted I can barely move. We may not suffer from future shock, but the act of time traveling still takes a toll on our bodies every time, putting us in a state almost like jet lag when we get back to the present. The best thing I can do is try to get a few hours of sleep, but I don't know if that will be possible. There's too much anxiety swirling through me, and I suspect it will keep me up all night.

Adam follows me to my car. "Elena…can we talk?"

I close my eyes for a moment, but then turn toward him, leaning back against my car. "Yeah."

"Are we okay?" he asks.

"I don't know." I want to say yes, but I can't predict what will happen to us if we fail to save Chris. I refuse to consider it. And from the glimpse I saw of our future, it won't be good.

He sighs and rakes a hand through his hair. "This last future, it wasn't the real one. That isn't going to be our fate."

"How do you know?"

Adam tentatively takes my hand in his. "When I saw we were married in that future, I wasn't surprised at all. And when we met Ava…" His voice gets choked up, and he swallows before continuing. "It felt *right*."

"But it didn't last. The future changed, and we weren't together anymore."

"No. I refuse to believe that what we have won't last."

I shake my head. "There's no way we can be sure that the future where we were married wasn't the fluke."

"I'm sure." He touches my face softly, trailing his knuckles down my cheek. "Some things won't ever change, like my feelings for you."

My gut clenches at his words, but I don't move away. "Don't say things like that. You might mean them now, but we're divorced in thirty years. You must not feel that way in the future, or you wouldn't have left."

"Elena, *you're* the one who left me in the future—not the other way around."

"Are you sure? How do you know?"

"I sent my future self a message and asked. I had to know." He watches me for a long moment, but I can't meet his eyes. "Is it really a surprise? You're the one who pushes me away time after time. Sometimes I wonder if you want to be with me at all."

"Of course I do. I just...I know it won't last. This past future we saw was proof of that."

"But there's a chance it will. We can still make the other future happen. The one where we're happy together." He cups my cheek in his hand, staring into my eyes. "Elena, I love you."

The words knock the breath out of me. No one has said those words to me before, not in that way. I know what the correct response should be, but I can't seem to speak it. My throat is tight, my mouth dry. He looks at me like I'm everything, when I know I'll never be enough. "Adam..."

"You don't need to say it back. I just wanted you to know."

I love Adam, I do. I want to tell him, but I...can't. Not now, not when I've just watched my friends die. Not when all I can think about is bringing them back this time. Not when I've seen how uncertain our future is.

He waits for some kind of response, but all I can do is shake my head. "I'm sorry. I'm...I'm really tired. I need to go."

His face falls, and I hate that I can't be the kind of girl who could run into his arms and profess my love for him. That's who Adam deserves to be with, not some messed-up girl like me. Adam's life is full of potential and the promise of greatness. My life's a loaded gun, and it won't take much to pull the trigger.

* * *

I leave him in the parking lot and drive home alone. Once there, all I want to do is shower and pass out, but there are a bunch of messages on my phone from one person: Shawnda.

Chris has been missing for over twenty-four hours now. I should call her back and reassure her…but how? I don't know what to tell her. The best thing I can do at this point is focus on getting Chris back, for her and for their son.

I lie on my bed and close my eyes, but I'm too haunted by the images behind them to sleep. I replay the second crime scene in my head, trying to look for clues and comparing it to the first one. They were set up in an almost identical way, even though Ken's body was in one and Zahra's was in the other. But now I know Ken killed himself in that other future, which means his death isn't related to Chris's at all. He was shot after he was already dead to make it look like he killed Chris and then himself—a cover-up for what really happened.

Chris was already dead, as far as I could tell, by the time he got to Griffith Observatory. They must have killed him somewhere else, which explains the lack of blood at the scene, especially in relation to Zahra's body that was shot then and there. But why would they take him to Griffith Observatory? Did they somehow know that Ken would die there?

Even though I stay up all night trying to put it together, I'm no closer to finding the truth by the time I have to meet the others.

SUNDAY

We can't get into the Aether lot through the normal security gate because there's still a guard there. We park at a nearby mini-mart, and Paige shows us a place we can sneak inside Aether's parking lot, where the fence has been chewed through by some animal and destroyed by the desert. I wonder how she knew this was here. Was she scoping the place out before? Planning to break in and steal something?

Dr. Campbell meets us in the lobby and lets us in, assuring us that the security cameras are all disabled. Even so, there's a very high chance we'll be found out, since we can't exactly hide that we're using the accelerator. We just need to be in the future before anyone can stop us.

Dr. Walters is in the basement already, waiting for us. His wrinkles seem more pronounced, his eyes tired. "The accelerator is ready. But you'll have to be fast. You'll only have one hour in the future this time."

"Will that be enough?" Paige asks.

"It has to be," I say. This is our last chance to save our friends. Our final chance to bring everyone back alive.

"We need to make a plan now, so we can find Chris immediately," Adam says.

"We know Chris goes to the graveyard while Jeremy is there," Ken says. "Maybe that's where we should go first."

"And Zahra?" Paige asks.

"She'll already be at the Griffith Observatory at that point."

Adam nods. "Okay, so we need to split up again. Elena and I can wait at the graveyard. Jeremy has to go to Griffith Observatory, since he can't overlap."

"Actually, I have another idea," Jeremy says. "I'm going to find my father in the future. If Aether is behind this, he might be the only person who can tell us what is going on."

Ken frowns and tilts his head. "That might be dangerous. If he's the one behind it all..."

"No, I think he's right," I say. "They didn't take Jeremy at the cemetery. It could be because Vincent won't harm his son."

"All right, just be careful, man," Ken says, slapping Jeremy on the back. "Paige and I will get Zahra."

Jeremy frowns. "You need to be careful too. Get out of there before those guys with the guns show up."

"Don't worry, we will."

"We're ready for you," Dr. Campbell says.

We move toward the accelerator for what I pray is the last time. If this trip doesn't work, I'm not sure what else we can do. We have to succeed. There's no other option.

I'm the last one to go in, but as I walk past Dr. Campbell, I pause. She's helping us even though it puts her career at risk, but perhaps I can make her future a little better. "There's something I need to tell you."

"What is it? Is everything all right?"

I should have told her sooner. I always planned to tell her, but with everything that happened with Chris, it somehow got lost in the shuffle. "Your future self told me she wished she could go back and change something that happened to her. But she couldn't go through the aperture."

"I always wondered if it would be possible to go back through an already open portal…"

"The answer seems to be no. But she did tell me what she wanted to go back and change."

She swallows, her eyes wide, but she nods. "What is it?"

"Are you sure you want to know? There's no guarantee you can change what happens. Some people might be happier to leave it to fate."

"I want to know."

"I would too. Which is why I keep getting into the same trouble again and again. But maybe this time my knowledge of the future can do more good than harm." I take a long breath and focus on the memory of what her future self said. "On your five-year wedding anniversary, your husband will go to the store to pick up champagne. He'll be mugged, and he won't make it. You need to make sure he stays home."

"Oh my gosh. Our anniversary is next month." She presses a hand to her heart, but then slowly nods. "Okay. Yes, I can do that."

"I hope you can save him."

"Me too." She wraps her arms around me in a tight hug. "Thank you. Thank you so much for this gift."

"Thank you for helping us. Both now and in the future."

I step inside the accelerator and take my place with the others. Dr. Campbell slams the door shut with a quiet, "Good luck."

The vibrating starts, and we crowd into the center of the

machine. Adam takes my hand, as he always does. No matter what's happened to our relationship, neither one of us wants to go into the future without the other by their side.

We're solemn as the countdown begins this time.

"Five."

We have no idea who killed Chris or Zahra, or why.

"Four."

We have no weapons and no way to protect ourselves.

"Three."

We have no clue what this next future will be like.

"Two."

We have no one to rely on but ourselves.

"One."

We have one hour to save them.

PART VI
THE THIRD FUTURE

00:00

This future is dim. My eyes adjust to the low light and my ears search for sounds, but I only hear footsteps echoing in the distance. The five of us are alone. There's no sign of Aether. No scientists. No futuristic technology. All of that is gone and has been replaced with large boxes and crates stacked around the basement.

"What happened?" Paige asks.

"Where is everyone?" Ken asks.

"Gone," I say. "Like in the original future Adam and I went to."

Adam approaches a stack of boxes and inspects them. "Pharmateka. They must have bought this building and turned it into a warehouse or something."

"What happened to Aether?" Jeremy asks.

Adam shrugs. "I guess we'll have to find out."

"We don't have much time," I say. "We need to get to the cemetery."

The footsteps get closer, and we turn toward them. I brace myself to get ready to run or to come up with a lie explaining why we're down here. But it's Dr. Campbell who approaches us, wearing a dark-blue uniform and a badge that says *Pharmateka* in LED lights.

"You're eight minutes early," she says. "I suppose that's my fault though. I programmed the accelerator, after all."

"What's going on?" Jeremy asks. "Where is Aether?"

She starts walking toward the elevator at a brisk pace, and we hurry to keep up with her. "Aether is gone. It went bankrupt a few years ago and Pharmateka bought it out. Now they're the leading technology and pharmaceutical company in the world."

"*What?*" Ken asks.

Bankrupt? I think back to the previous future, where Aether had fewer employees and less equipment, but still wasn't that bad off. Something has changed the timeline again.

"How did this happen?" Adam asks.

"After Vincent Sharp shut Project Chronos down, Aether spent billions of dollars trying to re-create all the technology you brought back. The design for the synthetic water generator was particularly problematic. Vincent refused to give up on it, but they could never get it to work, and the shareholders lost all faith in him after that. Especially when Pharmateka released one that *did* work."

Each of our heads snaps to look at Jeremy, who frowns. "Shit, that was my bad," he says. "I guess I should give my father the real design for the generator."

"You have the real one?" Paige asks.

"Yeah, I kept it. Just in case."

"I don't know if that will be enough," Dr. Campbell says, her voice laced with sadness. "There were so many other problems. So many projects failed. Stock prices plummeted. And for years, Pharmateka seemed to come out with the exact technology Aether was working on, but they were always a step ahead of us. Aether never had a chance."

"I'm on my way to talk to my father now," Jeremy says. "I'll try to figure out how we can stop this from happening."

"I hope you can find a way," Dr. Campbell says. "I didn't always agree with Aether's methods, but I can't deny they really were trying to make the world a better place. Pharmateka, on the other hand…" Her voice trails off, and she shakes her head. "They only care about profit and power."

"But you work for them anyway?" Adam asks.

"I took a job as a lab tech in this building for the sole purpose of being here to help you—and your other selves—when you came through the aperture. I knew no one else from Aether would do it, and I couldn't leave you without any guidance at all."

"Thank you," I say. It must have been tough for her to spend these years working for a company she hates just to help us.

"No, thank *you*. No matter how crappy my job is, my husband is still alive because of what you told me. We have five grandkids now. I will never forget that."

At least *something* has gone right in this future. It's proof that not everything I do to change the future makes it worse—and it gives me hope that maybe we can fix all of this somehow.

"Here, take these." Dr. Campbell hands us each a flexi and a neutralizer. "I have three cars ready on the roof. All of them have had their speed limit sensor disabled."

She leads us into the elevator, while we attach the flexis to our faces. This time, my flexi says *Welcome, Pharmateka employee.* There's another guy in the elevator in a uniform matching Dr. Campbell's, but he ignores us completely and gets out on the third floor.

The roof of this building is still a parking lot, but now it's full of Pharmateka cars. The surrounding area isn't as built up as it was in the previous future, with fewer buildings dotting the horizon. But the biggest change is that there's one of those force-field domes over the entire facility.

Three identical cars swoop down to us with the Pharmateka logo on them, their silver bodies glinting against the setting sun. "These cars can get in and out of Pharmateka's security domes," Dr. Campbell says. "Make sure you're back here in fifty-four minutes for the aperture. Good luck. I hope you can save them."

The remaining members of Team Delta and Team Echo look at each other for a heavy moment, like we all know this might be the last time we see each other alive. The fate of our friends and of this future rests on our shoulders, and we have less than an hour to succeed.

Paige and Ken hurry into one car, heading for the Griffith Observatory to rescue Zahra. Jeremy gets in the second, on his way to track down his father and find out what he can from him. Adam and I hop in the last car to head to the cemetery in hope of saving Chris.

As our car leaves the desert and zooms toward LA at top speed, we begin to notice more changes. There are tons of small force-field domes enclosing different parts of the city and even around certain buildings and homes. Pharmateka's logo is on everything. I can't turn my head without seeing the bright-green *P* of their name from the corner of my eye. I'm guessing Future Visions never happened in this future, since Chris is still dead. Which means that without Aether or Future Visions, Pharmateka would have a near-monopoly over the market.

Maybe we've been wrong all along, focusing on the enemy we know instead of the future threat we never could have seen coming. Pharmateka doesn't even exist in our time, but I'm starting to suspect they're behind all of this somehow.

"Look at that," Adam says, staring out the window at something below us. I lean over to follow his gaze and see a huge crowd in the street, outside a tall building with the Pharmateka logo on it. People are holding signs that I can't read from this high up and seem to be shouting, while the police push them back.

The building and surrounding areas are enclosed by a dome, but our car has access and we order it to quickly fly lower so we can see what is happening as we pass by. Some of the storefronts around the building have been smashed and vandalized. The mob is angry, surging forward toward the building, and their signs say things like "Free the cure!" and "We deserve to live!"

"What's that about?" I ask, although the cold pit in my stomach tells me I already know the awful truth.

"I..." Adam's voice is rough, and the look in his eyes is one of pure horror. "The cure...it has to be genicote they're talking about."

"We don't know that for sure."

He lets out a sad laugh. "What else could it be?"

I study the people in the crowd. Some of them have kids with them. Others are at least in their sixties, some even older. One woman with tear-streaked eyes holds up a sign that says "Pharmateka profits while our family members die." Another man has a sign that says "Medicine should save lives, not end them!"

Adam presses a hand to the glass as he takes it all in. "I have to know what this is about, but I'm too terrified to look."

"I'll look," I say, resting a hand on his knee.

"Thank you." He takes my hand and holds it tightly, his eyes never leaving the sight of the people below us, even as they fade into the distance.

It doesn't take me long to find out what is going on. It's all over the news. And the truth is so much worse than I could have imagined.

"Pharmateka, they..." I try to keep my voice steady, but it's hard. "They created the cure for cancer."

Adam's eyes practically bulge out of his sockets. "*They* created it?"

"That's what it says." I don't want to tell him the rest, but I have to. I fight back the lump in my throat and spit the next words out. "It's being used as a biological weapon by the United States in a war against China."

"No," he says, his voice barely above a whisper. "Please, no. Tell me that isn't true."

"I'm so sorry, Adam." Pharmateka has used the cure's side effect—how it causes horrible mutations and death in people who don't have cancer—to kill millions of people. It's something the Aether Corporation of the first future wanted to do, but Future-Adam fought them on it. But now, in this timeline, there's no one stopping Pharmateka from using it however they want.

Adam runs a shaking hand through his hair. "And the rioting?"

"Most of the cure being produced right now is being used in the war. No one can get it, even if they're sick, unless they have a lot of money or powerful connections."

"How did this happen?" He looks so lost, so helpless, so completely defeated that tears fill my eyes. His life's work has been stolen from him and perverted. The cure he developed is being used to cause death instead of preventing it. "There's no way I would have allowed this. I didn't create the cure to be used to end lives. I created it to *save* them."

"But you're not the one who created it in this future. They did."

"How is that possible?"

"I'll try to find out." I squeeze his hand. "Don't worry. Once we know, we can make sure this never comes to pass."

I look up information on the cure itself, but all I find is that it was developed by a team of scientists at Pharmateka. I search for

Adam next, to see if he was one of those scientists. But there's no Wikipedia page on him this time.

I finally find an article mentioning him, but what I read is so terrible, so shocking, so completely wrong that I refuse to believe it. I search for another, and another, and another, until I can't deny what they're all telling me, and the grim truth explaining why this future has gone so wrong.

Future-Adam is dead.

00:16

My heart seems to drop out of the car and fall all the way to the ground. Future-Adam was murdered over twenty years ago. A random shooting, the police say. But I know what it really was: an assassination. They killed him for the cure. His death was right around the time he was originally supposed to develop it. That can't be an accident.

If Adam was killed that long ago, then we never got married.

Which means Ava was never born.

"Oh God," I whisper.

"What is it?" Adam asks, but I shake my head. A tear slips out of my eye, but I'm too focused on my flexi to bother to wipe it away. I have to know if it's true, if Ava doesn't exist in this timeline.

The Elena Martinez of this future is in prison. Not for Adam's death—that was never solved. She broke into a Pharmateka facility, killed three guards, and attempted to steal something. Knowing me, it was probably some kind of proof about what they did to Adam or to the cure. But she got caught, and now she's in prison for life.

She never had any children.

"Elena," Adam says. "What do you see?"

I want to tell him, but it's too awful to say out loud because then it will become more real. All I can do is whisper his name and move into his arms. I press my face against his shoulder, and he holds me tight until the waves of panic and helplessness stop.

I quickly tell him what I learned, even though each revelation feels like it's ripping my heart out all over again. Adam takes it all better than I did, although by the end of it, he's holding on to me as much as I'm holding on to him.

"We can't let this happen," Adam says quietly. "This can't be our fate."

I draw in a long breath, trying to steady myself, and wipe at my eyes. "We have to figure out why this timeline is so much worse than the previous one. What changed between now and then?"

He considers it for a moment. "Zahra died, so she's not in this future anymore."

"Would that have changed the timeline that much?"

"No, probably not. She was an FBI agent in the other futures, but I can't imagine that would alter the world so much, in particular what happened to us."

I search my memories for what else it might be. "We saved Ken."

Adam nods slowly. "He's a chemist. His future self could steal the formula for the cure and develop it for Pharmateka."

"Maybe, although Ken seems more worried about curing Huntington's disease to save his mom's life and his own. I'm not sure what his motive would be for stealing the formula."

Adam takes off his glasses and cleans the fog off them with his shirt. "I don't know. But it's possible he's been a mole in Aether, feeding Pharmateka information until Aether collapsed. He would know about all the technology his team brought back to Aether."

I can't argue with that logic, but I'm not sure the boy I stopped from killing himself would do all of that. I look Future-Ken up, but find that he died at thirty-eight, like he did in the other timeline. He worked for Pharmateka before that, but was never able to cure the disease that eventually killed him.

I look up the others on Team Delta for good measure and to check that none of them have bought another lottery ticket or done anything drastic. But no, Paige is still married to her sketchy congressman husband, and Jeremy still works for Pharmateka. Zahra, of course, is dead, as is her brother.

But if it isn't Ken or the others, then I can't come up with any other explanation for what is causing this future, except…I pull away from Adam and look him in the eye. "Maybe it's us."

"Us?"

"Things have been…complicated between us lately. Since Chris died, it's only gotten worse. And each future has gotten worse too. I know it's arrogant to think we'd have such a huge effect on the fate of the world, but without our company and without you developing the cure…"

Adam stares at me for a heartbeat, and I wish I knew what he was thinking. "If you're right, then we have to fix it. We have to fix *us*."

"I don't know if we can be fixed." I can't meet his eyes any longer and turn to look out the window again. We've almost to the cemetery now. "We've visited four futures now, and we were only together in one of them. What if the two of us aren't meant to be?"

"No. I refuse to believe that." He takes my chin and guides my eyes back to him. "Elena, I love you now. I loved you six months ago. And I'll still love you in thirty years. Why is that so hard for you to accept?"

"I..." I swallow hard, staring into his perfect blue eyes. He's waiting for an answer and I wet my lips, trying to come up with one. Everything on the tip of my tongue is a lie or an excuse or a way to keep him at a distance some more. I can't tell him the truth: that I'm so scared to find happiness with him and then have it disappear as fast as it appeared. But if there's any hope for us and for the future, I have to be honest with him somehow. I have to stop pushing him away.

I trace a finger down his jaw, along the dark stubble there. He hasn't shaved in hours, maybe days, and it makes him even more handsome, especially in contrast with the glasses perched on his nose. That mix of geeky hotness and all-male ruggedness always gets me. But it's more than the way Adam looks. He's brilliant and determined, kind and confident, and no matter what, he always stands beside me. Even when I don't deserve it.

"I can't accept it because all my life, everyone I've ever loved has left me or been taken away from me," I say. "I never want to go through that again. I thought if I pushed you away first, there was no way you could leave me. Or that it would hurt less when you did."

"I understand," Adam says, smoothing back my hair. "But if there's one thing we both know, it's that the future isn't set. We control our fate. We choose our destiny. And I choose you, every time. In every future, it's *always* you. You're it for me. Now and forever."

He's so certain, so confident in our love. What am I waiting for? A sign from the universe that we're supposed to be together?

Didn't I already get one when we met our daughter?

I give up fighting my feelings for Adam any longer. I slide my arms around his neck, pulling him toward me, and the words come easily this time. "I love you, Adam."

He kisses me like he thought he would never get the chance again, and I kiss him with the passion of my pent-up emotions and the love I've tried to deny for months. His fingers tangle in my hair as he pulls me closer, his mouth demanding more, his tongue sliding against mine in a way that fills me with heat. I'm just as lost as he is, as decimated by this kiss as by our very first one in the rain.

But the happiness I feel at finally admitting to Adam how much I care for him is bittersweet, because I know I'll have to fight for this love now and every day of my life. Even in the best timeline, Future-Elena said it wasn't easy. But I won't give up on it. I won't give up on *us*.

00:22

We arrive at the cemetery as the sun sets fire to the horizon, casting the clouds above us in radiant purple and orange. Adam and I get out of the car beside Ken's grave, which shows he died at thirty-eight instead of eighteen, like in the first future. I scan the area while a soft breeze tickles my hair and sends shivers up my arms. Something's not right. I check the time on my watch again. The other Jeremy should be waiting here for Chris, before getting attacked by men in ski masks. But this place is empty. There's no sign of Jeremy anywhere.

"Where's Jeremy?" Adam asks, coming to the same conclusion as I did.

"He's gone."

"Do you think those guys with the guns took him?"

"No," I say, as a chill sinks into my bones that has nothing to do with the falling temperature. "I think he lied to us."

It all starts to come together in my head. Instead of looking at the differences in the timelines, I should have been looking at the things that remained constant. Future-Jeremy works for Pharmateka in every timeline, and in each one, the company gets more and more powerful while Aether gets weaker. And in each future we made decisions based on what Jeremy told us, believing all of his lies, chasing our tails while he carried out his own hidden agenda.

What else has he lied about?

And where is he now?

"We have to go," I say, as I turn back to the car.

Adam hurries after me. "Go? Where?"

"Back to the Pharmateka lab from the first future. The one Team Echo was supposed to break into. The one where Jeremy stole the design for the synthetic water generator."

"Why?"

"I think Chris is there. I think that's where he gets killed."

"I don't understand," Adam says, while we get back into the car and take off into the darkening sky.

I order the car to go to the Pharmateka lab at top speed, and it shoots forward into the invisible traffic lanes. "The last time we heard from Chris was when he was at Future-Jeremy's apartment. We assumed he was going to the cemetery after that, but maybe he never made it there. Maybe he found a clue at Future-Jeremy's place that led him back to the Pharmateka lab, where he uncovered something that led to his death. It's the only thing that makes sense. Aether wasn't behind their deaths; Pharmateka was. And Jeremy is at the center of it all."

Adam's eyes widen. "Why would Jeremy kill Chris?"

"I don't know. But I know he lied to us multiple times." I grip the edge of the leather seats, my heart racing as fast as the car. "I should have figured it out sooner, but they were such tiny things that they were easy to overlook. I didn't put them together until now."

"What did he lie about?"

"He told us he went to his future self's apartment and found Future-Jeremy passed out in a pool of alcohol and vomit. But Chris said when he went, no one was there."

"That doesn't mean anything. Future-Jeremy could have left his apartment by then."

"But there are other things. Like, he told us the car that took Chris was black, but the one that had his body was really silver."

Adam frowns and tilts his head skeptically. "Jeremy had just been hit with a neutralizer. It makes sense his memory would be scrambled a little."

"He was wearing a hospital wristband too. Why would he still be wearing that unless he'd gone to the hospital again for some reason?"

"Um, he probably forgot to take it off."

"That's what I assumed too, but now that I think about it, I remember seeing his arm without it back in the present." I shake my head. "Look, I can't explain it, but I feel it in my gut. Jeremy is behind this, and I have a feeling it all goes back to his parents and the synthetic water generator. That's why we need to get to Pharmateka." I quickly explain to Adam what Jeremy told me about his mom's death and how Jeremy kept the real design for himself.

Adam doesn't seem to believe me, but he sends a message to Jeremy, with me copied on it. Did you find your father?

Jeremy doesn't write back. Just like in the other futures, his flexi seems to be off-line. Which mean he's either in danger, or he *is* the danger.

We got Zahra, Ken sends. She's fine.

Thank God. They got to her in time. Now all we have to do is save Chris, and we can make things right with the future again.

Meet us at the Pharmateka lab, I tell them. And don't say anything to Jeremy about what we're doing.

I quickly explain my idea on the short flight out to the Pharmateka lab. None of them are happy about my suspicions, nor do they believe Jeremy is really the enemy, but no one offers any other explanation as to where Chris might be. In the end, they all reluctantly agree to my plan.

We're almost out of time. There's no way we're turning back now.

00:31

The Pharmateka lab in this future has been upgraded since we last saw it. The same grumpy security guard is out front, but now a force field covers the entire building. Our Pharmateka-owned cars are cleared for entry, but getting inside the building is still going to be tricky—especially since we have less than thirty minutes to get in and out and back to the aperture.

As we near the structure, we pass through the silvery dome without a problem. The guard looks up as I hop out of the car and walk over, but doesn't bother to stand. I head straight toward him, not slowing, neutralizer in my fist. The others are right behind me. He realizes something is wrong when I don't slow down, but by then it's too late. He stands up and reaches for a gun at his side, but I'm already on him. I deliver a swift jab to his jaw, and then I hit him with the neutralizer. He's out cold in less than thirty seconds of me getting out of the car.

"You're up," I say to Zahra.

She kneels by the guy and takes his wrist, using her imbed—which still works in this future—to hack in and get us inside the building.

Meanwhile, Ken starts removing the guard's uniform. "Sorry," he says to the guard. He leaves the guard in just an undershirt and boxers and dons the uniform himself.

"Got it," Zahra says. "I've shut down the entire security system in the building. I've also upgraded our employee status at Pharmateka. Now we each have the highest levels of clearance and should be able to get in any door."

"Does security have any record of Chris being here?" Adam asks.

"No, not that I see," Zahra says.

While Zahra waits with the guard and monitors security, the rest of us slip inside the building into a small reception area with a bored-looking woman at the desk. I grip my neutralizer, but as we walk past her, something automatically scans our flexis and grants us access. She doesn't even look up.

"Where to?" I ask the others.

"The lab with the synthetic water generator was this way," Ken says, turning down a corridor.

As we hurry down the hall, I worry that at any moment someone will run after us and tell us we're not supposed to be here. Or worse, shoot us. But Zahra's hacking skills protect us, and everyone we pass by ignores us, possibly because Ken is wearing the guard uniform.

We find the room with the synthetic water generator, but it's empty. No Chris. No Jeremy. It's a dead end.

"Now what?" Paige asks.

"We search the rest of this place quickly and pray we find something," Adam says.

We run down the halls, checking every room, trying to figure out where Chris is. There's nothing on this floor so we split up, with Adam and me taking the floor below and the others going up.

I'm getting desperate now, heart racing, worried we'll never find Chris or Jeremy. I must have made a mistake. I assumed they would be here, but I had no real proof. Now we're out of time and still haven't saved Chris.

We turn a corner and hear voices ahead. Adam grabs my arm and raises a finger to his lips.

"What are you doing here?" Jeremy asks, from a room down the hall. His voice is muffled and I can barely make it out, but I'm sure it's him.

"I'm here to bring you back to the present." That's Chris! He's still alive!

There's no reply from Jeremy, but then Chris asks, "What are you doing? Where's Ken? Is he here?"

"No. I don't know where he is. Why?"

"He's going to be found dead at Griffith Observatory soon, and I need to find him first," Chris says.

"Ken's *dead*?" Jeremy's voice gets higher, and Adam and I creep down the hall toward the sound. "How do you know?"

"I'll explain everything later. We need to get going."

"Not until I get what I came for."

"Hang on. That's genicote, isn't it? What are you—" Chris asks, and then he yells, "No, stop!"

There's a shuffle and a thump and the sound of glass breaking. Adam and I rush through the door, neutralizers in hand. We enter an antechamber with windows looking in on a large laboratory labeled with biohazard warning signs. Inside, a metal table is overturned with yellow liquid pooling around it and broken glass everywhere. Chris and Jeremy wrestle on the white linoleum floor.

"No!" Jeremy yells, reaching for a broken vial. "What have you done?"

He elbows Chris in the face and gets to his feet, while Adam and I make it into the lab. We move toward Jeremy with our neutralizers ready. He raids a nearby cabinet, shoving beakers and vials out of the way, then opens another and does the same. "There's no more," he says to himself. "He destroyed it all!"

"What are you looking for?" I ask.

Jeremy turns toward us with a frown. He's wearing a shirt I've never seen before. "Who are you?"

Right, this is the Jeremy from the first timeline, the one who got shot in the shoulder while breaking into Pharmateka. That's why I don't recognize his shirt—the hospital took it because it was covered in blood. But this Jeremy hasn't been shot, and he's never met me or Adam. None of that has happened yet.

Another man emerges from the back of the lab and shoves a gun at Chris's back. "Drop your neutralizers or I shoot him."

The man is older, late forties probably, with graying auburn hair. I've never seen him before, but he looks familiar. He looks like one of the other guys in the room, but with thirty years added to his face.

Jeremy isn't the murderer—his future self is.

I drop my neutralizer, and Adam does the same. "Look, we just want to get our friend so we can go home," Adam says.

Future-Jeremy shakes his head, his gun still trained on Chris. "I don't think that's possible now. I can't let you leave here alive. Luckily, I don't need you anymore."

There's a commotion outside the antechamber and the sound of footsteps. Ken yells, "You guys in here?"

He pops into the doorway, with Paige at his side. Future-Jeremy points the gun and fires. The blast is loud, and Paige screams as the bullet tears into Ken. I'm too far away from Future-Jeremy to stop him, but I use the distraction to bend down and grab a long, broken piece of glass off the floor. As Ken hits the floor, I grab the younger Jeremy's arm and hold the tip of the glass to his neck. Future-Jeremy moves the gun back to Chris's head immediately.

"Put the gun down," I say to Future-Jeremy.

"Or you'll what?" He shakes his head. "You're not a killer, Elena."

"You don't know me very well then."

"Oh, but I do. We were good friends for many years. Until I had your boyfriend murdered, stole his formula for the cancer cure, and made sure you went to prison. I apologize in advance for that, by the way. Nothing personal."

"Why would you do this?" Adam asks. He kneels by Ken and presses his hand against the gunshot wound. Paige takes off her sweater and hands it to Adam so he can try to stop the bleeding. Dammit, we need to get Ken out of here. We need to get all of us out of here.

"With the two of you gone, Pharmateka could make the cancer cure," Future-Jeremy says. "In every timeline I've convinced my younger self to bring the cure back to the present for that purpose, but Chris here always gets in the way."

"So you killed him and dumped his body where you knew Ken would be found to throw us off," I say.

"Essentially...yes."

"And Zahra?"

"I ordered my men to leave no witnesses. I didn't mean for her to be collateral damage, but sometimes shit happens." He presses the gun harder against Chris's temple, and Chris's eyes squeeze shut. "As you can see, I have no issue killing any of you. Now let my younger self go."

"If you fire that gun again, your younger self is dead." I press the glass into Jeremy's neck, making him cry out. "You just admitted to murdering my friends and sending me to prison, and you don't think I'll kill you?"

"Please don't hurt me," Jeremy whimpers in my arms. "I didn't know anyone would die!"

"You won't kill me," Future-Jeremy says. "Or at least, you won't kill *that* Jeremy. He's completely innocent. He hasn't become this man yet."

My fingers tighten around Jeremy's arm. "But he's going to become you one day."

"But will he? Or can he still change?" Future-Jeremy gives me a sardonic smile. "If you kill eighteen-year-old Jeremy, you'll have an innocent death on your hands. You'll always wonder if you could have done something differently. If you could have saved *everyone*, including him."

"Please," Jeremy says. "I had no idea what was going on. I was just following my future self's orders. I thought I was doing the right thing." Tears stream down his face, and he trembles slightly. It's hard to believe he could kill anyone, or that he'd ever become this cold-blooded monster in front of us, even if he is a liar.

Dammit. Future-Jeremy is right. I can't kill this guy. He hasn't killed anyone—his future self has. He isn't a murderer, not yet. The potential is inside him, but it's in *me* too. I made the choice to not purposefully kill Lynne. I'm making the choice now not to kill Jeremy. And he can make that choice too.

I can't kill him. But I can make Future-Jeremy *think* I will.

I dig the glass shard into Jeremy's arm, leaving a jagged cut along the skin. He screams, and his future self yells, "Stop!"

"I'll do it," I say, as Jeremy's blood spills all over my hand. "Let Chris go, or I'll keep cutting. I don't give a damn about you, now or in the past. And if you think I won't kill both of you to save my friends, you're wrong."

"Jesus." Future-Jeremy inspects his arm, where a jagged scar has shown up that wasn't there before.

I raise the glass shard to Jeremy's face. "Want another one?"

Future-Jeremy lets Chris go, shoving him forward and waving the gun at all of us. "Go then. Return to the present. It won't change anything. Things are already in motion that you won't be able to stop. I'll still control Pharmateka and bring Aether down. And I'll still get the cure in the end."

"No," Jeremy says, covering his arm to stop the blood seeping out of it. "I won't become a murderer like you. I won't do *any* of this."

"You—" Future-Jeremy says, but Paige comes out of nowhere and hits him with her neutralizer. The older man goes down, the gun skidding across the floor.

I let Jeremy go and drop the broken glass, now covered in his blood. I want to throttle him, but he still has his own timeline to complete, his own aperture to get back to. "Get out of here and find the rest of your team. And this time don't lie to our other selves about what happened here."

"I'm sorry," he says, his voice shaky. "I didn't know it would come to this." He dashes out of the room without another word.

I throw my arms around Chris. "You're alive."

He seems rattled, his breathing fast, but he hugs me back. "Thanks to you, it sounds like. You'll have to tell me everything that happened."

"Let's get home first."

While I grab Future-Jeremy's gun off the floor, Adam and Paige help Ken up. He's in a lot of pain, but Adam has turned Paige's sweater into a tourniquet and stopped the bleeding. "He'll be all right," Adam says. "Although as soon as we get back to the present he'll need medical attention."

We rush out of the building, into the car waiting for us, and make it back to the Aether-turned-Pharmateka building with two minutes to spare. We leap out of the car and hurry toward the elevator, which Dr. Campbell is already holding open. Jeremy—the one from this timeline, who supposedly went to visit his father—stands at her side, carrying a backpack, his face concerned. I'm tempted to grab him by the throat and shake him. To make him tell me why he lied to us and covered up what Future-Jeremy did. To ask him what he was doing while we were out there fighting his future and past selves. I won't though, not yet. First we have to get back to the present.

Dr. Campbell frantically waves us inside the elevator. "Hurry! The aperture is opening now!"

By the time we burst into the basement, the golden light is already there. There are only seconds left before the aperture closes. We run toward it, and all I can think is, *We're not going to make it.*

I step into the sparkling dome as it begins to fade, and the world bursts into light.

PART VII
THE PRESENT

SUNDAY

When the spots in my vision clear, I let out a long sigh. We made it.

I've never been happier to see the accelerator's metal walls. It's cramped inside with so many of us, seven total, but we're alive and back in the present—and that's all that matters. We can finally put all of this behind us. And we never have to go back to the future again.

The accelerator door opens, and Dr. Campbell stands on the other side. Her eyes travel over all of us, and then she smiles. "You did it. You're all back. Oh, thank heavens."

"Ken needs to get to a hospital," Paige says. "He was shot in the arm."

"No hospitals," Zahra says. "They'll file a police report because it's a gunshot wound."

"It's just a graze," Ken says, but his face is way too pale. "I'm okay, really."

"Get me a first aid kit, and I'll try to patch him up," Adam says.

Paige and Adam help Ken into a chair, while Dr. Campbell goes to fetch a first aid kit and Dr. Walters works to shut down the accelerator. We're still all wearing our flexis, still carrying our neutralizers, even though the accelerator has short-circuited all of them. Future-Jeremy's gun is still tucked in the back of my pants too. I take it out and set it on a nearby table, and then find the guy responsible for all of this mess.

I grab the collar of Jeremy's shirt and slam him against the outside wall of the accelerator dome, making a loud metallic *thud*. "You lied to us."

His eyes widen, but he doesn't fight me. "I'm sorry! I was only following my future self's orders, I swear! I thought I was doing the right thing!"

"Why?" I ask, slamming him back against the wall again. "Why didn't you tell us Future-Jeremy killed Chris?"

"I didn't know until we saw Chris's body! When I left the Pharmateka lab in that first timeline, Chris was still alive. And even then, I thought there had to be some other explanation. I didn't think I could ever be capable of killing someone."

Zahra moves to my side and stares Jeremy down. "Tell us exactly what happened."

"In the first future, the original one, the cure was developed by Future Visions, but Pharmateka had gotten hold of a sample and were trying to make their own version. They were modifying it somehow. I don't know. When I went to my future self's apartment, he had left me instructions for how to get the design for the synthetic water generator along with a fake design for my father. Then he told me to get the cancer cure from the lab and bring it back to the present. But Chris tracked me down at Pharmateka and destroyed all the genicote samples they had. Future-Jeremy told me he'd deal with everything, and then he shot me in the shoulder. I don't remember anything after that except waking up in the hospital. But I swear, I had no idea he killed Chris!"

"Not at first," Zahra says. "But you knew after we found Chris's body. You could have told us the truth then."

"I wanted to, but I was worried I would only make things worse. I thought I could fix things myself somehow. And I couldn't believe I was the killer. I really couldn't." His eyes close and his shoulders slump. "Guess I was wrong."

His voice seems sincere and what he's saying makes sense on some levels, but I'm still skeptical. "If all of that is true, then where were you in the second future when you said Chris was taken at the cemetery? Who hit you with the neutralizer?"

His eyes flick over to Adam. "I went back to the hospital and tried to get the cancer cure. I was still stupidly following my future-self's orders. But I failed. I went back to the cemetery and knocked myself out so you wouldn't suspect anything."

"And this last future?" I ask. "Where did you go while we were saving Chris and Zahra?"

"I really did go see my father. It was…rough." Jeremy shakes his head. "I'm just glad you were able to stop my future self. I never want to become that person."

"Make better choices in your future, and you won't become him," Adam says.

He nods and rubs his arm where I cut his other self, along the jagged scar that is now there. "My future self was obsessed with bringing down Aether and my father, but I'm not going that route anymore. I'll give my father the design for the synthetic water generator, but after that, I'm done trying to impress him. My future is my own, and I'm going to live it with or without his approval."

Zahra's lips press into a tight line, but she looks at me and shrugs. I reluctantly release Jeremy. He's an idiot and none of us will ever trust him again, but I don't think he's a killer.

Dr. Campbell comes out with a first aid kit, and Adam begins patching up Ken's arm. The bullet grazed him, so it looks worse than it really is, although Adam keeps trying to convince Ken to see a real doctor anyway.

Dr. Campbell gives Chris back his phone, which Aether confiscated when they locked us in the accelerator the first time. Chris checks it, and his eyes bulge. "Holy shit, I have a million messages from Shawnda. And it's Sunday? I missed *two days*?" He runs a hand over his shaved head. "Jesus, she is going to kill me."

"Sorry," I say. "She texted me, but I didn't know what to tell her. I just wanted to get you back alive."

"I'll figure something out. I don't even care if she's mad. I just want to go home to my girl and be there for my son's arrival. And maybe sleep for a week."

"That sounds nice. I'm Zahra, by the way. It's nice to finally meet you." She and Chris shake hands, and Ken and Paige introduce themselves to him as well.

"I'm curious..." Zahra says to Chris. "How did you know to find Jeremy at Pharmateka?"

"And how did you get inside?" Paige asks.

"I discovered a message at Future-Jeremy's house to his younger self telling him to get genicote from the Pharmateka lab, along with the design for the synthetic water generator. The message included access codes for the building, so I used them to sneak inside. That's when I found him in there." He glares at Jeremy who looks down at his feet, then turns back to us. "Where did you find Ken?"

I lean against a desk, relaxing for the first time in hours, while we catch Chris up on what he missed in the last two days. All seven of us made it back. It's hard to believe, but we did it. And now we can make the future right again.

"Your arm is done," Adam says to Ken. "But you need to get lots of rest, and you should really see a doctor."

Ken's face is still way too pale, but he manages to stand on his own. "Thanks."

"Adam and I can finish up here," I say. "The rest of you should take Chris and Ken home."

Chris grabs me in a hug and then pulls Adam in too. "What you did...I'm only now starting to understand everything you went through. Everything you almost sacrificed." His voice chokes up a little. "You came back for me, not once, but *twice*. Thank you."

"You're welcome," I say. "I know you would have done it for us too."

"That's what friends are for, right?" Adam asks.

He squeezes our arms, looking back and forth between us. "Not friends. You two are family."

We say our good-byes, but Jeremy stands apart from the rest of our group, waiting on the fringes with Dr. Campbell and Dr. Walters. He's an outsider now because of what he's done, and he's alienated everyone who once cared about him.

After Paige, Ken, Chris, and Zahra all disappear inside the elevator, Jeremy stays behind. "I want to make sure this is over," he says. "I want to make sure my father can't hurt anyone else."

Dr. Walters and Dr. Campbell open two large duffel bags, each one packed full of explosive charges. Dr. Walters briefly explains where to attach the charges to the accelerator and the surrounding equipment, and shows Adam how to set the timer.

"Where did you get all this?" I ask.

"I made it," Dr. Walters says. "I tried to use the explosives before, but Vincent stopped me. This time they'll do the job."

"You two should get out of here," Adam says to the scientists. "If you get caught, you could get fired or even go to prison."

"We can't leave you," Dr. Campbell says, frowning.

"No, you should go," I say. "If they find out we blew up the accelerator, we'll just threaten to tell everyone what they did to us."

"My father wouldn't dare go after Elena or Adam after what he's done to them," Jeremy says. "And I'm safe too. But he could make your professional lives hell."

The two scientists exchange a look, and Dr. Campbell reluctantly nods. "All right. Please be careful, and make sure you get out in time."

"Are you sure you know what to do?" Dr. Walters asks.

"We've got it," Adam says. "Just make sure the building is empty."

"Will do," Dr. Campbell says. She touches both of our arms, giving us a warm smile. "Good luck."

The scientists leave, and Adam, Jeremy, and I get to work, pulling out the explosive charges. But as we approach the accelerator, Adam stops and gazes up at its metal dome, his expression troubled.

"Second thoughts?" I ask.

He frowns, and I worry for a brief moment that he will change his mind. He never got the cancer cure from the future, and I know it's probably still haunting him, especially when he's seen what could happen if it's created by someone else. Is he tempted to return to the future one more time to try to get it? But he shakes his head. "No. Let's get this over with and get out of here. We have a future to start living."

We each take some of the charges and fix them to the side of the accelerator with duct tape. It takes us about fifteen minutes to rig the explosives, and when we're done, we stand back and look at our work, at the accelerator covered in the tools of its destruction. It seems a shame to destroy Dr. Walters's life's work, but it has to be done. We made a promise to him and to ourselves. We're not leaving until we make sure Aether can never send anyone to the future again.

"I'll set the timer," Adam says quietly.

The elevator door opens and Vincent steps out, wearing a rumpled suit. My hopes of destroying the machine plummet.

"What are you doing?" he asks, charging forward.

"We're destroying the accelerator," Jeremy says. "Once and for all."

"No! You can't." Vincent starts trying to pry one of the charges off the accelerator.

Jeremy grabs his backpack, the one he brought back with him from the future. He pulls out a gun, aims it at his father, and yells, "Stop!"

The gun looks exactly like the one his future self had. Exactly like the one that killed Chris and Zahra. Exactly like the one sitting on a nearby table, the one I took from Future-Jeremy.

"What are you doing?" I ask.

"I can't let him stop us," Jeremy says. "The accelerator has to be destroyed."

"Why do you have a gun?" Adam asks.

"To tie up loose ends. Now set the timer!"

Adam doesn't budge. He just stares at Jeremy like he's figured something out, something surprising yet inevitable.

So have I.

I try to grab Jeremy's arm, but he's too fast. He slams the gun against my forehead, hard. My head feels like it's being split open and stars fill my eyes, but I hear Adam yell my name.

"Stay back," Jeremy says, raising the gun at me. He waves it back and forth between me and Vincent. "Don't come any closer!"

I press a hand to my forehead and stare Jeremy down. So many lies. Why did I ever believe anything he said? "Your future self didn't kill Chris, *you* did. It was you all along. Not Future-Jeremy."

"My God, Jeremy," Vincent says. "What have you done?"

"What I had to do." He looks over his shoulder at Adam. "Now set the timer, or I shoot your girlfriend."

Adam shoots me a pained look, but he kneels beside the timer and starts working on it. I have to stall Jeremy somehow or distract him. I have to get that gun away from him. Or get the other one behind me. I take a step back toward the table. "Why are you doing all this? Why kill Chris?"

"Future-Jeremy is the one who created the synthetic water machine's design. Yeah, Aether didn't mention that, did they?" He shakes his head, scowling. "My mother started it, but thanks to my dad she died before she could see her life's work come to fruition. My future self spent his entire life trying to realize her dream. But my dad told Team Echo to steal it, to bring it back to this time, so that he could take it from *me*. He was going to take credit for *my* invention." He clutches the gun tighter, keeping it trained on his father. "No way in hell was my future self going to let that happen. Future-Jeremy told me what to do, told me to bring back a fake design and keep the real one, and to grab the cancer cure at the same time. But Chris got in the way, so he had to die. My future self just covered it up for me."

"What about everything you said about not going down your future self's path?" Adam asks.

"I'm *not* going down his path. I have the cure now, long before the other Future-Jeremy got it."

"You *what*?" My eyes hone in on his backpack, strapped to his shoulders. Is the cure in there too? Oh God, I have to get it away from him. I've seen what happens to the world when Pharmateka has the cure.

"I failed to get the cure from the first two futures, which is why I encouraged us to go back every time. Before we went to that third future, I made a new plan. I realized that if I became Adam's good friend over the years, my future self could kill him after he developed the cure and then steal it for Pharmateka. Then in thirty years, Future-Jeremy could leave the cure in his apartment for me to get while he took care of Chris at the Pharmateka lab with my other self from the first future. When I told you I went to see my father, I was really picking it up. Piece of cake."

Jeremy's betrayal is even bigger than I thought. He was going to keep deceiving us for years to come, pretending to be our friend so he could ruin our lives and steal Adam's cure. I remember what he once said about his father. *He always plays the long game, and when you add time travel to the mix*...But it wasn't Vincent with the long game, it was Jeremy. He has to be stopped, no matter what the cost. I take another step back, getting closer and closer to the gun behind me.

"Why do you want the cure so badly?" Adam asks. "Is someone you know sick?"

"No, no. I need it to beat *him*," Jeremy said, waving the gun at his father. "To bring Aether down for good. To make Pharmateka more powerful and more successful than anything my father has ever done." He chuckles softly. "I'm one of the founders of Pharmateka, you know. My future self kept that hidden from the public, but it's always been *mine*."

Vincent bows his head. "Jeremy, I know I haven't been the best father, but we can work this out. Just tell me what you need from me. Tell me what I can do."

"The only thing I want is for you to watch while your precious accelerator is destroyed."

Vincent takes one look around us, like he's just now seeing the horror he's responsible for. "Maybe that's for the best."

"How's that timer coming?" Jeremy asks over his shoulder.

But Adam's no longer working on the timer. While Jeremy was talking to his father, Adam crept up behind him. He tackles Jeremy, trying to wrestle the gun away from him, and my heart stops. I'm torn between rushing in to help Adam or darting back to grab the gun. But before I can move, Jeremy shoves Adam to the ground and aims the gun at him.

"You know what? Forget it," Jeremy says. "I can figure the timer out myself. I don't need *any* of you."

"Jeremy, don't do this," Vincent says, moving toward him.

Jeremy raises the gun at his father, and there's a split second for me to act. I turn and lunge for the gun behind me, then swivel around and aim it at Jeremy. But I'm too late, and a loud bang echoes through the basement. Vincent staggers back with a stunned expression before falling to the floor.

For a moment, Jeremy simply stares down at his father, his face impassive. Then he turns the gun on Adam again.

I don't think.

I point the gun.

I pull the trigger.

It isn't until the blood is seeping out of Jeremy, and the look in his eyes turns to surprise and horror, that I realize what I've done. He collapses, and I run toward him to check if he's alive, the gun still clutched in my hand.

"No..." His eyes fix on me as he coughs up some blood. "This wasn't...in any of the futures..."

And then he's gone. His body lies on the floor, his blood pooling under the accelerator he so badly wanted to destroy. I expect to feel some kind of guilt, or some regret, but all I feel is relief.

Turns out, I am a killer after all.

Adam rushes to Vincent and presses his hands to the gunshot wound, where blood rushes out in a steady stream. "He's still alive!"

I grab a lab coat off the back of an office chair and drop beside Adam. "Go. Set the timer. Then we'll all get out of here."

While Adam works to get the timer going, I hold the fabric to Vincent's wound. He moans and whispers, "Jeremy..."

"I'm sorry," I tell him. "I had to stop him."

He closes his eyes. "I know."

Once the timer has started, Adam sets off the fire alarm, in case there's anyone still in the building. We haul Vincent up and drag him into the elevator, leaving Jeremy's body there with the backpack still strapped to his back. I'm surprised Adam didn't try to take it, but perhaps he's realized that bringing the cure back might only create more problems for the future.

By the time we get to the lobby, there are ten minutes left on the countdown and Vincent has passed out from the pain or blood loss, or both. We stumble outside, putting as much distance between us and the building as possible. It's slow going, with his dead weight and exhaustion dragging us down, but we make it to the outer fence.

There's a loud boom deep within the earth. A low rumble begins under us, and the ground starts to shake. A huge plume of smoke rises up around the building, and flames quickly consume it. Within minutes, the lower floor begins to cave in on itself, starting a chain reaction that topples the entire building. I had no idea Dr. Walters's explosives would cause this much damage.

Vincent is awake again, and he watches his building collapse with a stunned expression. "Project Chronos is done," he whispers.

We're safe from this distance, and all we can do is stare at the destruction until the fire trucks and ambulances arrive. Adam wraps an arm around me and I lean against him, watching the sun rise over the rubble.

A new day is beginning. A new future where Aether doesn't control our fate.

SATURDAY

It's been almost a week since I killed Jeremy. I spent most of it alone, trying to rest and process what happened. To come to terms with the fact that I ended another life.

We never know what we're capable of until the future is barreling toward us and we have to make a choice. I didn't want to kill Jeremy, but I'd do it all over again to save Adam. To save the future.

There's blood on my hands, but the flashbacks have stopped, along with the nightmares and panic attacks. I'm not cured. I know that. I should probably go back to therapy at some point. But I'm learning to live with my memories and to not let them control me. I'm going to stop dwelling on the past, stop worrying about the future, and learn to live in the moment.

After we left Aether's ruins, I asked Adam to give me some space, and he did it without question. Every morning since then, I've found a different origami animal on my doorstep. I know it's his way of showing he loves me and is there for me if I need him. I lined each one up on the windowsill in my bedroom, creating my own little paper zoo.

On Saturday, I'm ready to face the world again.

First, I visit Chris and Shawnda and their new son in their beautiful house. I've never seen Chris so happy, and as I watch the way he dotes on his son and his wife, I know everything we went through to bring him back alive was worth it. His son will grow up with a father and go on to become a lawyer. Shawnda will never be a single mom or have to go to rehab. And Chris will found Future Visions with us and invent a machine that converts trash to energy in cars.

Adam is already there when I arrive, helping the new parents with whatever he can. Every time he smiles at me, my heart flip-flops like I'm some kid with a crush. Like I've fallen in love for the first time all over again. Maybe it's because our future is back on track now.

That night, he and I meet Paige, Ken, and Zahra for dinner at a Persian restaurant Zahra's cousin owns. We're seated in a back corner where we can talk privately about everything that happened during our multiple trips to the future and after we got back. Adam already gave them the complete rundown about what happened with Jeremy that night, but they want to hear it again from my perspective.

As I tell the story, I feel a huge weight lifted off my shoulders because I don't have to hide anything or hold anything back, unlike when I saw the therapist. It's not only me, Chris, and Adam who have lived through this crazy time-travel experience anymore. I have three new friends who understand what I've been through. Three friends I can talk to about it whenever I need to.

"It's so hard to believe Jeremy was such a stone-cold killer," Paige says, tugging on her long hair. "I knew he had a lot of issues with his dad, but I never imagined he would actually do all of this."

"I thought I knew him," Ken says. "But I didn't. Not at all."

"None of us did," Zahra says.

Paige lets out a dramatic sigh. "I'm just glad it's over."

Vincent Sharp recovered from his gunshot wound, and he promised all of us he would uphold his promise that Aether would stay out of our lives. I'm not sure I believe him, but we *did* save his life. Of course, we also got his son killed.

"It's strange," Zahra says. "We spent all this time going to these different futures, and yet I have no idea what will happen in mine now."

"Are you going to try to save your brother?" I ask. Last time she tried, it seemed to backfire on her.

Zahra's dark brows pinch together, and she considers her answer for a moment. "I think I'm going to get my brother some help for his gambling problem. Giving him more money didn't work. Neither did trying to stop his murder. I need to do something to fix the issue before it gets that bad. Maybe *that's* the way to save him."

Paige gives her a hug. "I think that's a great idea."

"What about you?" Zahra asks her. "What are you going to do about Brad?"

"That's easy. I've already dumped him once and for all. I won't get him in trouble, since that seemed to only make the future worse for everyone, but I won't help him either. I want my new future to have nothing to do with his. And from now on, I'm only dating good guys." Her eyes rest on Ken with a shy smile. He looks down, his cheeks flushing, but he has a grin on his face. Maybe the two of them don't need help from me or Zahra after all.

"Ken, what about you?" Adam asks.

"I'm not going to kill myself, if that's what you're worried about." He turns his fork over and over. "I'd still like to try to find a cure for Huntington's disease. I was planning to ask if you could help me someday."

Adam smiles at him. "I'd be happy to help. Maybe you can assist me with the cancer cure too."

"Sounds like a plan." He tilts his head and studies me and Adam. "What about you two?"

"We have a company to start with Chris," I say. There are other things in our future too—a wedding, a daughter, a life together. I don't know if it's possible to find our way back to the best timeline, but we're going to try.

"You know, one day we'll need smart people with unique skills for our company," Adam says, grinning at the others. "Any interest in joining us?"

Zahra flashes us a sly grin. "You know where to find us."

We all hug and say good-bye, but it doesn't feel like the end between us. It feels like the start of something big. New beginnings. New friends. New futures.

* * *

Adam studies the row of origami animals on my windowsill. The room is dark, illuminated only by the ambient light of a Los Angeles evening through the windows. I watch him from the doorway, admiring his broad shoulders, his slightly messy hair, and the way his jeans hug his perfect butt.

"You kept them," he says, picking up the dragon, his most recent addition.

"I've kept every single one you've ever made me." I move behind him and slide my arms around his waist, pressing my chest against his back, grazing his neck with my lips. "I love you," I whisper.

He turns to face me and brushes hair away from my eyes, tucking it behind my ear. "I love you too."

"I'll never get tired of hearing that."

"I hope not, because you'll be hearing it for a long time." He cups my face in his hands and kisses me slowly, leisurely, taking his time and making warmth spread from my lips all the way down to my toes. He's showing me that we don't have to rush, but I don't want to wait any longer.

I tug his shirt over his head, then slide my hands along his chest. My shirt comes off next, and then my bra. When we're skin to skin, Adam finds my mouth again and claims it in a desperate, hungry kiss, full of longing and passion. Time stops as his mouth moves across my jaw and to my ear, where he whispers again that he loves me before trailing kisses down my neck.

The rest of our clothes come off, and our hands roam each other's bodies. We've explored each other before, but this time it's different. This time we look at each other with new eyes, eyes that have seen our possible future together.

I open a drawer on my bedside table and fish out a condom. We're going to have a kid someday, but not now. Not anytime soon.

"Are you sure?" he asks.

I nod. "Are you?"

"God, yes." He pulls me closer, onto the bed, and then there are no more words.

It's Adam's first time, and our first time together. It might as well be my first time too, because none of the other guys meant anything to me. With Adam, it's real. And even though it's a little awkward and over too fast, it's still amazing, because it's *us*.

The second time is much better. Adam's a fast learner, after all.

While Adam rests, I head into the kitchen to get a glass of water. Adam's messenger bag lies on its side on the counter with a bunch of his huge science books spilling out of it. It's so full that a small notebook has fallen out. I start to push it back inside and note a green *P* on the corner of the cover. The Pharmateka logo.

I open the notebook with trembling hands. It's filled with handwriting I don't recognize and things I don't understand, pages and pages of scientific formulas and equations.

I slam the notebook shut and shove it back inside Adam's bag. But as I do, my fingers brush against something made of cool metal, something smooth and hard. A rectangular black, unmarked container.

I flip open the latches, and the box opens with an exhale. Cold air puffs out of it, and I'm frozen—not because of the chill, but because of what I see inside. A small vial of yellow liquid.

Genicote, the cure for cancer.

He must have taken all of this from Jeremy's backpack before we left. He promised he wouldn't get the cure from the future, and I guess technically he didn't, but he also said he wouldn't try to rush things either.

At first I'm mad, silently fuming at him for lying to me, for going behind my back, for doing the one thing I asked him not to do and then not telling me about it. I'm about to run in there and make him explain himself, but something stops me. And the more I think about it, the more I start to feel…oddly hopeful.

Would it really be so bad if Adam developed the cure early? He could save millions of lives, and we would make sure it never fell into the wrong hands. Maybe it's better if Adam creates it now, before anything else can go wrong with it.

Maybe the best way to predict the future is to invent it.

"Elena, come back to bed," Adam's sleepy voice calls from the bedroom.

I quickly close the box and place it in his bag, then return to bed beside him. He slides an arm around me, pulling me against him, and I melt into his embrace.

"Everything okay?" he asks, while his fingers trace circles around my origami unicorn tattoo.

I hesitate but decide to ask him about the cure in the morning. Tonight, I want to savor this moment. "Everything is great."

I don't know what the future will be like, or what will happen to me and Adam. All I know is that we're both going to fight for the best possible future—one where we're together.

I have all these memories of futures that will never happen. I have all these echoes of the past inside my head that I can't let go of. But the only thing real is the present.

The only thing that matters is now.